ROSAMUNDE BOTT

Legacies

'Walking, I am listening to a deeper way. Suddenly all my ancestors are behind me. Be still, they say. Watch and listen. You are the result of the love of thousands.'

Linda Hogan (b.1947) Native American Writer

PROLOGUE

The faceless man is there again, dressed in a cloak, and as so often before is trying to tell me something, but although he is standing in front of me, his voice seems to come from somewhere else, somewhere a long way off, or as if he is behind glass, and I cannot hear him.

He raises his arm as if to make a gesture, and I am distracted by something hanging round his neck on a chain. It is a large, long key, beautifully made, with a triple-ringed bow, and an intricate design on the shaft. It seems old, but looks new. I look up, and I know that he is smiling.

As always, when I woke from this dream, I felt happy. The man in the dream was like an old friend, and I knew I could trust him. I almost felt I could hold a conversation with him, right there and then. If only I could hear what he was saying.

Then, the sun began to shine in my eyes, and I crossed back from the dream into reality. I had been having this dream for some time. It was not like other dreams; it had a reality to it, and despite now being fully awake, I still could not shake off the feeling that the man was real. Yet, this morning, it had been different. The key was a new development. I had not seen it before, and its pewter grey remained clear in my mind as I turned over and looked at my clock radio.

I lay back and sighed, the dream falling away from me into oblivion.

I had just remembered that today I had to get up early to drive to Manchester for my uncle's funeral.

CHAPTER 1

March 1985

As I watched my uncle's coffin disappear behind the curtains, I considered that cremations were a lot tidier than burials, but I wasn't sure I liked them. Life is messy, and so is death. Funerals should be messy, with earth and spades and people weeping by a graveside in drizzling rain. Not this clinical end with everyone sitting on plastic chairs and on their best behaviour.

As the two curtains closed together, I resisted the urge to giggle. It was too theatrical, and yet, not in a good way. No-one applauded. There was just an awkward silence, as if a bad actor had just left the stage. Someone coughed politely.

I glanced around the room and, not for the first time in my life, wondered how I came to belong to this family. There was my Aunt Ada, sitting bolt upright in her smart and completely appropriate black suit, neat shoes and a modest hat, her face well powdered, showing no signs of grief or sadness. I decided to give her the benefit of the doubt: it was not that she did not feel it; it was just that emotion was for private life. In a social occasion such as a funeral one had to behave impeccably. One must not let the side down. The rest of the immediate family and friends all seemed to be of the same opinion. There were no sniffles, no sound of quiet, desperate sobbing, not even a baby crying. Just the mechanised sound of the curtains as they drew together in front of the disappearing coffin.

My mind drifted. I was at another funeral just five years ago in 1980. The rain dripped mournfully from the trees, the doleful sound of the vicar's voice fell flat in the damp air (I could not remember the words) and my two closest friends, Justin and Greta, stood on either side of me, ready to lend a steadying hand should I stumble or faint. I was still in deep shock.

The two coffins being laid to rest were my parents, dead in a pile-up on the M25 just one week before, and so I had not given much thought to what I should be wearing or putting on a brave face.

I was just twenty, and an only child; a late arrival after my parents had tried for a family for years and then given up, only to find that once they had let go of all hope of having a son or daughter, all their prayers and hopes were to be suddenly answered. My mother, Jennifer, had been a moderately successful writer of children's stories. My father, entranced by Jennifer Jepson's love of life and all things unconventional, had been rescued from a life of dreariness in a respectable banking firm, to get a job in a TV production company. This had raised some eyebrows within the ranks of the strait-laced Turvey family, who had thought the banking career a sound and sensible one. When Peter and Jennifer's only daughter had decided to become an actress, the eyebrows belonging to that branch of the family had raised even further. The Turveys had no interest in the theatre and that a career in it was for idiots.

The success of both my parents had allowed them to pay off their mortgage on the large old Victorian house just five minutes' walk from Hampstead Heath, leaving me the outright owner upon their untimely deaths.

For days after the funeral, I had wandered through the house, wearing one of my mother's old cardigans, which still retained the smell of Blue Grass, her favourite perfume. I opened doors as if hoping to still find my mother sitting writing at her desk, or my father working on some carpentry project in the basement. Justin and Greta brought food and bottles of wine, and we had sat holding hands on Parliament Hill, watching the sun go down over London, while I cried and talked. Eventually the house settled around me and finally became my own.

The cremation being over, and my thoughts back to the present, we all wandered severally back to Aunt Ada's house, where a buffet had been laid on. Filling my plate with as much as I could pile on (it was a long drive back to London from Manchester, and there was nothing in the fridge back home), I became aware that the person next to me kept looking at me. I turned to find a young, blond-haired man with sharp cheek bones and intense, questioning blue eyes. He smiled.

'Hi', he said, helping himself to slices of cold beef, 'good spread, eh?'

It wasn't the best opening introduction, but it was refreshing to see another young person here. Most of the people here were well over sixty, a whole contingency from my uncle's ex-RAF club, all blue-blazered and dapper looking, but a little on the fragile side. My uncle had been much older than my father and had served in the RAF during the war, a connection he had maintained for the rest of his life.

5

But this young man was different. He wore a grey suit and looked smart, but there was something slightly frayed at the edges about him. The suit was an old one, the trousers were flared and the cuffs on the jacket looked worn. He looked slightly out of place here, and perhaps, in my love of all things quirky, that was the reason I found myself attracted to him.

'May I join you?' he asked as I moved towards the one free table.

'Of course, please do.'

I had to admit to myself that I was pleased not to get stuck with my uncle's contemporaries and have to sit through discussions about the local bowling club, or whose arthritis was the worst.

'Are you family or...?' he asked.

'Family. He was my uncle. I'm Sarah, by the way.'

'Your uncle?' His eyes seemed to widen slightly. 'I didn't know he even had any... on which side?'

'Oh, my father's, but my parents died five years ago, and my father was much younger. You may not have...'

'So, you're a Turvey?'

'Yes,' I grinned, 'my mother wanted to call me Topsy, but Dad wouldn't have it.'

It was an old family joke, but he didn't seem to have noticed it. He seemed suddenly far away.

'What about you?' I asked.

He had stopped eating for a moment. But now he glanced back at me, his eyes distant and distracted. He then re-focused on his plate.

'Oh, me,' he moved some salad around with his fork, 'my grandfather was your grandfather's brother. I think that makes us second cousins.'

6

I felt a pang of guilt. I had never really kept up with my extended family.

'Oh, my goodness,' I said, chasing an olive round my plate with my fork, 'I'm not sure I even know what my grandfather's name was, let alone yours. I had no idea I had any cousins. I'm sorry, but I don't even know your name.'

'Well, that was mutual until a moment ago. My name is David Turvey. Pleased to meet you, cousin.'

His face had become friendly and focused again and he held out his hand. I took it, smiling back at him. His hand was warm and dry, but not very firm.

'I didn't even know there was anyone of my own generation in the family,' I said, 'the Turveys don't seem to have been blessed with the greatest ability to reproduce themselves.'

Before he could reply, our conversation was interrupted by the arrival of Aunt Ada who sat down next to me.

'Sarah dear, I just wanted to thank you for coming all this way...'

'Oh, that's quite all right Aunt Ada, I wouldn't have missed it...' I bit my lip, 'well, you know what I mean. I'm... I was so sorry about Uncle Charles. But you're looking... I mean, how are you bearing up?'

'Oh, I daresay I will be fine, once I can get rid of all these people and put my feet up with a nice cup of tea. So many people! It's just so exhausting!'

'Yes, of course. Uncle Charles must have had many friends'

'Sarah, dear. There was something I wanted to speak to you about. Now, your Uncle Charles, well you know there wasn't a great deal of... well, closeness between him and your father, but all the same, he was always very... well, you know, with your father passing away so suddenly. It was a shame, you know,

7

that they never really met that much after your father went to London.'

Call me paranoid, but I heard the unspoken criticism. London was where my father had met my mother.

'Yes,' I replied, with a smile, 'Mum was sad about it too. She would have liked to have known Dad's family better.'

'Well. Be that as it may. Your uncle wanted you to have something. Goodness knows why. I'm not even sure you will be interested, but it's because you're really the last of the Turveys.' She looked at David, who had coughed. 'Oh, well of course not quite, Hello David.'

'Ada,' he nodded, curtly.

'Well, David's a Turvey too, of course, but your uncle wanted you to have it because you are his brother's daughter after all, and David is...'

Enough of family politics. I was dying to get back home.

'But what is it Aunt Ada?' *Obviously not money*, I thought, allowing myself a distasteful feeling of disappointment. A financial legacy would have been very useful right now given the struggle I had to maintain the house on Hampstead Heath. The roof tiles had been looking exceedingly dodgy for some time, and the cost of heating the whole house meant I used only a small part of it, spending winters huddled in front of the gas fire in the living room.

'Oh, didn't I say? I really think my memory is going. Well, you'll think it odd, no doubt, but he wanted you to have all his notes on the Turvey family tree.'

At that moment, David dropped his fork on the floor, and dived under the table to retrieve it, and I was unable to give him the wry look of bemusement that I felt I wanted to share. I stared at my aunt instead.

8

'The family tree?'

'Yes. He's worked so hard on it for years, but it's all your side of the family, so it's of no interest to me. I've never really been into that kind of thing, anyway.'

'No. Of course not.'

'Oh, and I nearly forgot. Honestly, I think my mind is going...'

'Well, it's only to be expected,' I said, putting my hand on her arm, 'you've had a difficult time...'

'It's the silliest thing, but he was quite adamant about it. He said there was something that your father had in his keeping that you should know about, and you need to look at. Some items that were something to do with the family tree. I don't know... I'm sure there was something else too, but I can't quite...'

She sat staring at the ceiling. David had returned from under the table and was quietly moving food around on his plate.

'No, it's gone. Well, perhaps it will come back to me, and perhaps it wasn't that important, after all.'

'So, what exactly is it that my father had, and where would I find it?'

'That's just it. I don't know. Well, some box of something or other. He said your father would know, but of course... you know, I think he was rambling a bit towards the end, probably forgotten your father was no longer with us. I'm sure there was something else... but there you are, old age catching up with me. Probably nothing important. I will pop upstairs and get the papers for you before you go.'

I looked at David, who had abandoned his plate and was sitting very still.

'What do you make of that?' I said, as Ada went off to talk to Charles's RAF friends.

David shrugged and made a sort of half laugh.

I took a sip of wine. The Turvey family tree, and some kind of something that was in my father's keeping, but I didn't know what, or where. *Thanks for nothing, Uncle Charles*, I thought, and then mentally told myself not to be so mean. I'd quite liked Uncle Charles; he'd had a sense of humour, and I found myself feeling sad that I had never had a chance to know him properly.

Back home, Justin and Greta had turned up on my doorstep with an Indian takeaway, knowing I'd had a long drive and probably had nothing in the larder to eat, and we had demolished it quickly, with groans of enjoyment.

Justin topped up my glass from the second bottle of wine that evening and I sank back on the sofa.

'That was one of the best Indian meals ever. I feel like I don't need to eat for another week. Thanks guys.'

'Don't mention it,' said Greta, who was sitting, or half reclining, on a pile of cushions on the floor, 'that's what friends are for. We bring food, we eat, we drink; everybody is happy.' She waved her arm in the air as if dismissing any further comment, and a slight aroma of patchouli wafted into the air, mixing exotically with the smell of Tandoori chicken and onion bhajis.

Justin, having replenished all of our glasses, sat down on the ancient armchair on the other side of the gas fire that sat in front of the unused fireplace, crossing his legs and placing his glass carefully on the coaster he had put onto the coffee table next to him. He leaned back into the chair.

'What a mess,' he said, surveying the array of metal containers, half-eaten papadums and dirty plates and cutlery, 'we should clear up really.'

Nobody moved.

'In a little while,' I said, 'I just want to let that Tandoori chicken settle, and I might just finish off those papadums anyway... in a minute...'

'Ugh, how could you, 'groaned Greta, 'I have eaten too much. Always the eyes are too big for the stomach, and then... the suffering...'

I smiled. 'Ah yes, the suffering. We always have to have the suffering...' I clapped my hand to my head in mock drama.

Greta threw a cushion at me.

'Don't mock. I can't help it. Suffering is in my genes.'

Justin laughed.

'Honestly, Greta, you're a bigger drama queen than I am.'

'Life is a drama. Anyone who doesn't know that is already dead. Sarah, give me that cushion back, I need it.'

I threw the cushion back at her.

'So, how did the funeral go, Sarah?' asked Justin.

'Oi, how I hate funerals,' groaned Greta.

'Well, you would have found this one a little lacking in drama. My God, it was like everything was cling-film wrapped and served on a sterilised plate, and I'm not just talking about the food. Uncle Charles was sent off very tidily wrapped up and in an orderly fashion. There was no weeping or any emotional nonsense like that.'

'Oh well,' said Justin, 'I suppose that's the way some people like to deal with death. Make it into something they can handle; an event to be organised and prepared; it's the only way they can feel they're still in control. Don't forget, I've been to a few recently...' He looked away at the fire, and I knew that he was thinking of Mark, as well as a few other friends who had died of AIDS within the last couple of years.

'I know,' I reached over and touched his arm, 'but you're so sweet, Justin. You always see the best in people. I just wonder sometimes how this family is part of me. We're so different. Well, I don't know about David. He's a cousin I never knew I had. He was OK, I think. Anyway, he seemed to like me. He took my phone number anyway,' I ended, grinning into my wine.

Greta sat up and Justin looked up, twitching an eyebrow.

'Oh, really? Mm, now that sounds more interesting. Kissing cousins, eh?'

'Oh don't jump to conclusions, Justin. He lives miles away. He was quite good looking, I suppose, but...I don't know...'

'Well, sounds like this funeral had more drama in it than you're letting on. Anything else you'd like to tell us?'

'There was something a bit odd. My uncle left me something. But the most bizarre thing. I have no idea what I'm going to do with it.'

'What is it?'

'The Turvey family history.'

Greta sank back on her cushions with a disappointed grunt, but Justin leaned forward.

'Well, it may not be worth anything, but it might be interesting.'

'You think? Apparently, there's something I should look at that my father was in possession of, but Aunt Ada had no idea what it was. What good is that to me?'

'If it was important to your uncle, it might be worth finding out. Ooh, I do love a good mystery. Didn't she say anything else?'

'Not really. Just that there was something in a box. I suppose it could be something stored in the attic, but there could be hundreds of boxes up there. It might be like looking for a needle in a haystack.'

'It might be fun to look.'

'Perhaps...'

'Do you think it might be some dark family secret?'

'I've no idea. Aunt Ada didn't say. But why did he mention it as part of my grand legacy of the family tree, I wonder?'

'Darling, this is so exciting Let's have a look at it all and see if we can find something!'

Greta had been silent throughout this exchange. Now, she got up and started clearing up the food detritus.

'I am going to do the washing up. You children stay here and talk about your family histories. I don't want to know. It's just all dead people. What's the point? It's all in the past, dead and buried.'

'Oh Greta, we'll help...'

'No, no... I will be happy in the kitchen. It won't take long. Then I'll go home. It's getting on for eight, and I need to work on some designs. I've got a deadline to meet next week.'

After Greta had left the room, I exchanged looks with Justin.

'I'd forgotten what she's like about death and families and stuff. Do you think she's OK?'

Justin smiled. 'Greta's always more OK than she thinks she is. All the same, I can't imagine what it must be like to have all that in your background. Imagine if all of your grandparents had died in the gas chambers of Auschwitz, and your parents had only just managed to escape the same fate.'

'I can't even begin to. And they never knew what happened to the uncle did they?'

'Her father's uncle; he disappeared after he got her parents out of Germany. God knows what happened to him...'

We did not speak for a few minutes. Both Justin and I had suffered loss, but Greta's family had faired far worse.

I said, 'I'll wait until Greta's gone, and then we'll have a look at that tree.'

The family history papers that Ada had passed on to me consisted of a very large ring binder full of notes, a few sepia photographs of rather stiff looking people staring at the camera as if facing execution, and a long roll of paper which we laid out on the carpet, using a collection of ashtrays and mugs at the corners to hold it down.

Long horizontal lines sprawled across the paper, with each generation shown under short vertical lines. Hundreds of names and dates were written in small, neat handwriting.

'My God, he's done a lot of work,' I said, 'I wonder where he got all this information from.'

'Church records and Somerset House, most of it, or is it St Catherine's House now? It's where you can order birth and marriage certificates.'

'You seem to know a lot about it.'

'I know someone who is into genealogy. She's a friend of my mother's; in her forties; her husband's a lawyer. It started off as a hobby and now she gets paid to investigate other people's family history.'

I looked down at the tree, searching for my own name. It wasn't difficult to find; it stood out at the bottom; one little line coming down from Peter Turvey and Jennifer Jepson.

There were no other names on my generation, except, a few inches away, my newly discovered cousin David, son of David Turvey, the son of Stephen George Turvey, brother of Henry John Turvey, my grandfather.

14

'Wow,' said Justin, 'some of these lines go right back to the 17th century.'

I read the names at the top of the tree.

'Geoffrey Turvie. What does "bap" mean?'

'It's short for baptized, I think.'

'Ah, then baptized in 1639, Woburn. That's Bedfordshire, isn't it? Amazing. "M" must be short for married: 1660 to Agnis Field. I suppose that's how they spelled Agnes. Wow! Look at all those children. The old Turveys had a bit more lead in their pencils in those days obviously.'

'That's one way of putting it I suppose. And no family planning, of course. He's certainly got a lot of information on each person, particularly in the nineteenth century. All the wives have their surnames and parents written in, and they seem to be cross-referenced to the ring-binder with more notes and family trees on each one. Oh, except this one.' He flicked through the ring-binder again. 'No, there's nothing on her at all.'

He pointed to a single name on the page, five generations up from me, the wife of one of my direct ancestors, Edward Turvey. Unlike the other wives, she did not have a surname and no details of her birth or parents.

'Elizabeth. Nothing else. Looks like he wasn't able to find out anything about her. So she was my...' I counted up the generations, '...great-great-great grandmother.'

'That's odd. All the other direct female ancestors have lots of notes on when and where they were born, and some of them he's researched right back so they have trees of their own – but there's nothing for her, not even anything to say whether there were any clues. He's just put in Edward Turvey's notes that there's a possible marriage date of around 1853. He did not find a marriage certificate or anything in the registers. The census gives her place of birth as Gloucestershire in about 1827, but that's all he knows. A bit of a mystery, then.'

'Five children, and the first one was my great-great grandfather.'

For the first time, I felt a flutter of excitement in my stomach, but I could not explain why. 'It's funny, isn't it,' I said, 'all these people; just names and dates on a page. Seemingly meaningless. And yet they all had lives. They all had pain, suffered grief and loss, fell in love, out of love, married, had children, got ill, died. Some of them no doubt had secret love affairs, some perhaps committed crimes or inflicted cruelty. Perhaps some were heroes. They were all made of flesh, with thoughts and feelings and problems, just like you and me. Yet they've all been reduced to just this. A name on a piece of paper with dates attached and a few side notes. Do you think that's all we'll be one day?'

'What a depressing thought,' said Justin, 'I suppose the least we can hope for is to have more than a paragraph written about us in a scruffy ring binder.'

'Well, one paragraph is more than poor old Elizabeth Turvey got. I wonder who she was.'

'Perhaps you could find out.'

For a moment, I felt a tingle of excitement, but it soon disappeared.

'If Uncle Charles couldn't find out anything about her, I don't know how I could.'

'Hmm... I guess so. So what about that box? Do you think it has anything to do with all of this? Are you going to do anything about it tonight?'

'Like what? Anyway, I'm too tired, ' I yawned, 'It's been

a long day, and I don't see there's much point. It's probably nothing.'

Justin looked at me, barely hiding an expression of exasperation.

'Or it could be something.'

'But what?'

'My darling, I have absolutely no idea.' He rolled onto his back.

'Anyway, it's too late to go looking now. I forgot to tell you...'

'What?'

'I have a date.'

'What?' I sat up. Justin hadn't been on a date for two years. With the dreaded unmentionable virus that had been making its way through his circle of friends, it was terrifying to even contemplate any kind of relationship.

'Tell me all,' I said, 'who is he? Why didn't you tell me before?'

'I didn't tell you because I knew you'd be all "Tell me, tell me!", and of course I was right. Honestly, it's nothing. It's just a drink. We met at the Vauxhall Tavern, as you do. He works as a dresser at the Barbican, so he finishes work late, and I said I'd meet him in town for a quick drink after work. Really, it's nothing.'

'Then why did you tell me?' I teased, poking him in the stomach.

'Because I wanted to work on this with you, but I have to go, otherwise I'll be late.'

He got to his feet and held out his hand to help me up.

'What's his name?'

'Graham. Really, don't make anything of it. I think he's a bit flaky, anyway. I'm not sure he's really my type.'

I closed the front door after watching Justin walk up the road towards the tube station and offered a silent prayer for him to stay safe, then I came back to the family tree laid out on the floor. I looked at all those names, all those people who had had lives, all gone. What was the point of looking? There was enough to deal with in the present without digging up the past. Perhaps Greta was right.

There was another thing that disturbed me too. All the names on the paper seemed to be mocking me. Their lives were no doubt all filled with purpose and success. Even my parents, who had been different to the rest, had had shining, creative and successful lives, until they had been cruelly cut short. Why was I the black sheep?

What had all these people to do with me, really? Even if there was some family secret in a box somewhere in the attic, what good would that do me?

What I needed now was a job, something to tell me that I was on the right track. Something to tell me that I wasn't wasting my life, audition after audition, with no work to speak of except the occasional fringe production that promised a share of profits; profits that were usually non-existent. What use did I have for a family tree, no more than a list of dead people, as Greta would have said, and some box of boring documents that I would probably never find? And even if I did, what then? It was hardly going to be a treasure chest that would make my fortune, or some magic wand that would make me an overnight successful actress.

No. It wasn't worth it. It would mean a search through the attic; through my parents' things. Five years had gone by, but the thought of going through all those old documents and bits and pieces was still too much to bear.

I drained the dregs of my glass of wine, and took a last look at the family tree before rolling it up and putting it at the back of the cupboard at the bottom of the dresser. Then I turned off the light and went to bed.

CHAPTER 2

Two weeks later I was walking home after an audition for an Edinburgh fringe production; a musical based on the life of Florence Nightingale.

I'd been well prepared, and I had a good singing voice, but things began to go wrong when my nose started to bleed halfway through my number. The director had been perfectly nice about it and said it sometimes happened with nerves. He even made a joke about it and said that blood was something Florence had to deal with a lot, so it was quite appropriate, really. But I knew I didn't have the part, and anyway, I hadn't really believed myself to be right for it, and if I didn't believe it, no-one else was going to. I had only gone up for the part because my agent said there was just nothing else going at the moment.

All I could think about as I came out of Hampstead High Street station and walked through Flask Walk towards the Heath, was a hot bath and a glass of wine before Justin came over later. I was looking forward to seeing him. I'd not seen much of him since that night two weeks ago, and my guess was he'd been seeing Graham again, but when I asked him on the phone, he was a little cagey about it.

As I turned the corner and looked towards the house, I saw a car I did not recognize parked in the driveway. It was a rather ancient looking orange Hillman Avenger. Walking into the drive I saw a man sitting on my front doorstep. There was something slightly shabby about him that I vaguely recognized, but at first could not remember where I knew him from.

'Hello cousin Sarah!' he said, jumping up and walking towards me.

Of course, David. How could I have forgotten?

My feelings were mixed. I was exhausted and feeling rejected, and I'd wanted a relaxing evening with my closest friend, not the pressure to entertain family I hardly knew. All the same, he did have a very nice smile as he walked towards me, and I remembered that initial attraction, which perhaps was not something I should ignore, given the lack of romance in my life. I found myself smiling back, warmly.

'David, what on earth...?'

'I did leave a message on your answerphone but obviously you didn't get it. I'm just on my way to somewhere and I thought I'd drop in.'

'How did you find me?'

'Aunt Ada gave me your address. I hope you don't mind. I thought I'd just wait a while and if you didn't turn up, I'd go. But here you are.'

'Yes, here I am,' I said, fumbling for my keys and mentally waving goodbye to my hot bath. Well, I could offer some wine, anyway.

Except that when we got inside and I asked him if he'd like some, he said, 'Oh no, a cup of tea will be fine. I don't drink.'

Another mental adjustment. Was he really my type? Yet, losing an interest in someone just because they didn't drink seemed a little shallow. It didn't seem right to open a bottle just for myself; it perhaps wouldn't give the right impression, so I joined him in a cup of tea.

After the initial niceties where David remarked on what a lovely house I lived in and I asked him how he was and what he was doing in London (upon which he was rather vague), the conversation turned to my legacy from Uncle Charles.

'So, did you find anything interesting in the family history?' he asked, with a slightly dismissive little laugh.

'To tell you the truth, no,' I replied, 'I'm sure it's all very fascinating if you're into that kind of thing, but it's not really my cup of tea. I don't think I'll do anything with it, like try and add to it or anything. It looks pretty well researched already, anyway.'

'No,' he said, 'and I can't really see you grubbing around in dusty record offices and dark archives. It's very frustrating and difficult work anyway. Time consuming too.'

Something about this assumption about me, given we had only just met, put me on edge. I chided myself mentally, and told myself I should take it as a compliment.

'You seem to know more about it than I do,' I answered.

David put his mug of tea down and stared at it.

'I... had to do some research for something once. Nothing interesting; it was for work. So, did you find out what the thing your father had was?'

'Nope. I doubt if I will either. I'm sure it's nothing. Just Uncle Charles being... well, Uncle Charles. His mind was going perhaps; you know what I mean.'

David leaned back and smiled, 'yes, I think I do. Well, I'd better get going... I have to...'

He was interrupted by the doorbell.

'That will be Justin, my friend. You won't stay for a while?'

'No... I...'

I greeted Justin with a kiss at the door and introduced the two men as he came into the living room. They shook hands and Justin smiled, saying in a friendly way, 'Oh, you're Sarah's cousin, aren't you? From the funeral? You're a long way from home, aren't you? Down here on business or social?'

'Oh, well... kind of both. Just thought I'd drop in as I was passing. Sarah, I'll give you a ring. I've got your number...'

'Have you? Oh, sure. Yes, that would be lovely.'

'We could meet for coffee sometime.'

'Are you sure you won't stay?'

'No. Best be going.'

We kissed each other on the cheeks, and I watched him run down the three front steps and get into his car. He did have an attractive litheness about him, but I couldn't quite make up my mind about him.

Justin was sitting on the sofa and had picked up a magazine. Without looking up he said, 'He's not your type, really, is he?'

God, how I hated people making assumptions about me. I have to admit, after my disastrous audition, and missing out on my bath, I was feeling a little cranky. Justin's remark just wound me up further, and I did not reply.

Justin put the magazine down.

'So, how did your audition go, darling?'

'Best not to ask.'

'That bad? I am sorry, sweetheart. Do you need a hug?'

'I think I need some alcohol.' I opened the drinks cabinet and took out the only bottle of wine there. 'Here, open that will you?'

I handed him a bottle of Sauvignon and the corkscrew, and sat down on the other end of the sofa, watching him pop the cork and pour out two glasses.

I was still feeling pissed off, and I was looking to let off steam.

'So, you don't like my cousin, then?'

He had his glass at his mouth, but he paused for a moment and put the glass down.

'That's not quite what I said. I just said he didn't seem your type.'

'Seems everyone is deciding things for me today. He said I didn't seem the type to go grubbing around dusty record offices. Funny thing is, *he* was right.'

'It was just a remark, Sarah. I didn't mean to... I just felt...' he stopped.

'What?'

'Well, all right, if you have to ask, I know he's your cousin and everything, but no, I didn't like him.'

'For God's sake, you only met him for a few seconds!'

'I'm just being honest. I get feelings like that about people sometimes. There's something about him. I can't explain it. And I think he's homophobic anyway.'

'Oh, come off it! He doesn't even know you're gay, how could you possibly...?'

'Er, don't you think the earring, the moustache and the Pink Pride t-shirt is a bit of a give-away?'

'Well, I don't see how you could make that assumption within a few seconds.'

'He took my hand as if he'd just been handed a piece of rotting meat. There was distaste in his eyes.'

I looked away. Justin was over-sensitive, and he was exaggerating. All gays were over-sensitive these days. You could hardly blame them: the AIDS crisis had produced a lot of homophobic reactions. But David was my cousin and my new friend, and I was damned if I was going to let Justin spoil everything.

There was a long, uncomfortable silence.

'Did you look for the box yet?'

'No.'

Another silence.

'Seen anything of Graham again?'

'A little.'

The doorbell rang.

I let Greta in, who entered along with a chilly March wind, both hands full with carrier bags and her usual waft of patchouli.

In the living room she stopped.

'Oy vey, what is the matter? The atmosphere in here is so heavy! What's with you two, huh?'

Justin stood up.

'Sarah, has your loft got a ladder?'

'Why?'

'Just tell me.'

'Yes, but... you're not going to...'

'Yes I am. Where's the hatch?'

I told him, saying, 'you won't find anything,' but Justin said nothing and disappeared up the stairs.

Greta, muttering something under her breath that sounded pure Yiddish, took the bags into the kitchen and started unloading. I took her a glass of wine.

'What's the matter, liebling?'

I sat on a bar stool and told her what had happened, starting with the audition, while Greta rattled pots and pans, preparing us all a meal. When I'd finished, Greta stirred the contents of a saucepan thoughtfully.

'Well, it sounds like it was a bad day, but I've seen worse. I haven't met your cousin, so I can't comment, but I'll ask you this: how long have you known Justin?'

I thought back to my school days. Justin and I had met on the playground in the first year of secondary school, and I'd become his protector when some of the rougher kids had bullied him, teasing him because he was no good at football. I liked him because he loved music and art classes like I did. We both joined the school's drama group in the sixth form, which used to meet and rehearse after school hours, Justin designing sets and lighting and playing small parts. I was always playing the lead or main roles. My Lady Macbeth had got such good reviews in the school paper that my drama teacher had suggested acting as a career, and it hadn't taken much to persuade me. I was hooked.

After we left school, I managed to get a place at the Guildhall School of Performing Arts to train as an actress, and Justin went to Goldsmiths to study design. But we had always kept in touch and once we'd finished our training, we'd been able to meet up more and spend time together. Justin was now working as a buyer for Heal's Department store, and when I had spent a season doing the Edinburgh Festival with a small fringe company, I had met Greta, who was doing costume design. Dark, plump, and with a waft of the hippy about her, Greta lived with her aging orthodox Jewish parents in Golder's Green. Her heritage was always more pronounced when she had just been with them, but eased off after a few hours of being with us gentiles. Greta felt she owed it to her parents, who had suffered at the hands of the Nazis, to conform to tradition at home, but did not think of herself as truly orthodox.

'You know I've known Justin since I was 12,' I said, 'we met at school. We did drama together.'

'Well, it's not for me to say, but out of the two of them, I know which one I'd trust first. I'm not saying this cousin of yours is bad, but... well, Justin is just looking out for you, you know. He's very protective of you.'

I sighed. She was right. We'd always looked after each other.

'I know, I know. But I'm 25 and I really think I'm capable of looking after myself, and I should be able to choose who I spend time with.'

Greta threw her hands in the air.

'Who's stopping you? Anyway, I'm not saying any more. It's not for me to say. I'm sure it will sort itself out. Now, go and sit. Put your feet up.'

I wandered back into the living room and put a Barbra Streisand cassette into the cassette player. I sat down on the sofa, put my feet on the coffee table and shut my eyes, letting Barbra's smooth, soothing, rich voice wash over me as she sang the romantic lines of 'Guilty' with Barry Gibb. Nothing could ease my frazzled mind like Barbra.

It was a few minutes later when I felt a movement by my side. Something was placed on the table by my feet, and I felt the sofa sink next to me as Justin sat down.

I opened my eyes.

Next to my feet was a wooden box, about ten inches by five and four inches high. It was made from rosewood and was decorated on top by an inset of a coloured, but faded posy of flowers. On the front was a small lock, and inside the lock was a small, tarnished brass key.

I stared at it and blinked.

The song on the cassette finished, and before it moved to the next track, I got up and turned down the volume. I sat down again in front of the box and moved my fingers over the surface.

I looked at Justin and he looked at me.

'How do you know it's the right box?' I asked.

'Well, contrary to what we thought, there were not that many boxes up there that could be of any significance. Mainly cardboard boxes, old toys and bits of broken furniture. And spiders.' He brushed a few cobwebs off his arms. 'Oh, yes. And it was tied up in a plastic bag with a label on it saying 'Turvey box. My powers of deduction are legendary.'

I smiled. 'I'm sorry about before,' I said.

'Oh, don't worry. You've had a bad day. Sorry I spoke out of hand.' He pointed to the box. 'What do you think?'

'It's old,' I said, leaning over it.

'Typical Victorian,' said Justin.

I turned to look at him.

'Have you...?'

'No. I thought I'd leave you to do that. It's your legacy after all. I checked that the key works, the rest is up to you.'

'It's probably empty.'

'No. There's something in it. I gave it a little shake.'

I turned back to the box. Slowly, I put my hand on the key and gave it a turn. It yielded with a small click. We both leaned forward, and I slowly lifted the lid, my heart beating a little faster, which was surprising, considering I had not thought myself to be interested.

Inside were some folded pieces of paper, a roll of paper, creased at the edges where it had been tightly packed into the box, and at the bottom, what looked like a small book.

Justin got out a handkerchief and quickly dusted the coffee table and moved our wine glasses so I could lay the items out on it without damaging them.

I took out the papers one by one. They were of varying

28

sizes, from the scroll of paper, to a folded-up letter, and to the smallest, no more than a small scrap. The last two items were the book, which was a small, leather-bound book of the poetry of Shelley, and another piece of paper folded around something small and hard. Altogether there were seven items.

Justin picked up the small scrap of paper and studied it while I picked up the scroll.

'Good heavens!' he said.

'What?'

'It's a ticket stub.'

'A ticket stub? For what?'

Justin glanced at me.

'Drury Lane Theatre. The fifteenth of June 1851. The play is something called *The Queen of Spades.*'

'What...? You're kidding me...'

A theatrical connection from before my generation? I leaned over and took it from him, putting the scroll down on the table, where it quickly rolled itself up again.

'The theatre! What on earth...'

Justin picked up the scroll and unrolled it.

'But look at this! More theatrical stuff, Sarah. It's a poster, I think. Not Drury Lane this time but...'

I put down the ticket stub and turned to what he was looking at.

It was a long, yellowing piece of paper, about ten inches by two and a half feet. In large, bold letters at the top was written 'New Theatre', then in slightly smaller letters:

'On Monday Evening November 2nd, 1845, will be performed Shakespeare's Celebrated Comedy of...'

and then in very large, black letters:

'AS YOU LIKE IT, or What You Will'

Underneath there was a cast list, then more descriptions of the events of the evening: Dancing, comic songs, and the names of people who were going to perform them, followed by another name of a play:

MURDER IN THE RED BARN!

Again this was followed by a cast list. At the bottom were details on where to buy tickets, prices of tickets and other nights of performances.

I checked the date again. 'All this on one night?' I exclaimed.

'Poor Shakespeare must have been cut to shreds,' remarked Justin. Then he looked closer. 'Hey, I know where that is. That town is quite near where my parents live. I don't remember there being a theatre there though.'

He picked up another piece of paper.

'This looks like a kind of bill of fare from an inn called the Old Red Lion. Nothing theatrical this time, but it's a bit odd. It lists a pigeon pie and a strawberry tart, two pints of ale, two breakfasts and *midwifery* services, and then it says, 'Paid in Kind'! I know that pubs did all kinds of things, but childbirth?'

'How weird. Does it give a date?' I asked.

'Oh yes, at the top in the corner. Eleventh of July 1828. What are the other things?'

'A scrap of newspaper. Must be something significant... oh yes! Look! It's a review of a play. Theatre again! It mentions someone called Eliza Jayne: "Eliza Jayne is delightful as Lady

Teazle in *The School for Scandal...*'

'Eliza Jayne? Wait a minute...' Justin picked up the poster again. 'Look; there's an Eliza Jayne on the cast list of *As You Like It.* Played Rosalind, the lead role. Anything else with her name on?'

'Let's look at this.' I was fully engaged now, and I unfolded the letter as fast as I could without damaging it. 'Blimey, how can you read this?'

It was a letter, but the lines were written both across the page and vertically from top to bottom.

'Ah, yes,' said Justin, 'I've come across this before. If people were short of paper they'd write up and down the page after they'd used up all the space writing across. They can usually be deciphered with a bit of patience. Who is it addressed to?'

'Well, well, well! It starts, "My dearest Eliza".'

'From?'

I scanned down to the end of the letter.

'Someone called Bertie. Do you think that these things belonged to this person called Eliza Jayne? And what have they to do with my family? There's no mention of the name of Turvey so far.'

'Good question,' said Justin, picking up the poetry book. 'This has been well thumbed,' he said, opening the first page. 'Oh, look here: "To my dearest Eliza, from her Bertie. March 1849. Hail to thee, blithe spirit." That's a quote from Shelley isn't it? "Ode to a Skylark", I think.'

I looked at all the papers laid out on the table, and my eye fell on the paper that was wrapped around something. I picked it up, and as I did so, it unravelled, and something fell onto the table with a metallic ring. We both looked down.

A chill ran down the back of my neck, and I gasped.

31

'Another key!' said Justin, picking it up, but then I saw him turn to me, seeing the look on my face, my hand over my mouth.

'What on earth is the matter?'

Slowly, I took the key from his hand and turned it over and over. It felt cold, yet its significance seemed to be burning my skin. I moved my fingers over its triple-ringed bow. I felt slightly sick.

'It can't be.'

'Sarah?'

'It... it's the key; the key from my dream.'

Justin turned the key over in his hands. We had had dinner, and were now sitting again in front of the fire, each with a glass of wine. In front of us was the box with its contents laid out on the table.

'Are you absolutely sure this is the same key as the one in your dream?'

'I know it is. Not just because it's the same pattern and everything, but I just know it.'

'And... you say you've had the dream before?'

'Yes, but I'd never seen the key before until that night.'

We were all silent for a moment, Greta and I both leaning to look at the key in Justin's hands.

'It's very old,' he said, 'and pewter. I'm no expert, but I'd say this is Tudor... or Jacobean at the latest.' Justin had done some courses on history of design, and browsing antique shops was one of his favourite pastimes. 'It's rather beautiful. Not your everyday box key, I'd say. Are you sure you haven't seen it before - perhaps when you were young - and your dream has just dredged it up from memory? Perhaps your Dad showed it to you when you were a kid?'

I shook my head. 'I'm absolutely sure I've never seen it before, or anything else in the box. What do you think it means?' I was still feeling a little shaken.

Greta gave a little shiver.

'Someone is trying to tell you something,' she said.

'But who? And what? I don't really believe in spirits and stuff, but... I just can't explain it. And what about all the other stuff in the box, all the Victorian stuff? How are they connected? What does it all mean?' I huddled close to the fire. The whole thing was now making me feel a bit shivery.

'I don't know, but it's intriguing isn't it? Let's lay them all out in date order,' said Justin, 'and see exactly what we have.'

He laid out everything on the coffee table, starting with the pewter key. I got up and found a pen and paper from a drawer, and I wrote the following:

$16^{th}/17^{th}$ century? Pewter key
   1828 The Old Red Lion bill
   1845 New Theatre poster
   1848 Newspaper review
   1849 Poetry book – Shelley
   1850 Letter from 'Bertie'
   1851 Drury Lane Ticket stub

'What does that tell us?' said Justin.

'Well, the last five items all seem to be to do with this Eliza person, and I'm not sure how the inn bill fits in. The key is something else entirely. The inn bill is odd.' I picked it up and looked at it. 'Midwifery services. Someone was obviously born there. Do you think this is where Eliza was born?'

'Could be, Sherlock.'

'But why nothing after 1851? If she was the one born in 1828, she would be... 23. Why is there nothing else? And who is she anyway? What has she got to do with me? I don't understand.'

' I like the name Eliza', said Greta, 'isn't it short for Elizabeth?'

'Yes, of course... of course it is...'

Something clicked in my memory, and Justin and I looked at each other.

'Do you think...?'

'There was an Elizabeth on the tree,' said Justin, 'the one with no details. Elizabeth is a common name, so it could be coincidence, but... What was the date of the marriage? Sometime in the 1850s wasn't it? That would be after all these theatre dates, but it would fit in with her age, if she was born in 1828.'

'Now who's playing Sherlock? My God, Justin, if you're right, that means that I do have an ancestor who was in the theatre! It's in the blood after all! I knew I must have got it from somewhere. Let's get the tree out again!'

Justin looked at me and grinned.

'Oh, all right,' I said, 'I'm interested now... You were right. It is more interesting than I thought.'

CHAPTER 3

'Hi, David. It's Sarah here. Just thought I'd ring you and see how you are. Thought you'd be interested to know that I discovered something about one of our ancestors. Looks like I might be looking into those dusty record offices after all! Anyway, I hope you are well, and got back OK after your trip to London. Hope to speak to you soon. Bye.'

I hated answerphones, and leaving messages always felt cold and formal, and if you tried to make a joke or be more relaxed, it always sounded stupid and like you were trying too hard, and then you'd be cringing, knowing you couldn't change it and the person would think you were a complete idiot.

But they were a necessary part of life; well, my life anyway – the life of an actress. They were a complete godsend. It was no longer necessary to hover over the telephone, scared of going out in case your agent rang to tell you you'd got an audition for a part in some West End play.

After some hesitation, the reason for which I could not fathom, I had decided to ring David to tell him about the discovery about Elizabeth because I thought it only right, him being descended from her as well. I wasn't really sure he would be that interested. Something stopped me from mentioning the key and the dream. That part of it just sounded too loopy, and I didn't want him to think I was deluded.

Or, had I just wanted some excuse to ring him and... what? I wasn't sure of my feelings about him. It was nice to have a new person in my life, and if there was some attraction there, that would be a bonus. And why had he just turned up that day if he wasn't interested in me? OK, we were family, but only distantly... really. Who would call on a second cousin out of the blue unless they had some interest other than family?

He was quite attractive, in a kind of pale, off-key kind of way. Certainly more appealing than anyone I'd met recently. And the last time I had been in any kind of serious relationship was far too long ago. At least five months. He was an actor I'd met in a low paid fringe play a year ago and I had really thought the relationship might become serious. I had allowed myself the luxury of imagining a permanent arrangement. Then he had got a repertory theatre job in Bristol and I never heard from him again. No letter, no phone calls. Nothing. After leaving several messages for him that were not replied to, I realised that he had used the job as a way of breaking up with me without actually having to do the deed. I'd been humiliated and deeply upset for weeks. I was both hurt and angry with myself for not having seen the signs. Until I came to my senses and realised what a terrible cowardly bastard he had been, and I'd had a lucky escape. So much for actors.

It was about time I had someone new in my life, and the fact that David wasn't involved in the theatre was perhaps in his favour after all. Actors, even the nicest ones, could be unreliable. Far too many of my friends in the business had been in relationships that had not survived the necessities of being apart for lengthy periods of time, especially long runs where you were forced to work closely with other, often extremely attractive, actors and actresses. Jealousies and affairs were common, but even if your partner was faithful, it needed a lot of strength to ride the financial ups and downs of being in and out of work.

So a relationship with someone not involved in the theatre could be an advantage. But there was a niggle at the back of my mind. What Justin had said had annoyed me, and I was still sure he was wrong. He was just being paranoid. And yet, and yet...

I wouldn't mention David to him again, though it would be a bit awkward if I started going out with him. Still, maybe Justin would change his mind if he got to know him...

I sighed. I grudgingly admitted that a small part of me was jealous that Justin had someone new in his life, even if he was in denial about it. I was sure that he was seeing this guy, Graham, more than he was letting on. I was pleased for him, if this was the case, but it put my own sense of loneliness into sharp focus.

I needed to think about something else.

I picked up the small card that Justin had given me in The Flask last night when we had met for a couple of beers. It had a picture of a tree on it and a woman's name: *Georgina Hall, Professional Genealogist.* She had some letters after her name, which looked impressive, and I hoped she wasn't going to be too expensive. I picked up the phone again, and dialled the number on the card.

Another answerphone.

'Is everyone out doing exciting things except me?' I said out loud, before the woman's voice announced her name and request for the caller to leave a message.

'Oh, hi. My name's Sarah Turvey, and I was given your

number by Justin Lacey. I am interested in finding out about someone in my family tree, and I wonder if you could ring me....'

April had arrived with fickle promises of warmer days and then had turned cold and wet. All the same, I could not help smiling when I looked out of my window to see cherry blossoms beginning to come into flower down the street, and daffodils providing a cheery boundary to the edge of the Heath. And yet, I could not shake off a feeling of sadness. Spring was here, people were out and about, doing things, having a purpose. Even nature itself knew what it was up to and where it was going. I could not help feeling that things were moving forward without me. My life was stuck; a monotonous routine of writing letters, ringing my agent, preparing auditions, occasionally going to an audition and then the disappointment of the rejection letter.

Unlike other actors I knew, I was lucky enough not to have to pay rent or a mortgage, so I had avoided the need for a full-time job or being dependent on unemployment benefit. But I did need to eat and pay bills, so I spent three lunchtimes and two evenings a week waitressing at a local trendy wine bar/restaurant. I dreaded Saturday nights, when, after a whirlwind night of serving ungrateful, demanding customers, I would walk home on aching feet, desperate just to fall into my bed and slope off into oblivion.

It was on such a Saturday night that I arrived home at midnight, even more exhausted than usual. There had been a birthday party at the wine bar, and the group had been particularly rowdy, ordering never-ending rounds of wine bottles, burgers and cheesecakes. I'd had to clean up two lots

38

of broken glass, and I stank of red wine. I could not wait to get out of my clothes and sink into the peaceful sanctuary of duvet and pillows.

The first thing I noticed when I got through the door was the answerphone winking continuously, telling me of several phone calls. For a split second, I toyed with the idea of ignoring them, but I could not help wondering whether it might be my agent; though why she would be ringing on a Saturday, I could not imagine. All the same, best to be sure.

Justin's voice was shaking, and he sounded on the verge of tears.

'Sarah, something terrible has happened. I'm at the Whittington Hospital at Highgate. It's Graham, the guy I've been seeing. He... he's been beaten up by thugs. He's in Emergency. Please come. I don't think I can bear it on my own if... Oh God, please come as soon as you can.'

I didn't wait to hear the other messages. Grabbing the jacket I had just thrown onto a chair, I ran back out of the front door, mentally checking I'd got an *A to Z* in the car.

After nearly ripping the pages trying to find the right place, I was glad to see it was a straightforward drive round the top of the heath.

I drove dangerously fast, screeching the brakes at several corners and shouting abuse at traffic lights.

I had not met Graham, but I had noticed that Justin had been in a particularly good mood lately, and I knew that things were going well with this new man in his life.

A few days ago, I had broached the subject again, casually asking whether he'd seen Graham lately.

'Yeah, a few times.'

'And...?'

39

Justin had looked thoughtful for a few seconds.

'He's nice. Not my usual type; more flamboyant and camper than I usually like, but he's sensitive too. Probably too sensitive. I just don't know. It probably won't last. I'm not sure we're right for each other. I'm not sure I want to get into anything right now, and the trouble is, I think he's more into this relationship than I am, and I don't want to hurt his feelings. So, I'm trying to keep a distance.'

As I turned into the car park of the hospital, I remembered these words, and then thought of Justin's voice on the answer-phone just now.

'"Keep a distance", my arse!' I said, 'Justin, my friend, I think you are more into this guy than you're letting on!'

I was angry too, at the mindless bullies that had attacked Graham.

'Such ignorance,' was all I could think, 'such stupid, narrow-minded pig-ignorance.'

Thankfully, the traffic wasn't too bad at this time of night and the hospital was well sign-posted, so fifteen minutes after leaving the house, I swerved into the hospital car park. I parked, paid the extortionate parking fee and ran to the main entrance.

Justin looked pale but calm when I saw him in the Casualty waiting room. I rushed towards him and he threw his arms around me.

'Darling, thank you so much for coming. Sorry about all the messages – I was distraught. I forgot you work on Saturdays.'

'I only got one – I didn't wait to listen to the rest. How is he? Is he going to be...?'

'Yes, he's going to be all right. They were worried he might have internal bleeding, but he's just got lots of bruises and of course he's going to be really shaken up for a while. But he'll be fine – they're just going to keep him overnight to be on the safe side, but he'll be home tomorrow.'

'Oh, thank God! I'm so relieved, Justin.'

A few seats away I noticed a couple in their 50s looking towards us, and then quickly looking away when I saw them.

Justin leaned over and whispered in my ear.

'Graham's parents. He told me that they're not happy about him being gay, and they've been looking daggers at me all evening. They probably think that somehow it's all my fault.'

I sighed and squeezed his hand.

'Well, that doesn't make things easier, does it?'

'Tell me about it. I've only been able to find out what's going on by earwigging, and nabbing the occasional nurse going by.'

'Well, at least you know he'll be OK. How did you find out, I mean about what happened?'

'After some passer-by called the ambulance, his parents were notified at first, being next of kin, of course. But when he got to the hospital, he revived enough to ask them to call me.'

We sat down on two plastic red seats.

'Tell me what happened, or do you know? Have the police been called?'

'Ye-es, but I doubt they'll do anything. It was a queer-bashing, without a doubt. The police are just not interested. They'll do the paperwork, and that's it. They'd be more likely to arrest Graham for cruising; poor sod was only walking home from work. I've warned him about walking home through that park at night. I've been there, and there's loads of anti-gay graffiti around, but what can you do?'

I looked at his face, so tense with worry.

'You're really into this guy, aren't you?'

He gave me a wry smile.

41

'Against my better judgment. He's kind of grown on me, and there's nothing like a drama to make you get clear about your feelings!'

I looked back at Graham's parents, who also looked tense and anxious, but refusing to acknowledge Justin's presence. It made me feel profoundly sad.

I turned back to Justin.

'So what will happen? Will he go and stay at his parents for a while? I suppose he'll need a bit of looking after?'

'If I know him at all, he'll probably refuse to stay with his parents.'

'Could he stay with you?'

I felt him stiffen slightly.

'I... it might be too soon to... Oh, I don't know Sarah. You know, I wasn't looking for a serious relationship. I don't want to... I might see if I can go and stay with him at his flat. You know, make sure he's comfortable and he eats properly.'

I smiled. He was hooked, but he still didn't know it.

'Can I get you some coffee?'

He laughed.

'If I have one more coffee, I'll be climbing the walls. It's pretty revolting anyway. No, darling, but, listen. Can I ask you a favour?'

'Of course. Anything.'

'I'm going to wait a while longer, just to see if there's any more news, and then I might as well go. They won't let me see him 'cos I'm not family. I was wondering if I could kip at your place tonight? I think I need the company. Stupid, I know, but the whole thing has left me feeling a bit shaken.'

'Of course you can, darling, and it's not stupid at all. I'll give you a lift into the hospital tomorrow, and if he's going back to his place, I could take you both in the car if you like. That will save you a taxi.'

'You're an angel. I don't know what I'd do without you.'

It wasn't until the next morning that I listened to the rest of the phone messages.

After we had arrived home the night before, we had both felt the need of a strong drink and had had two large whiskies each before I found I couldn't keep my eyes open any longer, and I just managed to make up the spare bed for Justin before crashing into my own.

So it was only the next day, as we were getting ready to go back to the hospital that I remembered I had not listened to the rest of the messages, so I played them while Justin washed up the breakfast things.

Most of the messages had been from Justin asking me to come to the hospital as soon as I could, the last two with tangible relief in his voice as he knew the danger was over.

There was also a phone call from a woman with a very educated, middle-aged voice, and for a few moments I couldn't think what she was talking about, everything having been forgotten with the events of the last few hours.

'Yes, this is a message for Miss – or is it Mrs? – Turvey. I would be interested in the work you suggest. I charge £6 per hour plus expenses, and I will need a little more information in order to begin the research. I wonder if you would kindly call me again at around 6 o'clock and we can discuss the details. Thank you so much. Goodbye.'

Oh, of course. The genealogist. I immediately wondered if I could afford £6 per hour, and just how many hours would be needed, and what the expenses would be. Justin would be

43

interested, but it wasn't the time to talk about it now. I would ring her another time and tell Justin later.

There was one last message.

'Sarah? Hello. It's David. Turvey. I got your message.'

Brief silence.

'I hate these machines.'

Pause.

'So, you're looking into the family tree after all? Just wondering what you found out. Sounds interesting. Er... yeah, I'd like to know what you're up to. We must try and arrange something... Anyway... Cheerio.'

I smiled, and then quickly turned the machine off as Justin appeared.

'Ready?' I asked.

'As I'll ever be. Any interesting calls?'

'Not really. Oh, that genealogist you told me about. But we'll talk about that another time.'

Justin gave me a quick smile.

'Let's go.'

It seemed unfair to meet someone for the first time when their face was all bruised and swollen. Graham tried to smile at me, but it was obviously painful.

'Justin's told me all about you,' he said.

'All?' I said, with a quizzical smile.

'Well... all the decent stuff. I'm sure I'll get to hear the indecent stuff sooner or later.'

Although he was speaking without smiling, he made me laugh, and I instantly warmed to him.

But despite his obvious sense of humour, he looked grim. It wasn't just the bruises, the red, swollen eye and the bandage round his sprained wrist. He looked shell-shocked; haunted.

I noticed that his parents were no longer around to see him leave the hospital.

I watched them both in my rear-view mirror as they got into the back of the car. Graham was quiet and thoughtful, and I had the feeling this was a little out of character. Justin looked pale and tight-lipped.

We drove mainly in silence.

Sitting at a red traffic light, I glanced in the mirror. Graham was leaning on Justin's shoulder and they were both gazing out of the same window with their own thoughts. Or the same thoughts? Was there some silent communication going on?

I felt a pang of envy.

How wonderful to have someone's shoulder to lean on, to have someone to support you and look after you when things go wrong. Especially, when you couldn't rely on your parents...

I looked back at the traffic lights. They were changing to amber and green, but looked slightly misty.

I cleared my throat and blinked. The mist cleared and I drove on.

Graham lived just south of the river, in a flat in Lambeth. I dropped them off outside the sixties block, and Justin squeezed my hand through the window.

'Thanks darling. I'll ring you later, OK? Take care, doll.'

When I got home, I felt flat and depressed. The house was cold and empty, and I was vaguely disturbed and out of love with the world. I telephoned Greta, hoping that she might be able to meet later and talk and drink too much.

'Oh, Sarah, is everything OK? Justin rang me from the

hospital. I was so sorry about what happened; such a terrible thing. I would have come but my mother has the 'flu, and I cannot leave her.'

So much for an indulgent evening.

'Oh, I am sorry, Greta. I hope she's better soon.'

I told Greta about the hospital visit and taking them both back to Lambeth, and my impressions of Graham, and Justin's feeling about him. We spoke for a while but there was no point in trying to arrange anything.

I idled round the house aimlessly, wandering into my parents' old bedroom, touching the furniture lightly with my fingers, and opening the wardrobe to brush my hands through my mother's old dresses. I should have got rid of them by now, but I had never been able to bring myself to throw them out. I buried my nose in a camel coat and breathed in the faint, but still recognisable smell of Blue Grass. It had almost faded completely, and very soon it would disappear for good.

It was the same with my father's tweed jacket. It still had a slight cigar smell, and a whisper of the aftershave that my mother had always bought him for Christmas. A wonderful, comforting smell that was almost gone.

I shivered.

Looking out of the window, I saw daffodils bordering the lawn, blossom on the old apple tree. It was a pretty sight, but the lawn would need mowing soon, and somehow my depression deepened. I pressed my forehead against the cold glass. I felt tearful, yet no tears would come.

I went downstairs to make a cup of tea, and as I moved through the living-room I remembered the box and the large sheet of paper in the drawer of the old dresser.

Forgetting my tea, I opened the drawer and took out the

box. I sat down at the dining table, opened it and withdrew the contents. I looked at each little item, wondering what it all meant and how it related to me. Lastly, I picked up the pewter key and rolled it round in my hand, the dream coming back to me in all its clarity at its touch. It had a pleasing heaviness, and it sent shivers down my spine to think how old it was. What did it open? A box? Some ancient chest? Probably something that no longer existed, but it was a lovely, well-made key, satisfying to look at and to hold. I had not dreamed again since that night, and I wondered whether I would again.

I read through all the Victorian papers again, except for the cross-letter, which I could not begin to decipher.

'Eliza Jayne. Who are you?' I whispered.

Two minutes later I was on the telephone.

'Mrs Hall? It's Sarah Turvey here. I wonder if you would like to meet so we could discuss my possible ancestor? I have some documents you might find interesting.'

CHAPTER 4

July 1828

The afternoon sun blazed down on the dusty track and caused the man to stop and wipe the sweat from his face. The horse he was leading softly whinnied and hung his head. He patted his neck.

'Not far now, Shadow. There'll be water soon.'

From the cart came a woman's low moan of pain.

'George? Where are we? It's getting worse…'

'Not far now, love. Hold on; we'll be there soon.'

Heat rose from the ground along with the intense, warm, green smell of nettle and meadow grass.

A few more steps and he saw the wall of a house at the end of the lane. A few more, and on his left, he could see farm buildings set back from the lane. It was no good stopping there. He knew the place they had to stop.

'The Red Lion is your best place,' Old Henry had said after George's wife had announced that the baby was starting early. 'The landlord there is all right, if you make it worth his while. Better than having the little'un on the road, being the first one and all. You never know when you might need a physic. In this heat, you need somewhere cool where you can get fresh water.'

'What about tonight?' George had said.

'Don't worry, we'll cover. We'll cut your song and Helen can do the dance she's been rehearsing. As for the play, Harry's been learning your part and should be good enough to step in. We'll expect you for rehearsals in the morning, mind. Take Shadow and the small cart; Sarah won't be able to walk the two miles, and the stabling there is the best in the area.'

They were approaching the centre of the village, and as he turned the cart round a bend, he saw the small village green and next to it, the sign of the Old Red Lion. Some children were playing tag on the green and as he approached, they stopped what they were doing and stood staring at him and the horse and cart.

The cart was painted brightly with theatrical masks, musical instruments and colourful curlicues, and across the centre was written the words: *Henry Holland's Travelling Theatre Company.*

George supposed that the children would not be able to read the words, but they did seem fascinated by the colourful decorations. A couple of old men sitting outside of the inn, smoking pipes, also seemed intrigued by this strange appearance, and also probably could not read, but would be able to guess at his profession, and they viewed George and his cart with more suspicion than the children did. One turned to the other and said something in his ear, and they both grinned and sniggered.

George nodded towards them, and they looked uncomfortable, looking away and pretending they hadn't seen him. George smiled to himself. He was used to such reactions.

Inside the inn, he approached the innkeeper, a large red-cheeked man, who had obviously seen his approach from the window, and probably could read, and looked him up and down with a look of distaste as he cleaned a tankard with a cloth.

George took his cap off.

'Good day to you, sir. I hope it would not be too much of an inconvenience to you if I should ask for a room and some assistance for myself and my good wife, who is at this moment in labour with our first child.'

The landlord showed no surprise at this piece of information, and did not reply to George's speech, only looked at him for a few moments, continuing with his cleaning, and then turned around and called out: 'Lizzie!'

A woman of equal proportions to her husband appeared from a doorway and looked George up and down just as he had done.

George made the same appeal, and the innkeeper and his wife looked at each other briefly, and then he nodded. She turned to George.

'Well, you had better bring her in. I will get water and linen. Is she strong?'

'Oh, as strong as they come,' George replied.

Her face twitched. 'She should be all right, then. Best get her up the stairs.'

Between them they managed to help Sarah out of the cart, whilst the children on the green looked on with wide eyes.

'Meg,' said Lizzie the landlord's wife to the oldest girl, 'run up to Betty Ballard's and see if she can come quickly. If not, knock on Martha Brown's door. Then come back and help your Da with serving.' She turned to George, 'Betty's the local midwife, but Martha will serve well enough if she's not free. They'll expect some compensation, though.'

George nodded. 'Of course.'

'My horse needs water,' he said, after they had seen Sarah safely upstairs.

'It will be taken care of,' said the landlord, 'we provide good stabling here.'

'So I've been told,' said George.

He sat in a dark corner of the bar, going over his lines for the new play they would be showing in a few days, *Luke the Labourer*, in which he was to play the eponymous villain. There were not many people in the bar, it being late afternoon and the labourers being all out in the fields, but there were a few elderly men and women who came in to pass the time, drink ale and make conversation. They occasionally cast odd glances at George as he sat there, mouthing his lines, but he just winked and nodded back, and they would quickly turn away and exchange glances with each other instead. Shortly after he sat down, a portly woman came bustling through carrying a large bag, closely followed by Meg, who joined her father behind the bar. The landlord greeted the woman as Betty, had a few words with her, and they both turned to George. She gave him a cursory nod, being the husband and of little importance to her, and then headed up the stairs, panting and wheezing at the effort. George felt a sense of relief that Sarah would be attended by a local midwife as well as the landlord's wife.

It seemed very strange to George to be able to sit for a while and do nothing but go over his lines. On any normal day, when the company was not walking from town to town, he would be rehearsing with the other actors, perhaps practising or choreographing a sword fight or a comic dance. At other times he might find himself painting scenery, and if it was his benefit night, he might be out selling and advertising tickets to be sure of a good house. Every night there would be several performances: a new play, perhaps a Shakespeare piece, and several songs and dances and comic turns. And on top of all this

51

there would always be lines to learn. It was hard, sometimes, to keep up with all that needed doing, and many a night he would sit up in bed trying to cram in the lines he had to remember for the next evening's performances, while his wife sat up mending a tear in his breeches and learning her own lines at the same time. With a small grin, he thought it was a wonder they had had time to make a child at all.

It was hard work being an actor. Yet he would not trade it in for any other job in the world. Yes, it was physically exhausting, but the work of the agricultural labourer was even more so, and did not have the mental challenge that was involved in learning a part and portraying a character. The work was varied and interesting, unlike that of the tradesman who might do the same thing every day of his life.

Although the licensing of players towards the end of the last century had made the actor's life a more respectable one in the eyes of the law, it was not unusual for all 'theatricals' to be viewed with suspicion and distrust. The label of 'rogue and vagabond' was still attached in many people's minds to the strolling player. George looked up at the scowling faces across the bar, and then thought of all the labourers that would soon be coming in for their tankard of ale to refresh them after the day's work under the hot, parching sun. Then he smiled to himself.

Finishing his own tankard, he walked out of the bar and round to the stables. He stopped at Shadow's stable to give him a nuzzle and make sure he was being properly looked after. He was no ordinary horse, this. He was not just a cart horse; he appeared on stage many times, and had often times been responsible for reviving a flagging season as there was nothing that sold tickets like a live animal on stage. A theatrical horse like this had to be looked after properly.

Henry had been right about the quality of the stabling. Shadow had fresh hay and a full water bucket, and had been given a brush down by the groom. He patted his neck, and then walked over to the cart which had been stowed in a corner of the stable yard. The younger two of the landlord's children were there, fascinated by the patterns on the side, and one of them was standing on tiptoe, trying to peer underneath the canvas cover.

'Hey,' said George, softly, and the boy stepped away guiltily.

'I wasn't doing nothing, sir,' he said, 'just wanted to see inside.'

'I'll show you,' said George.

He undid the ties on the canvas, withdrew a large travelling carpet bag and laid it on the ground. The children stared at the bag. He opened it and took out a strangely shaped leather case that was covered in scratches and scuffs, which he also opened. The children's eyes widened when they saw the smooth wooden object that emerged. It had a long neck with strings of metal down the centre.

'What is it?' cried the young girl.

'It's a fiddle,' said George.

'What do you do with it?'

'This.' George took up a bow, put the fiddle under his chin, and stroked the bow across the strings, playing a jaunty little tune.

The children laughed and clapped their hands, and followed him back into the inn.

'Pa! Pa! He's got a fiddle! It makes music!'

The landlord was polishing another tankard.

'Whoa there! What's this now?'

George gestured to his instrument.

'Would you allow me to play a few tunes for a while? I'll stop if they don't like it.' He nodded towards the other patrons, who were trying not to look interested.

'Go on Pa! It's very good music!' said the girl.

'Well... I don't suppose it would do any harm,' he said, winking at his daughter, 'just for a while.'

George stood at the edge of the bar, and started to play an Irish jig. The children immediately joined hands and started dancing round and round.

George's hearing was sharp, and he could tell that the group of people in the bar had stopped talking. He glanced very quickly towards them and saw the old man who had been scowling at him before was trying to pretend he was not listening, and concentrating on drinking his ale, but underneath the table George saw that his foot had started to tap. The woman sitting next to him was looking towards him, and without smiling her head started to bob up and down, almost as if she was unaware she was doing it.

George smiled and played on, getting more and more vigorous, and playing faster and faster, until he ended with a swift upward swing of the bow, and the children fell on the floor, gasping.

George looked at the landlord, and was glad to see that he was smiling.

'Well, that was something,' he said, 'what else can you play?'

'Oh, many things. Songs and ballads and dances. Music to make you laugh, music to make you cry. Whatever mood takes you.'

'I prefer to laugh, myself,' said the landlord, 'but either way, people will buy more beer! Look, the workers are coming in.

Can you play something cheery and suited to the end of the day's work?'

'I certainly can,' said George, and raised his bow.

He played the old folk tune, 'John Barleycorn', an old Scottish song about the growing of barley, and the turning of it into beer.

As the men came in, dirty, sweaty and grim looking from the day's labour, they turned to look at him, surprised by the sound of music. They grinned at each other, slightly embarrassed at first, as they ordered their drinks, then downed their pints quickly to slake their thirst.

A few of them ignored him, and went over to the quieter end of the bar to sit and chew over the day's work. Most of them stayed near the bar to listen to the music.

And then one of them started to sing.

''Twill make a man forget his woe;
'Twill heighten all his joy;
'Twill make the widow's heart to sing,
Though the tear were in her eye.'

A few of them joined in for the last verse, raising their tankards, and laughing as the ballad came to an end. More beers were ordered, and George began again with 'Gaily the Troubadour', and a few who knew the song joined in again.

The inn began to fill up as more labourers came in, and those who lived nearby arriving to see what was going on, having heard the music. The landlord's children were all now either helping behind the bar, or serving patrons. Soon, the inn was alive with people. George played another Irish jig, and people started to lose their inhibitions and dance with each other, and laugh at each other as they danced. What would normally have been a normal, quiet evening became a village party, with people dancing and spilling out onto the village green, and small children running around between their legs. A few people even brought in their own instruments so the music could be heard outside as well as in.

It was late in the evening when the landlord's wife came into the bar and whispered into her husband's ear, and the landlord filled George's empty tankard up to the top with ale and said, 'Your wife has given birth to a healthy baby girl. This is on the house.'

A few people heard what he had said, and the news spread around the inn. Suddenly, people were shaking George's hand and wishing him well, and George beamed and blushed and thanked them.

The landlord beckoned him over.

'I've done more business tonight than I usually do in a week. Whatever you want to eat is yours. Whatever you want: mutton chops, pigeon pie, cold ham, and there is a strawberry tart if you wish. My wife makes the best strawberry tart in the county. I've never seen the place so lively. When you've been up to see your wife and babe, I will have it ready for you in the snug. And anything your wife wants too.'

George thanked him and ordered a pigeon pie and tart. Leaping two steps at a time up the stairs, he came into the little room where his daughter had just been born. Sarah smiled weakly at him from the bed, and beside her was a small bundle that fidgeted and grunted.

A small fist appeared from the blankets, and George peered down into a cross-looking, little scrunched up face.

'Eliza,' he said, taking her hand. The baby opened one eye

and squinted at him vaguely.

'Eliza?' said his wife. 'Not Elizabeth, after my mother?'

'It's still after your mother,' said George, 'but she'll be christened Eliza. It has a better sound. Eliza Jayne. It has a good ring. Perhaps she'll be a famous actress one day.'

He put his hand to his chest and felt the solid shape of the old key that hung round his neck. As often happened when he felt it, a small shiver went down his spine. One day, it would belong to this small child.

Sarah looked at her husband and nodded.

'You've been entertaining,' she said, 'I could hear the commotion. Did you do well, George? Was it a good house?'

'It was good, Sarah,' he said, 'the landlord's giving us free food and drink for the business it brought in. I'm so hungry I could eat three pigeon pies in one swallow, and a whole strawberry tart. What would you like, Sarah? Some cold ham? A pint of ale?'

Sarah sighed and laid back on the pillow.

'I think I would like a cup of tea,' she said, and promptly fell asleep.

CHAPTER 5

May 1985

'The baptism actually gives the date of birth, which is definitely the 11th July,' said Georgina Hall, 'but the baptism itself is on August 21st in Leamington. Eliza Jayne, daughter of George and Sarah Jayne, and his profession is given as "theatrical", and their abode, Warwick Street. This is definitely her.'

I looked at the photocopy of the baptism that Georgina had brought with her.

'Leamington? That's quite a way from where she was born...' I said, tentatively. I found Georgina Hall slightly intimidating. She was smartly turned out in a dress suit with shoulder pads, a chunky gold necklace (real gold), and dyed hair cut in a straight-cut bob. She had a demeanour of confident efficiency. I remembered what Justin had told me about her being a lawyer's wife.

'Yes, but I've done a little bit of research on the theatre at this time, and there was a theatre in Leamington in that period. If they were a theatrical family, they were probably part of a travelling company and would have been moving from place to place. It looks as though Eliza was born between venues.

Warwick Street is probably the place where they were staying at the time of the baptism, presumably in another inn. I found a book at the library on travelling theatre companies,' she added, with a sudden smile. I smiled back, instantly warming to her, despite my initial trepidation.

'Wow. That's amazing,' I said, rather impressed that she had carried out extra background research to work out how they would have lived and worked.

It was several weeks since I had met her, and she had told me that due to having several clients, it would be a few weeks before she could report back to me. Obviously, this genealogy stuff was a game of patience. We had now met up again in the first week of May.

'So what next? How do we find out whether she is the Elizabeth who married Edward Turvey?'

'Yes, we definitely need to prove she is the right Eliza before going further. Well, I'd normally search the marriage registers at St. Catherine's House, but you say your uncle already did that?'

'I think so; well, he says in his notes that it wasn't found, so I assume that's what he did.'

'Hm. Very strange. It could be that they were never married, but it seems unlikely in this case with all those children. Perhaps they weren't married in England. The census records that your uncle found for Edward and Eliza in 1861 and 1871 were a bit vague about Eliza's place of birth, and just say Gloucestershire, which certainly fits, but it's a shame it's not more specific. The couple were living in Clapham, so I could have a look for a marriage in the parish registers there, but they didn't necessarily marry in the same place they were living. Often, it was in the bride's parish, but if Eliza's early years

59

were so peripatetic, she probably didn't have a home parish as such.

'It says in the notes that their children were all born in Clapham.'

'Yes, but I'm not holding out much hope we'll find the marriage there. If it turned up in the registers, then why is it not in the civil registration indexes? And if they didn't marry in Clapham anyway, it's a real needle in a haystack.'

I swallowed. Because the baptism and birth were in different counties, Georgina had had to search several county indexes before she had found the baptism of Eliza Jayne, and then there were the expenses involved in obtaining a photocopy from the county record office, and I had just paid her a cheque that I couldn't really afford.

'Perhaps I should leave it for a while... I'm so sure it is her...'

Georgina gave a wry smile. 'Professionally, I wouldn't want to do any further research until we have documented evidence.'

Yes, definitely a lawyer's wife, I thought.

But why shouldn't I carry out some research on my own? I did have a bit of an opportunity. Last night Justin had rung to tell me that his parents were going overseas for a few weeks and he was going to be staying at their house in the country while they were away. He had been staying on and off with Graham, and 'in a mad moment', he said, had invited him to spend some time there with him. Graham was still on sick leave, and Justin had taken a couple of weeks off work, so it seemed like a good idea at the time, so when he asked me if I wanted to come and stay too, I had the feeling that he was feeling a little jittery about having asked Graham to stay so soon in their relationship, and needed someone to play gooseberry.

I had hesitated when he asked me, wondering whether I

should just leave them to get on with it and work out what they wanted from each other on their own. But during my meeting with Georgina, I remembered that Justin's parents lived very near to the town where the theatre poster was from and it might be fun to take a trip into the town and just have a look round.

'Can we leave it for a while?' I said to Georgina, 'I'm going away for a few days and I'll call you when I get back.'

'This is very civilized', I said, sipping a glass of chilled Frascati.

We were sitting on the patio of Justin's parents' well-kept back garden, on white wrought iron chairs. Bowls of olives, a home-made guacamole and wholemeal pitta bread sat on the table, also white, wrought iron, along with the almost empty bottle in a bucket of ice. A few steps led down onto a freshly mown lawn (Justin had obviously been busy), and neat borders full of roses and other plants I could not name, shrubs and at the bottom of the garden, several apple trees in blossom.

'It certainly is,' agreed Justin, 'but it helps that you brought the sun with you.'

It was true that after weeks of glowering clouds and showers, the sun had begun to shine. I had seen the blue sky start to appear as I drove up the M40, and by the time I had arrived at the Laceys' 18th century Cotswold stone house, the temperature had soared into the low 80s, and I found Justin and Graham both dressed in shorts and t-shirts and setting the table on the patio.

I stretched my legs and arms, enjoying the luxury of feeling the sun's warmth on my skin again. I sighed deeply and began to relax, turning my face to the sun.

'Oh, this is good. I feel like I'm on holiday. I think I needed a break. From what, I don't know. It's not as if I'm working!'

'You don't have to be working to need a holiday, sweetheart,' said Justin, 'sometimes you just need to get away from normal life.'

'Mm... true...' I said, thinking of the problems with the house, and my never-ending quest to find work.

'I see you've become attached to that key...'

I looked down at the pewter key which I had attached to a chain round my neck.

'Yes. I think it's rather lovely. It kind of makes a nice pendant. I brought the box of stuff, too. I thought Graham might be interested.'

'Good idea. He loves all things theatrical as well as a good mystery. Might take his mind off things.'

The sound of pots and cutlery being moved around came through the open kitchen doors.

In sotto voice, I said, 'How's he doing? And, apart from that, how are you two doing?'

'We're OK,' said Justin, cocking his head to one side, 'I'm still not sure whether this relationship has got legs, but I think he needed someone to look after him for the time being. And, he's fine – just a little bruised, both figuratively and literally. I needed a break from normal life too, whatever that is. Oh, and Greta's coming over the day after tomorrow. She thought as we're all up here she might as well come up for the weekend.'

I resisted the urge to point out that inviting your boyfriend of just a few weeks over to your parents' house for several days, albeit the parents being away, and you invite your other friends too, was a pretty relationship-y thing to do. But I was certainly pleased to hear about Greta.

'Brilliant!'

62

Graham stepped out onto the patio, quickly dropping his sunglasses down from on top of his head back onto his nose. I wondered whether he was still self-conscious about the slight bruising round his eyes, or he was just sensitive to the sun.

'Lasagne will be ready in about ten minutes, my darlings,' he said, picking up the bottle of wine and sharing out the remains into our glasses. 'We're going to need another one of these, aren't we?'

There had been no awkwardness when I met Graham for the second time, even though our first encounter at the hospital could hardly be called a proper meeting. He was one of those people who greeted new people with instant warmth and enthusiasm, and he immediately treated me as an old friend.

'Hang loose,' said Justin, 'there's another one in the fridge. I'll get it in a min. Sit down relax for a minute. You've been working all day.'

Once again, I could not help thinking that Justin was perhaps in denial about the seriousness of his relationship with Graham. I reached out and took Graham's hand.

'Thanks so much Graham, this is lovely. You really are a star.'

'Wait 'til you see dessert!' said Justin.

'Oh, thank you, gorgeous,' replied Graham, beaming at me. He squeezed my hand back and took an olive with the other one. 'Oh, is that the famous key? It's lovely! Justin told me about the family mystery. How divinely intriguing!'

While we were eating our lasagne and salad, I told them both about what Georgina Hall had said about Eliza's birth, and her theatrical family.

'"*Curiouser and curiouser, said Alice!*", and how exciting! And you're going to go and see if you can find where this theatre

63

was tomorrow?'

For a moment, by the excited look in his eyes, I thought he was going to ask to come with me, and I would have liked the company, but then his eyes kind of clouded over, and he said, 'You'll probably be best on your own, though. I'll go and get dessert and coffee. You do like cheesecake, don't you?'

'Love it!' I said, and I turned to Justin as Graham went indoors, raising my eyebrows.

'Anything wrong? I know I've not known him long, but that seemed a little out of character.'

'Yeah,' said Justin, 'since the thing that happened last month, he seems to have developed a form of agoraphobia or something. He just wants to stay in all the time.'

'He probably just needs a bit of time. I wouldn't worry too much.'

'Yeah, I know. I'm glad you're here though; I don't want him to lean too much on me, and it's good for him to socialise with other people.'

'Actually,' I said, suddenly remembering something, 'I nearly didn't make it. The weirdest thing happened last night. I won't mention it in front of Graham, but I was very nearly taken out by some lunatic in a car as I was walking to work. I just managed to jump over a hedge – he came right up onto the pavement. Must have been drunk.' Remembering this incident again, I recalled how shaken up I'd been, and I had had to pull myself together to get on with serving customers at the wine bar. Thinking of it again now, I realised what a close shave I had had, and I shuddered.

'Darling, that's terrible. Are you OK? Did you tell the police?'

'No good. It was too dark to get a reg number anyway, and what could they do?'

'Well, I'm glad you're here, unscathed. You take care, all right?'

Graham returned at that moment and I changed the subject to my plans for tomorrow. I didn't mention what I'd just said to him, as he was obviously still in a sensitive state, and it could have been upsetting. Anyway, it was something best forgotten. I'd just ended up with a few scratches from the hedge so there was no harm done, and it would be best just to let it go.

In the morning after breakfast, Justin found a map of Shipsford, and we sat pouring over it at the table, trying to locate the site of the theatre that was in the poster, which I had brought with me.

'No theatre, as I thought,' said Justin, 'I'm sure I would have known if there was. But there's a museum on New Street, which is where the theatre was supposed to be according to the poster. They might have some information.'

'OK,' I said, feeling a little disappointed, 'I suppose it's worth a try.' I was beginning to wonder whether the trip into town would be worth it. What could I possibly find out from just looking at a building, even if it did still exist? Still, perhaps I could just enjoy the little trip and perhaps do some window shopping while I was there.

It was another warm day, and I sang to myself as I drove into town, noticing with a smile how the sun had brought everyone out onto the streets, and how happy and relaxed they looked. I was glad I had worn my pale-yellow cropped cotton trousers and the striped yellow and grey top I'd bought in a sale at the end of last summer, and my spirits began to rise at the thought of spending a few hours just mooching round. Perhaps I wouldn't spend too much time looking for the theatre. I'd just pop into the museum, and then go into the town centre, maybe get some lunch to eat in the park, and then do some serious window shopping; maybe even buy something. I was on a kind of holiday, after all, and I could do with spending a bit of money on myself, whether I could afford it or not.

I drove slowly down New Street, which turned out to be a mishmash of old and new buildings, mostly new. It had lost any feeling of its Victorian past due to the neon signs, glass-fronted chain stores and untidy street furniture that dominated the area. Despite its touristy focus, there were parts of the street where you could be in any town, anywhere.

I only just spotted the Museum and Tourist Centre, as it was set back a little from the road, and almost swallowed up between a modern office block and a Spud-u-Like. It was a small building, independent of the larger and newer buildings around it, with a gabled frontage. I wasn't an expert in architecture, but I could see straight away that it was a much older building than those around it. I found the nearest parking space down a side street, fed the meter, and walked to the front of the building, where there was a big notice board proclaiming the opening hours, and posters of upcoming exhibitions.

I walked through the wooden swing doors into the reception, where there was a shop area in a corner selling postcards, stationery and leaflets about the locality, and went straight to the reception desk.

The receptionist was busy talking to a couple of American tourists who were asking about coach trips to Stratford-upon-Avon. I looked around while I waited, and noticed some old photographs of the town on the walls, dating from the late nineteenth century. I studied them for a while, fascinated by the sight of streets I had just driven through, looking almost unrecognisable, filled with horses, trams and men and women dressed in top hats and long dresses.

In one of the photographs I recognised one of the buildings as being the museum itself, looking very much as it did now. Only when I looked closer, I saw something that made me tingle all over.

Above the door of the building, instead of the modern sign that was there now, there was some black lettering painted onto the red brick, which said "New Theatre".

Feeling the hairs rise on the back of my neck, I looked around with new eyes. There was nothing that gave any clue that this building had once been a theatre. The walls and ceiling were plain, painted pale green, and with no decoration of any sort.

The American tourists wandered off happily loaded with leaflets, maps and postcards, and I approached the receptionist. She was a middle-aged woman with short hair and large glasses attached to a chain round her neck.

'Excuse me, but I've been trying to find out where the old theatre was, and I've just noticed that photograph over there. Am I right in thinking that this was actually once the theatre?'

The woman smiled. 'Yes, I believe so. I think it's had a few incarnations, but... now let me see...somewhere...' she riffled in a drawer and put her glasses on to read some papers, '...ah yes, we had this leaflet about the history of the building itself, but of course most people here are more interested in finding out about other places, so we don't usually display it, but you can have that. And we do have a few theatre items in the museum, but I would have to charge you for entrance. It's 80p for one adult.'

'Thank you,' I said, instantly laying aside my window-shopping plans for the moment, 'yes I'll do that. This is really exciting; you see I think that one of my ancestors actually played here as an actress. I have a poster... actually I have a copy with me.'

I drew the pieces of A4 out of my bag. Because of the size and shape of the poster, it had had to be copied onto three sheets. I handed them to the woman.

'Oh yes, that's a lovely example. I don't think we have a copy of this one here – would you mind if I took a copy?'

'Not at all.'

'It was only a theatre for a short period, of course – you'll see in the leaflet – these small provincial theatres mainly catered for the travelling theatre companies. I believe they went into decline after the railways came and people could travel to the larger theatres in the big towns. It was a Quaker meeting house for a while, and then a lecture hall. During the war it was a dance hall, which continued until the Tourist Board took it over in the 1960s. Here's your ticket. I hope you enjoy your tour – we've a nice collection of local bronzeware and ancient jewellery found in a recent dig, if that interests you.'

I took my ticket, although there was no-one to hand it to, and went through a squeaky door into a semi-dark room full of display cabinets lit from within. I walked slowly through the museum, trying to take an interest in bronze and iron-age bits of cooking pot, spear heads and bracelets, through Roman tiles and beads, Medieval tools of the local wool & weaving industry, Tudor coins, furnishings and local hand-knitted stockings, Civil War armour, drums, pikes and muskets, restoration wigs & costumes, elegant Georgian porcelain & woodwork, more about the local wool industry with the development of mechanised looms in the industrial revolution, and then, at last, I came to a small display cabinet showing theatre posters very much like the one I owned. Next to the display was the same information sheet the woman had just given me which explained how the building had started off as a theatre where the local travelling theatre company would appear two or three times a year on its way through the provincial theatres and fitted-up barns of the West Midland circuit.

My heart beating a little faster, I peered through the glass, looking at each item intensely, hoping that there might be some sign of my elusive ancestor. There were three posters, each of them written in the similar style as mine, a stage prompt book that was nearly falling to pieces, filled with stage directions and underlinings, some old theatre tickets and a pair of shoes supposedly worn by Fanny Kemble. There was also a faded garland of flowers made of silk which was labelled as a possible piece of costume dated to the early nineteenth century. It was all very interesting, but I could see nothing that obviously related to Eliza Jayne, except that these were all types of things she may have been familiar with.

I looked up at the walls and ceiling, trying to imagine the building as it would have been as a theatre, but it was impossible. There had been too many changes over the years.

Feeling more intrigued than ever by my acting ancestor, I left the museum and found the nearest bookshop where I headed for the history section. After a bit of a search I found a book on the history of travelling actors in England, and spent the money I had half been planning to spend on clothes.

The sun blinded me as I came out of the dark bookshop, and it felt as warm as high summer, even though it was still only early May. I breathed in with a sense of sudden inspiration, and getting a tuna sandwich and a carton of juice from a near-by bakery, I headed off to the park, where I sat and read my book.

CHAPTER 6

November 1845

Eliza ran off the stage and threw herself into the arms of her father. As she did so, the small garland of silk flowers that she had worn on her head for the last scene in *As You Like It* fell from her head.

'Well, father, do you think your daughter now a proper actress? Ten good houses for the whole run and the last few sold out? What do you think?'

'I think,' said George, squeezing his daughter affectionately, 'that you will do very well. You have brought in the mob for the Shakespeare piece who would normally only arrive for the dancing, songs and the melodrama. You have proved yourself in the comic role...'

Eliza broke away and looked him in the eye.

'...but not yet the tragedy? Do you think Old Henry will try me for Juliet? Oh, please pa, you will speak to him?'

George laughed. 'He can see as well as anyone else the talent you have. Nothing I say will make any difference to that. And you've certainly been good for business, there's no doubt about that. But... there is plenty of time to talk about that.' He nodded towards the stage. 'Let's listen to your mother.'

Eliza turned to look back at the small stage, where the applause had finally died down and her mother, Sarah, was now in the centre, beginning her ballad, a romantic song. She had a beautiful voice, and had the ability to so affect the audience that they would become hushed during her performance. This was almost unheard of in provincial theatres where audiences came to have a good time and comment on the performances while they were performing rather than sit and listen patiently all the way through. Eliza stood leaning against her father as she listened to her mother's voice.

She was tired, yet exhilarated. Her first acting debut as Rosalind had come to the end of its run, and she had proved herself a success; had made the transition from child performer to real actress. It was an important rite of passage for all children born into acting companies, and did not always pay off. But she had done it; the audience had loved her.

In the wings on the other side of the stage, she could see the flashing smile of Abe, the Negro dancer. She smiled back. She loved to watch him dance. The acrobatic way he could turn somersaults and flip himself over with grace and ease, made everyone else seem almost clumsy in comparison.

Abe fascinated audiences, and there was no denying that he packed the houses. People would come to see his amazing rhythmic slave dance, and would gasp when they realized that he was a real negro, not a white man painted with burnt cork as was often done in the popular minstrel shows. When he sang and danced 'Jim Crow' the audience would cheer and stamp their feet with delight.

But Eliza knew that an audience is a strange, fickle animal, and showed a different face in the daylight, street hours. She had once walked down the street with Abe, and people looked at him with distaste and fear as they walked past, men taking women's elbows to guide them across the street, rather than to run the risk of brushing up against the negro. They even looked at her as if there was something wrong with her to be walking with the companionship of a dark man. Yet, Abe didn't seem to mind. When Eliza mentioned it, he flashed those white teeth and laughed his booming laugh.

'Don't you mind it, Abe?'

'Well, Mizz Eliza... the way I sees it is this. I would rather be ignored in the street as a free man, than tol' what to do as a slave!' and he again burst into peals of laughter until tears came out of his eyes, and Eliza laughed too, and the scandalized looks of passers-by made her laugh even more.

Abe had been born into slavery on a Virginia cotton plantation. He had been bought by a trader and arrived in England with his new master as a boy of 14. Because England had abolished slavery in 1807 his master had been forced to free him, but rather than let him loose, illiterate and without any form of income, he had employed him as a servant and had him educated to read and write. At the age of 21, Abe chose a new life when he had seen an acting troupe performing and knew that he had found his future.

Eliza watched him now, as her mother left the stage, leaping on with a somersault and mid-air pirouette that had the audience gasping and squealing with surprise and delight. Those same people who would not walk on the same side of the street as Abe yesterday, were now laughing and clapping and shouting for more.

Eliza kissed her mother and they both turned to watch Abe go into his dance called the 'Virginia Breakdown'. Danced to the music of a fiddle, Eliza thought it was very much like an

Irish jig, except that his feet would tap and shuffle on the stage to create a complicated rhythm, and he would whirl round and jump in the air. Abe had told her he had learned it from an old riverboat man back in Virginia. On his plantation the slaves used to have dancing contests, just to see whose feet could tap the fastest, and Abe was one of the youngest to take part, and sometimes won.

She sensed someone standing beside her and turned to see Old Henry, as the company's manager, Henry Holland, was affectionately known. He had been called 'Old Henry' since he was quite young because he was so clever and seemed to have an old head on young shoulders. But now he really was beginning to look like an old man, his shock of wild hair, white and grown wispy, a combination of laughter and care lines worn into his face like a map of roads travelled. He was smiling at Abe's antics, but Eliza could see something else behind the smile, the businessman behind the showman, weighing things up, something playing on his mind.

'It's been a good house, has it not, Mr Holland? Here at Shipsford.'

Holland turned to her with kind eyes.

'Yes, it has been a good house here at Shipsford, thanks to yourself, and,' he nodded towards the stage, 'our dark friend over there.' He was quiet for a few moments, and then almost to himself he said, 'It might be another story in the days to come.'

Eliza turned to him, a small note of apprehension cutting into her feelings of happiness, 'Why, do you not think we will have good houses at Wolverhampton...or the rest of the circuit?'

Holland sighed and again looked at her kindly, and with, Eliza suddenly thought, a sadness, almost pity.

'My dear Eliza. Do not let the ruminations of an old man worry you too much. But there are things that need to be discussed. We actors are a vulnerable species. Talk to your parents. They know what the problems are that face us in the coming years. But for tonight, enjoy yourself; enjoy your success. You deserve it.'

She turned back to the stage to watch the rest of Abe's act, but Old Henry's words hung in her mind, like a shadow that had crept into the corner of a bright room.

'Henry is worried about the railways, Eliza.'

They were sitting in the snug at the Horseshoe Inn. Having had a beef pie and some apple pudding, they were now sharing a flask of ale, and Eliza had told her parents of her conversation with Old Henry and what they thought it meant.

'The railways? Why, what has that to do with anything? Will they not bring more people to the theatres?'

'Well, yes, 'replied her father, 'but Henry believes that what will happen is that people will start to visit the larger, more luxurious theatres in the big towns and cities, instead of the little draughty barns in their own small towns. We travelling actors have always brought theatre to the public. But it may be that in the future the public will travel further afield for their entertainment, and we will not be able to compete with the resident stock companies in places like Birmingham and London, where they can offer comfortable, warm theatres and better lighting and scenery.'

Eliza felt, for the first time in her life, a sense of helplessness; of events moving in the bigger world that would affect her and her family in a personal way.

'So, what will happen, father? What will happen to us? What

will we do?'

George smiled and patted her hand. 'Do not worry too much yet, my daughter. It will take time before we start to see the serious consequences, and time enough for you still to further your own career. And, then perhaps, who knows? Perhaps you will be able to apply to a big company as a permanent actor. Perhaps even you might find yourself becoming a star in London. There is always a silver lining...'

'But you are just talking about me. What about you and mother? '

George and Sarah exchanged glances.

'We're not getting any younger, child,' said her mother, 'if things change as Henry thinks they will, it would be too late for us to start again. The big theatres want fresh, young blood who will bring them money for many years to come. We're too old to start looking for new work.'

Eliza felt that her happy, carefree world was crumbling.

'But it's not fair!' she cried, tears suddenly smarting in her eyes, 'why should everything change! Why can't things just continue as they are? Stupid railways!' She kicked the leg of the table. 'Why do they have to spoil everything!'

'Child, everything changes', said her father. 'Mr Brunel is not building his railway tracks just to vex you personally. For most people they are going to be a good thing. Imagine, you can now travel from Birmingham to London in less than six hours. You will be able to go to London without having to stop overnight. Yes, it will mean a big change for us, but that has always been the nature of our business, and we must try and adapt to the times we live in.'

Sarah, Eliza's mother, turned and smiled at her philosopher husband.

Eliza sniffed and blinked her eyes, trying to keep her tears in check and to calm her sense of everything around her shattering. How could her parents be so calm about it? Why should things change? Why shouldn't Henry Holland's Travelling Theatre go on and on? She was happy here. She did not want to go to London and play in a big theatre. She liked the small, intimate places they played in, the way the audiences knew them all and welcomed them back each year.

'I like the life we have,' she said, her voice low and shaky.

'Perhaps it will be a while before things change,' said her mother, her own eyes looking a little moist, 'but your father's right. Change is difficult, but it's not always for the bad. Just think, not so long ago, the drama was banned completely. We have been blessed with a freedom those before us did not have, and perhaps this gives us all new opportunities. We live in exciting times, that's for sure. We must try and make the best of things.'

'What are you going to do father, if you cannot work in the theatre?'

'Well, now,' he said, 'that is a question I have been considering for some time, long before the railways started to change things. Your mother and I have found the long walks between towns to be getting quite tiresome, and we knew there would come a time when it may not be possible for us anymore, whatever happens in the outside world. There was a time when I thought of trying for the London stage, but I think that time is against me now. My idea is, Eliza, that your mother and I should look for an inn that is in need of a landlord in some up and coming town where the railways will create visitors. A place where we could put on small entertainments, and perhaps get up a play or two now and then. We could sing, and play music, and perhaps dance. If it was in a town with its own theatre, we could provide accommodation for guest actors and musicians, and they might add to the provision of entertainments. I do not know yet if the plan would work, but that is what I have in mind. If the houses start to fail, as Henry thinks they will, I will start to make enquiries. What do you think of that, Eliza?'

Despite her fear of losing the life she was currently living, Eliza could not help feeling that it was a reasonable plan. Perhaps there was something to be said for staying in one place after all.

'Well, father, it sounds like it would be a very nice inn. Would you consider occasionally employing a young actress who can sing and dance a little, and perhaps stay in the inn when she's not otherwise engaged?'

'What? You mean the great star of Drury Lane, the Incomparable Eliza Jayne?' her father said, putting his hand on his chest and feigning great wonder and astonishment, 'why, do you think that such a great actress would lower herself to step into our parlour and entertain our guests with her great presence? Oh, Mrs Jayne, that we should be so honoured...'

Eliza and her mother both laughed. 'Oh, George, stop teasing her. Of course you will, Eliza,' she said, 'that is part of the plan. But what your father is saying in his own naughty way is that perhaps you will by then have become a star and will be very busy elsewhere. We know you have the talent, so why should it not be possible?' She grinned, and leaned towards Eliza, winking at her husband, 'and of course, you already have your very own admirer. That's a good start.'

Eliza blushed and squirmed in her seat. 'Oh, the both of you are impossible. That young Turvey is a fool. He is just a pompous ass and knows nothing of the theatre. I would not have anything to do with him, but that he will send me letters and flowers, and I cannot help that.'

Sarah smiled, 'I know that, but it maybe something you will have to get used to. In my younger days, I had many a young admirer who used to linger at the theatre doors and write me love letters indeed! As if they thought they knew me. Of course,' she glanced slyly at George, who was rolling his eyes, 'your father put an end to all that when he joined the company and swept me off my feet. Quite literally, of course. We did a dance together and he used to throw me into the air. I can still remember how the audience gasped. I was much lighter then. And then, of course we married, and then much later, you came along, born in an inn while your father entertained the guests with the fiddle, and now I doubt he could throw me over his shoulder, let alone in the air...'

'Do not tempt me, woman, I may try it right here in front of everyone.'

'Oh, stop it at once!' cried Eliza, embarrassed and yet giggling now, her tears almost forgotten. 'How did I ever deserve such terrible parents? You are always determined to embarrass me!'

They continued to laugh and joke, but even in the midst of her laughter, Eliza began to think again of how she was to make her way in the world if Henry's fears proved to be true.

CHAPTER 7

May 1985

I sat on the patio reading the book I had bought in Shipsford. Justin and Graham lay on loungers in shorts and sunglasses, soaking up the sun. A jug of iced white wine spritzer was on the table along with bowls of corn chips and dips.

'In all my time in the theatre,' I remarked, 'I never knew much about the travelling theatre circuits. Apparently, they were big in the early nineteenth century, but were really affected by the rise of the railways. The whole system just declined over the 1840s and 50s.'

'So that would have affected your ancestor, wouldn't it?' said Graham.

'Yes, it must have. I wonder what happened. The theatre poster is dated 1845 so that was just about the time things were starting to change. No wonder the museum I visited was a theatre for only a short period of time.'

Justin got up and topped up the glasses with spritzer.

'So, what was the next item in the box? That might be a clue to what happened next.'

'It was a newspaper review I think, but it was only dated a

few years later. They were probably still going as a travelling theatre. All the items might be from that time. Perhaps the reason there is nothing after 1851 is because the company she was in had to close. Oh, if only we had something from later on.'

'Hmm... from after her marriage then,' said Justin, it could be that we have nothing after that date because she changed her name...' he looked up at the sky. 'Do you know, I think it's clouding over. Looks like our little taste of summer might be coming to an end. I'd better go and sort out some tea. Greta will be here soon. You two staying out here?'

I looked up at the sun, which had disappeared behind large banks of grey cloud building up from the east, and felt a sudden chill. 'No, I don't think that sun's going to re-appear. Come on Graham, let's get all this stuff in too; it looks like it might rain.'

'Well, my darlings, such news! Such news I have to tell you. But first, Sarah, I went over to your house to check your phone and post and water your plants, and here is your post.'

We were sitting in the front room with a pot of tea and crumpets. Greta had arrived just ten minutes beforehand, complaining that she had brought the bad weather with her.

'No phone calls from your agent, I'm afraid, but while I was in the house the phone rang and I answered it. It was a male voice. He just said, "Sarah?", and I said, "No – she's not here right now", and he said nothing. I asked him if he wanted to leave a message, but he just said "No". and put the phone down. No please or thank you. I think he was very rude. I tell you; I did not have a good feeling about it. The man's voice gave me goose bumps...'

I was only half listening as I went through my post, and I could not help thinking that Greta was such a drama queen. I thought the phone call might have been David, but I was sure he hadn't meant to be rude; he was just a bit shy. However, I did not want to bring up the subject of David in front of Justin. It was still a bit of a taboo subject, and he might see it as a reason to dislike my cousin even more.

'I'm sorry Greta, I wouldn't worry about it. I'm sure he'll ring back if it's important, whoever... Hello! What's this?' I picked out an envelope that I recognised as bearing the franking mark of my mother's agent's. I ripped it open, and immediately sat down.

Inside was a cheque for seven hundred and eighty-seven pounds.

'Oh my word. This is brilliant!'

'What is it?' asked Justin.

'It's a royalty cheque for my mother's estate.' I quickly looked through the statement. 'Yes, that's it. One of my mother's stories was filmed some time ago for children's television, and I occasionally get a few pounds for it. But they've just sold it abroad and it's also been repeated here. I didn't even know. It means I've got a cheque for nearly eight hundred pounds!'

'Oh, Sarah, that's wonderful. Congratulations!'

'Hee hee!' I cried, getting up and doing a little dance round the room. 'This means I can stop worrying, at least for a few weeks. Thanks mum!'

'You see, she's still watching over you,' said Justin, giving her a hug.

'Have we got any champagne?' asked Graham.

'No, but this definitely calls for something,' said Justin,

'I don't think my dad would mind if we raided the drinks cupboard. He rummaged in the corner cabinet. 'Sherry, Glenmorangie or Gordons... Oh well, better than nothing I suppose. Who's for a gin and tonic?'

I wallowed on the large sofa, enjoying the soft kick of the spirit and the mellow mood that was creeping over me. Justin had put some Mozart on his parents' gramophone which was playing quietly in the background. He and Graham were in the kitchen washing up and Greta had gone upstairs to unpack.

For a while, the day to day worry of the lack of work and the need to get by had been erased. My mind and body were slowly relaxing, and I allowed my thoughts to free-fall.

As an out-of-work actress, you might think that my first thoughts after a little windfall would be to use some of it to further my career. Get some new promotional photographs taken, perhaps, or enrol in some classes at the Actor's Centre. But to be honest, these were not my first thoughts. In fact, all I could think about was my theatrical ancestors, and the key around my neck. Of course, then I felt guilty and started questioning my own priorities.

When Justin came back into the room and sat down, I told him my thoughts, and asked him if he thought I'd got my priorities all wrong.

'Nothing in the pipeline at all?'

'No. Do you know, Justin, I sometimes wonder whether...' I stopped, not daring to voice what was at the back of my mind.

'Go on. Say what you were going to say.'

'Well, it sounds silly. I love the theatre, and I love acting. I love the creative buzz of the rehearsal room, the camaraderie of being in a theatre company, and the excitement of being on stage. But the periods in between are getting me down, and I just sometimes wonder whether it's worth it. I've been wondering whether there is something else I should be doing. Something more worthwhile, perhaps. Sometimes just the thought of going to another audition and sitting in a waiting room with countless other actresses who you KNOW are better suited to the part than you are, I just feel I want to run away. So, perhaps I'm not really cut out for the ruthless competitiveness of this business. But I have absolutely no idea what else I would do. I just feel a bit lost. No confidence...'

To my annoyance, my eyes had suddenly brimmed with tears.

'Sounds like that money has come at exactly the right time. Forget about the photos and the acting classes. If you're not feeling motivated to do all that stuff, it's obvious you need some time out from it all. Just relax and try not to think about it. Sometimes that's the best way to deal with a problem – don't think about it for a while. It can just sort itself out.'

I sat up. He had said exactly the right thing. I had just needed to give myself permission to take a break, and he had given me just the nudge I needed.

'In that case, can I ask you a favour?'

'Ask ahead, sweetheart. If it's possible, I'll do it.'

'Well, I was just wondering whether I could stay on here for a while with you guys. I don't need to go back home for a couple of weeks. I'd like to stay up here and do a bit of research on my family history. Would that be OK? I'll pitch in with the shopping of course.'

'You'd be more than welcome, darling. We'll give you a hand, if you like. What are you going to do next?'

'I thought I'd find out about the other venue, the one with the newspaper review. I brought everything with me in case we felt like looking at them, but I could drive over to the place where it was and have a mooch round. I don't know whether any of it will amount to anything but as I've now got some time, it would be fun to try and solve a little bit of the mystery perhaps.'

Justin grinned. 'You're really hooked, aren't you?'

'Well, just a little bit,' I replied, my hand moving to the key hanging from my neck, 'I'm kind of fascinated by what this key is, and what the link is with my ancestor. I don't suppose I'll ever find out, but it's just a little project that seems to have presented itself to me, and it's just a nicer thing than the daily grind of trying to find work all the time.'

At that moment, Greta came through the door, followed by Graham with a tray of tea and biscuits.

I suddenly remembered Greta's words when she had arrived earlier.

'Greta, you were going to tell us something weren't you? Didn't you say you had some news when you came in? I'm so sorry, it's my fault; we all got distracted with my cheque. Why don't you tell us what it was?'

'Oh, that's all right. I am so pleased for you. But, yes, I do have some news.' She looked around at everyone sitting looking at her in anticipation. 'You remember my telling you about my great-uncle? The one who helped to get my parents out of Germany in the war? They were very young then of course, but the two families were very close and Great Uncle Otto took the children before... Well, he got them out just before the war started and the barriers came down. Not only my family, but other people's children too. He was in contact with the British Government and had to arrange to find them homes and everything. He then went back to try and find the rest of

85

our family, but they had all been arrested by then, and he was then captured himself. Nothing more was heard about him. We all thought that he had probably died in a concentration camp himself. But my father has always been trying to find out more, and eventually we have heard... we have heard that he survived the death camps. He left Germany and came to England. He's alive!'

'Oh my God, Greta, that's wonderful news! What happened to him?' I asked.

'That part is not so good. After he was released from that terrible place – I won't even say the name – he made his way to England. He had no money. He had lost everything. He had no home, no family except for my parents who were just children; everyone he knew had died – murdered - in the holocaust. Can you imagine? He was in a displaced person camp for a while, but there was nothing left for him in Germany or Poland. Every single one of the family he tried to find turned out to be dead. He decided to come here and try to work, but his health was terrible, and he could only find low paying work. He's now too old to work, and he is living on a tiny pension. This man, who should be a hero, is living in poverty in a Birmingham bedsit. My father went to see him. He said it is terrible where he lives. A great tragedy that such a man should live like this; he saved their lives. My parents, and many others, would not be here if it was not for him.' Her eyes filled with tears. 'Imagine. Imagine what he has been through, this wonderful man.'

It was difficult to know what to say. I sat next to her and embraced her.

'My... my father said the meeting was overwhelming. When Uncle Otto realised who it was, he burst into tears and wept on his shoulder. For forty years he has not seen any member of his family. He was completely alone. Forty years.' She shook her head.

'What will happen to him now Greta?' asked Graham, wiping his eyes, 'How old is he?'

'He is in his 70s. I don't know, my parents are discussing it. It may be that I will move out of the house and he will have my room. We cannot leave him where he is.'

'Oh Greta, you can move in with me a while,' I said, 'I've got plenty of room.'

'Oh, my dear, that is perhaps a good idea. But let's not be hasty. We'll see what happens. Thank you so much.' She rummaged in her handbag and pulled out a handkerchief, and then blew her nose. 'I'm sorry, this is all very emotional. I did not mean to be so...'

'Oh, darling, of course it's OK. This is a really big thing,' said Justin. 'It's difficult for any of us to imagine what he has been through. I just find it hard to contemplate...' he threw his hands in the air shaking his head, unable to find the right words.

'You know, I've never wanted to talk about... the whole thing. What happened to my family in the war. The thought of discussing ancestry and family was just too painful.' She turned away and sighed, trying to find the right words. 'It's just... too big...too terrible...'

Justin put his arm around her.

My thoughts turned to the terrible pictures I had seen of concentration camps at the end of the war. Knowing someone whose family had suffered in those places made it somehow more real. There was very little one could say.

I said, 'You know, Greta, we'll do whatever we can to support you, and your family. That's what friends do, right? That's what's important.'

Greta squeezed her hand.

'Thank you darling. It means a lot to me. Friends and family. They are the most important things in life, don't you think? Perhaps this family history thing is a good thing after all. Keeping the memories alive of those who have gone, eh?'

We all smiled. I too was beginning to think along the same lines.

Graham said, 'It would be nice to know that when I'm gone someone cared enough to look at my life. Though it's unlikely; I'm not going to have any descendants, am I? I might be someone's great uncle though. It's a funny thought – some great-grandchild of my niece compiling a tree and adding my name, and wondering who I was. Quite nice, really.'

The next day, I got out the small scrap of newspaper with the review and noted the details. The theatre mentioned was in a town near Oxford, and the review described Eliza as a rising star, and her performance of Ophelia in Shakespeare's *Hamlet* as 'stunning and entrancing'. It also went on to praise the 'guest star from the London theatres, Bertrand McDougal, whose performance of Hamlet was of such poignance that even the most boisterous members of the audience were quieted.'

'Bertrand McDougal?', I said out loud to myself, 'I am sure I have heard of him. Wasn't he a member of one of those big acting families in Victorian times? Oh, if only I had my *Who's Who in the Theatre* with me. So, Eliza acted with him... oh! Wait a minute!'

Out of the box I picked up the poetry book and looked again at the inscription. 'To my dearest Eliza, from her Bertie. March 1848. Hail to thee, Blithe Spirit.'

Bertie... Could that be the great Bertrand McDougal? And he

was 'her Bertie'! So, if I was right, it looked as though Eliza and Bertrand had some kind of relationship... but wasn't he married? This was getting even more interesting!

I got out the Yellow Pages and looked up theatres in Oxfordshire but, not surprisingly, there was no theatre listed that matched that of the review. I then looked up the Oxfordshire Record Office and picked up the telephone.

'Hello. I was wondering if you could tell me about the old theatre in Kidlington – are there any records for it, and does the building still exist?'

The archivist asked her to hold the line, and then came back to her.

'Yes, there are a few posters for the theatre, but as far as I can see it was only a theatre for a short time. It was turned into an assembly hall in 1860, and was a cinema for a short time. It was pulled down in 1967. I know the area myself; I think it's now the site of the local Tesco's. You're welcome to come and have a look at the posters, but that's all we've got I'm afraid.'

I thanked her and put down the phone, feeling a little deflated. Would it really be worth going all the way to Oxford just to look at a Tesco and more posters? Posters would tell me nothing other than dates and who played what. While that was quite interesting, I needed more than that.

I picked up the cross-letter, the one written from Bertie to Eliza. This would contain some information, surely? But apart from the occasional word, it seemed impossible to read.

'Eliza must have been able to read it,' I said to myself, 'so surely it can't be that difficult.'

I wandered into the kitchen where Justin was stirring the contents of a large pot.

'Carrot and coriander soup, darling,' he said in response to her sniffing the air, 'it's the new soup taste sensation! Thought I'd give it a go, and soup is easy to feed several people with, as long as you have lots of garlic bread, which we do, so, hurrah!'

'Smells gorgeous,' I said. 'Justin, do you know if there's a magnifying glass anywhere in the house?'

Justin glanced at me with a grin.

'Sounds like you're doing a bit of detective work again. Ooh! The letter? Hey, let me put this on to simmer and I'll come and help. My mum uses a magnifying glass when she's reading the paper sometimes. I should be able to find it. Just hang on a mo. Don't start without me!'

CHAPTER 8

August 1848

'A toast! A toast to a new star!' said Bertrand McDougal from the top of the table. He was looking at her, and everyone at the table turned towards her. She blushed as everyone applauded and laughed at her discomfort.

But it was not just modesty that was making her blush and wish she could be somewhere else in that moment. It was Bertrand.

When he joined the theatre company in spring as the guest star, everyone was very excited about working with him, although there were some in the company that grumbled and called him too conceited, but even they admitted that he would be useful to bring in more audiences and perhaps bolster falling attendance.

Bertrand McDougal was the son of a famous actor-manager, Edmund McDougal, who had arrived in London from Edinburgh in the 1810s along with his pretty actress wife, whose portrayal of Juliet had turned the heads of all the normally cynical reviewers, and so brought this acting family fame and success; rivals of the established Kembles. By the time Bertrand was old enough to tread the boards, he was guaranteed stardom just for being his mother's son. Some were keen to point out that he may have inherited his handsome looks from his parents, but not, perhaps, the same level of talent. No-one, however, could deny that he had a dynamic presence on the stage, and women had been known to swoon if he turned his gaze upon them in the course of a soliloquy. Despite some mediocre reviews, audiences, the male content of which perhaps having been encouraged by their female companions, flocked to see him play Benedict or Antonio, though even the most ardent followers admitted he might be just a little too mature to play Romeo by the late 1840s.

Eliza was the happiest she had ever been. She had proven herself as a rising star and her career was heading for great success. Her parents had now retired and were running an inn in Stratford upon Avon, employing Abe, the negro dancer, as a star attraction. Although she missed them, she now felt a great sense of autonomy working in a theatre without them watching over her and telling her when it was time to sleep or get up. And while it seemed likely that the traveling theatre company may not last for many more years, she knew she would be able to get work in London as her reviews and the general esteem in which she was held would no doubt get her work in the capital without too much trouble. On top of everything, Bertrand McDougal, the handsome and rich actor whose fame was established not only in London but throughout the country, Scotland and across the Atlantic, was paying her much attention, and not just when they worked together.

She had never had such attention from any man before. Oh, there was that silly Turvey man who followed her round and waited for her outside stage doors, but how could she possibly be interested in any man who did not share her life in the theatre? She knew that hers was a charmed life; a life very different from the vast majority of women; women who were owned by their fathers and husbands, who were not expected to have a career, women who would shock and swoon at the idea of dancing on a stage in scanty clothing. How ridiculous. How hypocritical! These very same women would think nothing of accompanying their husbands who came to the theatre to ogle at her dancing on the stage. How could she possibly be interested in a man who lived in that world?

But Bertrand was not only handsome and kind, he had been brought up in the theatre, just like her. They shared the same experiences and they understood each other's lives. What a couple they would make!

Eliza blushed at her own thoughts. She could not help her mind racing ahead of itself and thinking all kinds of future scenarios where she and Bertrand would be the leading lights of the theatre, rearing another acting dynasty...

'I must stop this!' she said to herself, over and over again. But every time he looked at her, she felt him looking right into her very soul. Only the other day in rehearsals he had suddenly taken a lock of her hair and studied it as he let it fall through his fingers. It was not part of the scene they were playing. Then he had looked at her and smiled with a twinkle in his eye before continuing with the scene. That night she had not been able to sleep for running this moment through her head repeatedly. What did it mean?

He was of course much older than her. This was the only sticking point. A great difference in age was frowned upon in marriage. But so what if it was? She was a theatrical. She did not conform to the normal rules of society. The question of his age occurred to her several times, but each time she tossed it aside as of no importance.

He was a very private person. She respected that. He did not speak of a past life. She wondered if he had been married before, and perhaps some great tragedy had befallen his wife, leaving him a widower. It was obvious that he had no wife, as he never spoke of her and nor did anyone else.

Eliza's happiness lasted for several months, until one day she received a letter from an uncle informing her that both of her parents had been killed in a railway accident, when several carriages had become de-railed and rolled down the side of an embankment. George and Sarah had been on their way to London to visit friends and were both killed outright.

So sudden a shock was this that Eliza was unable to take it in properly. She took the letter to Henry Holland, to ask him to read it to her again, hoping that he would tell her she was mistaken. But he shook his head, and said, 'Oh, my poor girl; this is terrible news. George and Sarah! Oh, my dear. Sit down, you look quite pale. John! Bring Miss Jayne some brandy at once! I think she may faint.'

After a few moments he had said to her, 'Of course we will cancel tonight's show. And for the rest of the week, Miss Leyton will take your part. You will need to go home for the funeral, and... I will try to come myself. You will need time to sort things out.'

'Funeral?' said Eliza, frowning, still not fully understanding.

'Yes, my dear. Er, do you have any other family, apart from this uncle?'

'No.'

'Well, we can travel to Stratford together. My wife will look after you.'

'But... but... surely, this cannot be. There must be some mistake. Why, I had a letter from my mother only two days ago. Please. Read the letter again. It must be wrong...'

'I am so sorry my dear. This is a terrible shock for you, and for all of us.' He patted her shoulder. 'There, there. This is a terrible calamity, but everyone here will look after you.'

Eliza went through the next few days in a kind of stupor, and a constant state of bewilderment. Mrs Holland was very kind, but Eliza could not make any conversation nor respond to any questions beyond a simple yes or no.

It was not until she arrived at the inn in Stratford and found that it had been closed temporarily due to the untimely deaths of its landlords that she began to understand that her parents no longer existed, and that she was alone with no family, apart from the uncle who had written the letter, and with whom she was very little acquainted.

After the Hollands had left her to settle into their rooms in another part of town, she wandered through the rooms at the inn, for a while, looking for signs that her parents might still be alive, and it was all a terrible mistake. She looked through every room, opening closets and drawers as if looking for something mislaid. After going through all the rooms, she eventually wearily sat down upon her parents' bed, and the tears arrived, and she thought they would never stop.

The following morning, the day of the funeral, there was a knock at the door, and Eliza opened it, expecting it to be the Hollands to pick her up, but there, looking as sorrowful as a homeless puppy, was her old friend, Abe.

She threw herself into his arms and wept on his shoulder, ignoring the shocked glances from passers-by.

95

'Oh, Mizz Eliza, I don't know what to say!'

She invited him inside, and after they had sat down, Eliza asked Abe what he was going to do now.

'I sure don't know, Mizz Eliza,' he said, wiping another tear from his eye, 'I can't even think straight. Perhaps I'll make my way to London and see if there's any company that needs a niggur who can sing a dance a little.'

Eliza hugged him again.

'I wish you well, Abe.'

Her parents had never had much money, and so Eliza was left with very little after the funeral expenses and business debts, including Abe's wages, had been paid. The inn was taken over by new landlords, and so she was alone, reliant upon herself to earn a living with nowhere to go if anything went wrong.

Her father had left a will, but it was a very simple one, leaving all residual items after the payment of debts, to his wife, and after her death, to Eliza. The only item that was mentioned separately in the will, so that there was no doubt over its fate, was a large, pewter key. This was to be given to Eliza to be kept safely as part of the family's heritage, though there was no clue to what lock it would open. Eliza had seen the key before, hanging on a chain on her father's neck, and when she had asked about it, he had only said that it had been passed to him from his father to be kept safely in the hopes of one day finding the thing that it opened. According to family legend, there was some mystery attached to it, some important legacy that one day would bring fame and fortune to the Jayne family; yet no-one knew where it had come from or even what kind of thing it would open; a door? A box or chest?

As the train rattled along slowly, taking her back to her

working life, Eliza held the key in her hands, feeling its weight, and admiring the quality of its work. It was a finely made item, and obviously quite old. But what good could it possibly be to her? What hope was there of ever finding what it opened, if no-one knew where it had come from? Whatever it was must be lost and forgotten, and perhaps no longer exist. It was certainly no good to her in practical terms.

But it was something that had belonged to her father. And as such, she treasured it. The will had said it must be looked after, and so she would honour her father's wishes, and in time, pass it on to her own children.

CHAPTER 9

November 1848

Eliza went back to work, and impressed the whole company by the professional way in which she carried on, despite the terrible tragedy that had befallen her. She was not quite the sparkling, cheerful soul that she had been before, and that was only to be expected, but she did not allow it to affect her performances, and in fact, seemed to have improved and deepened them. Off stage, she was quieter and more thoughtful. She seemed to have grown from child to adult very suddenly, and those of the company who had felt the need to protect and counsel her before as the youngest independent member of the company, suddenly felt that their patronage was no longer needed. Far from needing support and succour after the death of her parents, she felt more the need to be alone, and to allow her grief to go through its natural course on her own terms. She had no desire for sympathy or long discussions on the vicissitudes of life. Any hint of a pitying eye or well-meaning question about her well-being, and she would, albeit politely, leave the room and seek solitude. She wished for no-one's company, for no-one could make her feel any better.

Except for Bertie.

His friendship and nearness were a great comfort to her, and he put no pressure on her to talk about her parents or to offer too much sympathy, which only made the tears come to her eyes if anyone did so. After she had returned, he had touched her hand and said, 'You poor girl', and it had meant the world to her.

Bertie seemed like a rock. While the death of her parents had left her with nothing to fall back on if anything went wrong, in her mind, he took their place. Everything would be all right as long as Bertie was there. Perhaps soon he would tell her his feelings, and perhaps they would marry. To Eliza it seemed inevitable. For now, he was being quiet, and allowing her time to grieve, before he pushed her to make any big decisions. She appreciated that. It was just part of his kindness and protectiveness. What a wonderful man he was.

As the weeks went by, however, Eliza became anxious. Bertie was a guest performer and would soon be leaving the company and going back to London as he was contracted to play at Drury Lane Theatre. Surely, soon he would declare himself? Yet, the day of his leaving came ever closer, and although he was attentive to her as always, he made no sign of wanting to become more intimate or speak with her privately.

And then, with just one week before the end of his contract, he turned to her at the side of the stage one evening and said, 'Miss Jayne, if you would honour me with your presence this evening at my rooms in the inn, I have something I would like to give to you.'

Eliza's heart skipped a beat, and she looked down, trying to hide the blush that she felt spreading across her cheeks.

'I will be there,' she said, unable to say more without him

hearing the tremble in her voice.

Bertie met her at the entrance to the inn.

'I realised that it would not look quite right for you to come to my rooms,' he said with a smile, 'Someone might get the wrong idea, and I would not want to compromise your reputation. But I have arranged a table in the snug, so we can be quite private.'

Eliza blushed and said nothing, but she smiled at his thoughtfulness and followed him to the dark little area, out of sight of prying eyes. Her heart was beating so loudly she could hardly hear her own thoughts. She hoped she had dressed properly for the occasion. She did not think a décolleté would be quite the thing, so she was wearing her best yellow day dress, bulked out with petticoats, a silk shoulder wrap, and a new bonnet, coloured a demure pale yellow, with a pale pink silk rose as decoration and a velvet ribbon. Yellow was one of her favourite colours, and with her dark hair, fair skin and red lips, she knew it suited her very well.

Bertie had arranged a light meal for them, with a flagon of wine. The snug was dimly lit with a single oil lamp hanging from the ceiling, and a candle in the middle of the table.

'Oh Bertie, this is lovely,' she exclaimed as they sat down.

'Let me pour you some wine,' he said. As he picked up the flagon, he looked at her a little shyly and said, 'I must say, you look very becoming tonight... not that you do not any night but... this is most definitely your colour. There are not many women who can wear yellow, though many try...'

Eliza giggled. 'Don't be naughty Bertie. Now you are trying to have me believe you are a man of the world. I will not have it!'

He looked away and cleared his throat, and then started

rummaging in his waistcoat pocket. Eliza's hand went to her chest. Was this the moment?

'I, um... well, as I will be returning to London shortly, I er... wanted to give you something... to remember me by.'

Eliza looked up at him. Remember him by? *Remember* him by? This did not sound like the beginnings of a marriage proposal. This sounded like a farewell. Her throat felt like it was closing up, and she could not breathe. Surely, after all, after their closeness and friendship, he could not be saying goodbye? Perhaps she had mis-heard him? That must be it. Or perhaps it was a kind of joke? She breathed out in a kind of half laugh. Yes, it must be a joke.

He pulled something out of his pocket, and it was larger than a ring box. It was a book. She stared at it. A book. Not a ring. A book.

He was talking. She must listen.

'....one of my favourite poets. And this poem makes me think of you. Here, I have marked the page: "Ode to a Skylark" – and here on the front page I have written the first line: 'Hail to thee, blithe spirit!' That is you, my dear little Eliza – a blithe spirit. It will always make me think of you.'

Eliza took the book and stared at where he had written the first line of the poem.

'Oh...!' she said.

'You do like it?'

'Oh... oh, yes, of course! It's lovely, Bertie. How kind.'

All she could think about was that when Bertie left, she would be utterly alone.

'You seem a little pale, my dear. Here, have a little wine. You need to build yourself up. You probably have not been eating enough. Do you feel quite well?'

'Yes, I am perfectly well, thank you. I felt a little dizzy. You are probably right. I have not felt much like eating lately.'

They were interrupted by the lady of the house who brought them roast beef, gravy, carrots, and potatoes. Eliza's heart sank as her appetite seemed to have deserted her completely.

While she picked at her food, Bertie tucked in like a man who had not seen food for weeks, and told her about his contract at Drury Lane, and the parts he would be playing. He went on to talk about other actors he had seen: Kean, Kemble, Macready and their various merits, and faults. Eliza tried to concentrate on what he was saying, and make the appropriate comments and responses when necessary, but all the while she felt as though there was a terrible abyss opening up underneath her. Her future seemed uncertain. Would she just continue to be an actress in a company, alone and single? What would happen if she could not work? What if they no longer wanted her, when the company no longer existed? The kind of life that could be for a one-time actress who could not get work and had no husband was not to be contemplated. While Bertie eulogised about Macready's great stage presence, Eliza saw herself destitute. She had no parents, no brothers or sisters, and no-one else to turn to. Her one friend, Abe, had disappeared into the city, and she had not heard from him. Of course, he could not read or write, so it was unlikely that she ever would.

With the slim possibilities of a guaranteed permanent income in the profession she was in, she realised on what shaky ground she trod. Up until now she had felt secure. She had had her parents who were always there for her, and now they were not. She had no money except what she earned, which usually ran out at the end of the week. She thought then she had Bertie, but now she was beginning to think that she did not. For the first time in her life, she saw that her life was not secure; there was a darkness on the other side of this happy, carefree life, and it would be so easy to slide into it...

But perhaps... perhaps not all was lost as far as Bertie was concerned. He was obviously fond of her. He had bought her the lovely book, and had written in it so sweetly. Perhaps he just needed a little gentle persuasion to do the right thing. Men were sometimes shy, were they not? Was it not Mrs Shipley in the company who had joked how she had virtually had to propose to her husband before he got the idea?

She was suddenly aware that Bertie was asking her a question.

'...I have noticed it quite often, since you returned from Stratford. Is there any significance in it?'

'I... I am sorry Bertie, what did you ask me?'

'The key. The key that you often wear on a chain. I presume it is of some importance to you?'

'Oh, yes...' her hand went to where it usually sat against her breast, but of course she was not wearing it today. So heavy a thing would not have been right against the delicate gown she was wearing, the gown that seemed rather inappropriate now for a simple supper in an inn, not a marriage proposal. 'It was my father's, and he got it from his father, and now it is handed down to me. But there is a mystery about it. No-one now knows what lock it opens or opened; but it has some importance about it. Each generation is supposed to look after it until the mystery is somehow uncovered. But it seems nonsensical to me. It is unlikely that anyone will ever find the lock it opens wherever that may be, or indeed if it still exists. But it is a pretty thing, and well crafted...'

'...and very old.'

'Yes, it must have been in my family for many generations. It is worth keeping for its own sake, and because it belonged to my father, of course.'

'Of course. But is that all? Is there nothing else, no clue to tell you anything about the key?'

'No, nothing.' Just then, a memory came back to her. 'Oh, now I think of it, my father once said something about a dream he once had, and that someone in the dream had been wearing a key round his neck just like this. It seems silly now, but he was quite sure that the dream was telling him that the key must never be lost. How strange, I have only just remembered that. It seems terribly unlikely, but my father was quite adamant about it.'

'How interesting,' said Bertie, 'you know, dreams can be very powerful and important. Who knows what they are trying to tell us...'?

'Do you really think there is something in it?'

He thought for a moment, as if remembering a dream of his own, but then shrugged and smiled.

'"There are more things in heaven and earth...", but it is not for me to say. If it is somehow important to your family, then you must hold on to it, and one day pass it on. But I would have liked to see it again. Such a pretty thing. What a shame I am due to leave for London tomorrow.'

Eliza lowered her eyes for a moment while she considered this opportunity that had arisen. Without raising her eyes, she said,

'Why not now?'

'You have it with you?'

'No, it is in my rooms.' And then she raised her eyes, and

saw that he understood.

The following day Eliza sat alone in her room, holding the key that he had held.

'Yes,' he had said, 'it is quite old. Beautifully made. How curious... there is something about it that...'

'What, Bertie?'

He looked at her, and laughed.

'You will think me quite strange, but it gives me an odd feeling. I have always felt so when I saw it on you. Almost as if there was something familiar about it, but of course I have never seen it before in my life.'

'Perhaps you have seen one like it?'

'Perhaps.'

'Take it,' she said, suddenly.

'What?'

'Take it. It's yours. I... I feel it belongs to you.'

He frowned, turning the key over again in his hands. He looked up at Eliza, and seemed about to say something, but when their eyes met he seemed to forget all about the key, and instead was looking at her in a very different way, a way that made her heart beat fast and she too forgot all about the key.

Remembering all this, Eliza's heart beat fast again, and she blushed and smiled to herself, hugging herself as she thought of all they had done and said. Everything had changed. She was a woman now. Bertie was surely hers. He was gone to London today, but surely he would send for her soon.

Afterwards, he had picked up the little book of poetry that he given her, and opened a page at random, reading in his beautiful rich and resonant voice:

Music, when soft voices die,
  Vibrates in the memory—
  Odours, when sweet violets sicken,
  Live within the sense they quicken.
  Rose leaves, when the rose is dead,
  Are heaped for the belovèd's bed;
  And so thy thoughts, when thou art gone,
  Love itself shall slumber on.

She had thought it rather a melancholy little verse, for the circumstances, and they had both been silent for a while afterwards. Then he had said that he must go, and had dressed, while she watched him from the bed.

'When will I see you Bertie?'

Not meeting her eyes, he had replied, 'In good time, in good time.'

And she took that to mean that he would call for her soon.

It was only later that she realised that the key was still with her, lying on the bedside table where he had left it.

CHAPTER 10

May 1985

We laid the letter out on the table, arranged an angle-poise lamp to give us as much light as possible, and I had a notebook and pen by my side.

'Right-ho, here we go,' said Justin, taking up the magnifying glass and leaning over the table to view the top of the page.

It was painstaking work, and we spent a long time trying to decipher some of the words. But slowly, with many crossings out, a few gaps, and interruptions while Justin went to turn the heat off under the soup and answer a telephone call, we put together a letter that looked like the following:

London
  Theatre Royal, Drury Lane

My dearest Eliza
  Thank you so much for your sweet letter. I am of course missing your company also, but I am very much distracted by work at present. I have so much to do what with learning lines and rehearsing new plays. There are one or two very fresh new actors in the company who need 'settling in', and of course I do my best

to take them under my wing and instruct them.

I do not think it would be such a good idea for you to come to London at present my dear. The cholera is very bad here, and I would not want you to put yourself in any danger. I do not go out anywhere except to travel between the theatre and home. The audiences ———- and managers are putting all kinds of spectacle and ———— ———— entice them to come out. Bunn is going all out. I worry that if his plans do not come off, he may go bankrupt again. I am writing to ———— ————— Covent Garden, or I may try for America.

I do not think it expedient for you to visit me at home, particularly ———- my <u>wife</u> being so fragile and finds visitors rather tiring. So you see, my dear <u>friend</u>, we have ———- ———— and our lives are not our own. But I would be delighted for you to continue to write – address to Drury Lane (until further notice) – and I will endeavour to write too, when I am able to get a moment to myself. But you know how it is in this business, and I have so many different kinds of friends like you, both male and female. But the freedoms we enjoy in this business, can never be spoken elsewhere.

The play here continues to bring in the audiences, and I am pleased to say we opened to good reviews, on the whole.

I went to see Macready at the Garden last week, but it was a very poor play, though Macready, as usual was excellent.

The letter meandered on about plays he had seen, and people he had met, and how the weather had been, until he ended abruptly with:

I am running out of paper and of time! I hope you will be able to read this. Now I must rush and catch the post.

Do keep hold of that key. It was kind of you to offer it to me, but I

do not know what I would do with it. Keep it. I feel, somehow, it is
important.

   Affectionately yours
   Bertie.

'Well,' said Justin, 'what a cad and a bounder! Reading between the lines I would say he had seduced poor Eliza before going home to his wife, and if you read 'actresses' instead of 'actors' in that first paragraph, he probably went on to seduce a few more.'

'You're probably right,' I said, 'the way he underlines "wife", and then "friend" in the next line is making the message very clear. I wonder if Eliza knew he had a wife before this letter. But what about that last line when he mentions the key? Do you think he is talking about my key? What do you think it means?'

'It's very interesting. I wonder why he had such a strange feeling about it. Eliza had obviously shown it to him, and they had discussed it – and she had tried to give it to him.'

I took the key, that was still held around my neck on a chain, and gazed at it again. A shiver crossed my shoulders.

'Oh, this is so weird,' I said, 'to think that my ancestor, Eliza, was holding this and discussing it with Bertrand McDougal, just as we are now. I wonder if she had dreams too...'

'Well, if she did, she never found out herself what it was for, otherwise it would never have come down to you on its own. It's a puzzle still to be solved.'

'Yes, it looks as though she just put everything in a box and left it for someone else to sort it out. And now it's come to me.' I shuddered again.

'You OK?'

'Yes. I just suddenly got chills down my spine. I mean, well, this could either be a complete wild goose chase and all nonsense. But if it isn't, it seems there is something important here, important to my family. And I'm the keyholder. It feels like a big responsibility.'

Justin sat back in his chair and looked thoughtful. Then he said, 'I think we both need to eat. I'm starving. I'll go and heat the soup up and then we'll talk some more if you like.'

Graham joined us for lunch, and afterwards he also read through their transcription of Bertie's letter.

'Hmm....' he muttered, 'he certainly is a bit of a cad, and doesn't this bit hint to something more?'

Justin grinned. 'I know. It seems fairly obvious to me, and perhaps he was trying to tell her something about himself, without actually saying it?'

I looked at them both. 'What are you guys talking about?'

Justin nodded to Graham.

'Go on.'

'This bit in the letter at the end where he talks about friends "both male and female" and that statement about the freedoms of the business. Surely, he is warning Eliza that she is not the only one, other than his wife. And not only that, she is not the only sex, either. In other words, to use a more modern term, this guy would screw anything that moved, darling.'

Sarah looked at the letter again.

'Wow. Of course, I think you're probably right. Poor Eliza. I wonder if she realised what he was saying. I suppose he couldn't say too much in a letter, in case it fell into the wrong hands.'

'Well, the arts have always been the place for free-thinkers and, I suppose, therefore, a kind of haven for anyone who lives outside the normal rules of society. I mean, look at the women in theatre, for one thing. They had an autonomy and more freedom of expression than any other women in society in the nineteenth century, who saw them as no more than prostitutes in the main. But what about gay men – or gay women for that matter? The theatre has always been a place where they can enjoy the tolerance of their workmates, with the exception of a few I suppose. But in a society where homosexuality was a criminal offence, the theatre was the place where they too could enjoy a certain amount of freedom, whilst hiding their true nature from the rest of the world. I think Bertie is warning her that she is just one of many, but even he is a little wary of writing it down. He might have been afraid to offend Eliza, who is still too young and innocent, despite her years in the theatre, to know so much.'

'Yes,' said Justin, 'very eloquently put, and exactly what I was thinking.'

'Wow,' I said, 'do you know, I was so busy thinking about poor Eliza finding out that Bertie was married, I didn't get that reference, but you could be right. And then I got a real jolt when he mentioned the key. I wonder why he felt it was so important. I mean, what would it mean to him?'

No-one had the answer.

'If only we knew what that key opens,' said Graham.

'Oh, it's so frustrating,' I said, 'I'm no closer to finding out any answers than I was at the start!'

'What about those dreams of yours,' said Justin, 'was there anything else in them that could be a clue?'

I shook my head.

'No. Just the man in a cloak. I like him, though. The dream

is always pleasant, and he seems benevolent.'

'What does he look like?' asked Graham.

'Well, I never see much of his face, but I have a feeling he has a beard – one of those neat, close ones. And a big collar. The cloak is not full length, but short and swishy.'

'Similar period to the key, perhaps,' said Justin.

'Sarah,' said Graham, 'how's it going with tracing the family tree? Since the key has come through your family, perhaps tracing back further than Eliza might help?'

'Oh!' I exclaimed, 'Of course! The genealogist! I told her not to do any more for the present, because it was rather expensive and I was running out of money, but now, with the money from my mother, I could tell her to do some more. Graham, you're a genius!'

'Are you really up for this?' said Justin to Graham, 'It could be a bit of a treasure hunt, I suppose. You know, getting out a bit.'

Graham clapped his hands. 'Oh, but yes - this is exciting. If it gets us out and about and digging up graves in the moonlight, then I'm definitely up for it!'

'I hope it won't come to that!' I said.

But I could see that Justin was surprised at Graham's response, and he was looking at him with a kind of curiosity. Then he turned back to me.

'Well then,' he said, 'the games afoot!'

CHAPTER 11

Before anything else, I decided I ought to touch base and go back home for a night or two, so I could pick up some clean clothes and my post and sort out anything that might be needed. I left the box and its contents with Justin.

As I pulled into my drive, looking forward to a hot bath and a glass of wine, I knew something was wrong. There was something odd about the angle of my front door, and as I got out of the car and approached the front step, I realised with a chill down my spine that it was slightly ajar.

Could Greta have been careless enough not to close it properly after she had visited to water the plants? But... that did not sound like Greta, who was so meticulous and careful in most things.

I pushed the door slowly open and entered the small entrance hall. The door to the living room was open. I stood and listened. I could hear nothing except the slow dripping of a tap in the downstairs cloakroom that I had been meaning to get fixed for ages. I waited a while, just to be sure, but the house felt empty.

Leaving the front door wide open just in case I needed to get out quickly, I opened the door into the living room, and froze where I stood, my eyes wide open.

The drawers and cupboards were all open, their contents

strewn around the room. A painting on the wall was crooked. The door through to the kitchen/diner was open and I could see that it was the same in there.

I was unable to move for several moments. My hands were on my face. I whispered to myself, 'Oh no... oh no...'

Then I stumbled to the telephone and called the police.

Two hours later I was on the phone to Justin. I would not be returning to Gloucestershire for the time being.

'Nothing was taken, Justin. Nothing. There were so many things they could have taken: the television, stereo, my mother's jewellery. But the police say it was obvious that whoever broke in was looking for something, and they weren't interested in anything else.'

Greta and I were sitting in the living room, a half-consumed bottle of wine between us. Greta had brought food to pick at, so we didn't have to use the kitchen before it had been tidied up.

'My God, Sarah,' said Justin, 'what on earth were they looking for?'

'I don't know. Whatever it was, they obviously didn't find it. I'm scared. Something weird is going on.'

'Are you going to be OK tonight? Are you alone?'

'Greta's here. She's going to stay the night. But I don't think I'll get much sleep. I've had the locks changed already; the police said it was a good idea. Apparently, whoever did this got in through a back window and left through the front door. All the same, I just feel terribly vulnerable. I think I'd feel better if they had stolen something. That would be that. But this is different. If they're looking for something, they'll come back, won't they?'

'Shit. Yeah, I can understand how you feel, but now you've been alerted, I doubt anyone would be stupid enough. Look, would you like me to come over and stay for a few days? We were going to stay on here, as I said, but Graham's feeling better, and he's thinking of getting back to London and getting on with things. I would have stayed up here if you were coming back, but I could come and help you clear up instead. I'll bring all your stuff back for you.'

'That sounds wonderful, Justin. You're so kind. I would really like that. What about Graham? Why don't you bring him over too, if he's coming back to London anyway.'

There was a brief silence.

'I'll see what he says. I'll be driving down tomorrow. I'll stop at the flat to pick up some stuff then be with you around lunch time. Don't worry, darling, we'll sort it all out. You'll be fine. It's just a horrible thing to happen and you're bound to feel shaky. See you tomorrow, OK?'

I said goodbye and put the phone down. Then I burst into tears.

Greta handed me a glass of wine and a tissue, and sitting down next to me, put her arm round my shoulders. Her familiar, warm smell of patchouli was comforting.

'You poor old thing,' she said.

I blew my nose. 'Thanks Greta. Sorry. Being really silly. It was just – everyone being so kind. I'm so lucky...' and my voice went all squeaky as the tears started again, '...I'm so lucky to have... such... good friends.'

As I had expected, it took me a while to fall asleep that night, but eventually I fell into a deep sleep.

I am walking through a forest. All the trees around me stand so tall, I cannot see their tops, but I can hear the sound of the leaves as a soft breeze blows through them. I reach a clearing, and in the centre is a large tree, and I know that it is my tree; my special tree. I smile, remembering how I loved to climb trees when I was a child. The branches are high, but someone has placed a ladder so that I can reach the lowest ones, and I start to climb.

The tree becomes a maze, and I am walking through dark corridors, lined with books. A sense of foreboding comes over me. I feel I am being followed, and I start to panic, going down passages, not knowing whether I am going the right way. Ahead of me, I see a familiar figure. The man with the cloak and the key. He smiles, and beckons me, and then he points towards a door, encouraging me to open it and go through. Above the door is a name.

The man looks behind me, as if he too senses danger, and then he looks at me again and nods in encouragement, saying 'Be careful...' I turn to walk through the door...

I awoke, and lay for several minutes, trying to remember each part of the dream before it faded, so I could describe it to the others. Frustratingly, I could not remember the name above the doorway. But, for the first time, the dream disturbed me. When I had dreamed of the man with the key before, I had always felt comfortable and happy, but this dream had been different. That sense of foreboding followed me out of the dream and into my waking consciousness.

Then I remembered the events of yesterday, and it seemed fitting that my dreams should be troubled. With the sense of foreboding still upon me, I got up quickly, and went downstairs to make myself a strong cup of tea.

It would be several hours before Justin arrived, and Greta

was at work all day, so I decided to call Georgina while I was waiting. Perhaps concentrating on the family tree business would take my mind off the break-in.

'I've decided to continue a bit more with the family tree,' I said, 'I'd like to see if we can trace Eliza's line back; the Jayne family tree.'

'Well,' said Georgina, 'I did have another look for Eliza's marriage after we last spoke. I happened to be at St. Catherine's House, and thought I'd double check it while I was waiting for some certificates for another client. As you said, your uncle had searched for it without any luck, and I have to say I came to a dead end as well. I tried several variations on her surname without any joy. Unless there's been a clerical error somewhere, it's possible she married abroad, or perhaps she was living with Edward Turvey as a wife but without being married to him. It happened more often than you might think in Victorian times. It's a huge problem when that happens. The marriage certificate would confirm her father's name, and then we'd know we have the right person.'

'Oh bother,' I said, feeling disappointed, 'all the same, I feel certain that Eliza is my ancestor, and that we have the right baptism for her.' I told Georgina about the cross-written letter and her possible relationship with Bertrand McDougal. As I spoke his name, I clapped my hand to my mouth as I remembered my dream again. Until now, I had not remembered what the name was above the door, but as I talked about Bertrand, I now remembered that the name was McDougal.

My mind was racing, but I said nothing to Georgina, and she spoke again.

'Very interesting; it does sound possible that she did not

know Bertrand was married when they formed their relationship. Of course, we cannot know for sure, but it makes me wonder...'

I sat up. I was hoping Georgina's mind was working in the same way as mine.

'What are you thinking?'

'Well, of course, it's something that can probably never be proved, so I can't say this without a great deal of caution, but it is entirely possible that Eliza had become pregnant with Bertie's child.'

'Yes...go on...'

'And if she married Edward Turvey soon afterwards, then that would mean that her first child, your direct ancestor, was the child of Bertrand, and not Edward's.'

I let out my breath, realising I had been holding it for the last few moments.

Georgina continued: 'But of course, this kind of thing can almost never be proven.'

'No,' I said, 'I understand that. But I really do feel that you are onto something. It feels right to me.'

Georgina sighed. 'I am sure it does, but if only I could tell you how many times I have felt that something is "right" and then been proved wrong! But in this case, I doubt we can prove anything one way or another. If we could find the marriage, then the date might give us a clue, if it was less than nine months before her son's birth, but I have looked at all possible dates, including a late marriage. Though that still wouldn't prove anything.'

'Oh, how frustrating!' I said. For the moment I had forgotten all about the break-in.

'Do you want me to do anything else? I can look at the Jayne line, of course, if you think it's right, though of course I cannot advise you that this is one hundred per cent certain...'

I thought for a moment.

'Yes. Yes, please do. I'm certain. Why else would her letters and personal things have come through my family? But... I wonder if you could do something else for me?'

'Certainly, if it's possible!'

'Could you have a look at Bertie's – I mean, Bertrand Mc-Dougal's line? I know we can't prove he is my ancestor, but I am interested in him anyway.' I was not going to tell her about the dream, but the symbolism of the name above the door seemed to suggest that what she had suggested was right. 'I'm assuming, with that name, there's a Scottish connection?'

'Hm. Yes. Hopefully, as he had some degree of fame, there might be some information on his family anyway, but after that, I might have to contact a colleague of mine in Edinburgh. It might add up to some expense. How much do you want to spend on this?'

'Let's say, up to £150 for now,' I said, 'I've had a bit of a windfall, and I really want to find out more. I'm really intrigued. Would that be enough for now?'

'Indeed it would. It might take a few weeks, but I will be in touch.'

I finished the phone call and sat on the sofa for a while, thinking about what Georgina had said. How exciting it would be to be descended from a theatrical family like Bertrand McDougal's! It seemed possible that this was what that part of the dream was trying to tell me. Symbolically, the tree in the dream seemed, fairly obviously, to be my family tree, and if so, I had been shown a 'branch' of that tree with the name McDougal. But could it ever be proven, and what was the significance of it? And why was I having these dreams, anyway? Why was it so important?

I jumped as the postman posted several envelopes through the door, and the current reality came back to me. Since yesterday, I had felt vulnerable and was reacting nervously to any little noise in the house. I was alone, and it was still a couple of hours before Justin was due to get here. The thought of being on my own even for just two hours was giving me the creeps, but I didn't want to go out, leaving the house empty again. Besides, the weather was gloomy, with heavy clouds creating a claustrophobic mugginess to the warm May day, and the thought of coming back to what I had come back to yesterday terrified me. I knew this was irrational, and the likelihood of the same thing happening again was very slim, but I did not feel very rational. I felt scared and threatened. I wished I could speak to someone, but who? Justin would be traveling by now and Greta was at work.

I went into the kitchen to make a cup of tea, picking up my post and throwing it onto the coffee table to look at while I drank. The telephone rang just as I was coming back in with my mug.

'Hello?'

'Sarah? It's David.'

I smiled. How timely. I had needed a distraction, and someone to talk to; he was just the right person.

'How nice to hear from you. I needed a chat.'

'Really? Anything wrong?'

'Yes. I've had a break in. Nothing taken, but such a horrible experience. Feeling a bit vulnerable alone... silly really...!'

There was a slight pause on the other end.

'Do you want me to come over?'

I was confused. Didn't he live in Manchester?

'Oh... no! No... thanks for the offer, but my friend Justin – you remember you met him? He is coming over and probably staying for a few days, so there's no need. Thanks all the same.'

Surely, she thought, he must like her if he was offering to come all the way from Manchester?

'I see. Well, it would have been nice to see you. I suppose the police have been...'

'Yes. They've taken fingerprints, but whoever it was, was probably wearing gloves. They asked me if I knew of anything that someone might want, but I can't really think of anything. Weird, isn't it?'

'Yes.' Another pause. 'Anyway, I haven't heard from you since our answerphone messages. How's your family tree going?'

At the time, I barely registered the sudden change of subject from something so important. I was just glad to have the distraction from the emptiness and vulnerability of my threatened world.

'Yes, sorry I didn't get back to you again. I've been staying in the Cotswolds with Justin. Oh, I have lots to tell you...!' I proceeded to tell him all about the letter and what I had found out about Eliza and Bertie, and the possibility that Bertie might be an ancestor. I did not tell him about the dreams. David listened patiently without speaking, and when I had finished, just quietly said, 'Wow.'

'Well, I know you're not as interested in the family history as I am, but I thought you should know anyway. For me, it's nice to know I come from at least one theatrical family.'

'Well,' said David, 'thanks for all the news. I have to go now. It's been nice talking to you. I'll call again soon.'

I put the phone down feeling deflated. Had I gone on a bit much about the family history? Some people just find it boring. Perhaps I had put David off? He certainly hadn't sounded very warm when he had closed the conversation like that.

I picked up my tea, which had turned lukewarm. I put it down again and picked up the post. Most of it was junk, but there was a hand-written large letter from Manchester. I opened it. It contained a short letter from Aunt Ada, and another sealed envelope with my name on it.

Dear Sarah

I hope you are well and enjoying this spring weather! I looked out of the window and the dark clouds. It must be sunny in Manchester.

You are going to think me an absent-minded old thing – but that is what old age does to you. I was going through some of Charles's things, and I found the enclosed envelope. Of course, it all came back to me then. When he left you the family history, he also said there was a letter he had left for you to read after his passing. I knew there had been something else, but at the time of the funeral, it had completely gone out of my mind. I do hope it is not too important, though I cannot think it will be anything to worry about. Probably just some notes on the Turvey family. Anyway, please find it enclosed.

Things are mostly sorted out now, and I am getting used to the empty house. Do visit if you are up this way.

Kind regards

Your Aunt Ada

I picked up the envelope from Uncle Charles. What on earth could it be? I tore it open and read the enclosed letter.

My Dear Sarah

If you are reading this, then I will have passed on and this message comes to you from beyond the grave – or I should probably say 'beyond the urn'!

I half smiled. Uncle Charles always had had a rather warped sense of humour.

Anyway, I do hope that Ada has remembered to give you the things I left for you, including this letter. In fact, this letter may be the most important thing of all. None of it is in the will because I did not want it to be public, so I have had to trust to Ada's memory, which is a risk I have to take.

Now, you should have received the family tree stuff, and I hope that Ada told you about the box that was in your father's keeping. I gave it to him some time ago for reasons that should become clear. In that box you will find some items relating to a female ancestor of ours.

You are probably going to think that your ageing uncle was going a bit gaga. Well, perhaps. But it seems important to me, so here goes.

For some time now, I have had strange dreams...

I sat up, nearly choking on my cold tea.

...that seem to suggest the importance of the large key you will find in the box. These dreams – or perhaps I should call them visions of some kind – have led me to believe that there is some importance around Elizabeth's line. You will see her on the tree. The documents in the box I believe belonged to her, and that she began life as Eliza Jayne, and that she was once an actress – that

should interest you Sarah!

Dreams and visions? If anyone had said the same to me, I would have thought them completely barmy and deluded. And here is your very sensible old uncle saying he believes in such things! All I can say is, if something like that can convince me, then you know there must be something in it!

But I am also beginning to believe that there is something odd about Eliza's marriage to Edward Turvey. The letter in the box shows she had some kind of intimate relationship with the Victorian actor, Bertrand McDougal, and I began to wonder...

I am sure you will follow my train of thought.

I am sure most families have lines coming from the wrong side of the bedsheets, as it were, and we are no different it seems. But my investigations have led me to believe there might be some inheritance involved. Alas, my age and growing infirmities have put an end to my ability to follow this up – and that is why I am passing all of this on to you, dear niece.

One more thing – and this is most important.

You will probably meet your 2nd cousin David at the funeral. I don't know if you've ever met him before, but he is the grandchild of my father's brother Stephen. He came to visit once, and I told him all about the family tree and the items in the box, which he showed great interest in.

Really? That didn't sound like the David I knew.

I didn't tell him about my dreams, but I did express my thoughts on the possibility of an inheritance. But afterwards, I wished I hadn't mentioned it. He kept ringing me and asking about what I had found out, but I've always been a bit vague about it, and started to play it down. I think he has in mind that if there is anything to inherit, it should be him, but I have never told him that you were more likely to inherit, and I'm not sure he knew that you existed. Not that there is anything to inherit as far as I know, but whatever all this leads to, who knows what might come of it?

The thing is, I have come to distrust him. His father, my cousin David, was an odd-ball, and deserted his wife and David when David was very young. David seems very like him to my mind. To me, he has all the hallmarks of a sociopath.

So, you may think me paranoid or over-cautious, but I would advise telling David nothing about the box and the tree, or the fact that I have given it to you. If you do ever speak to him, whatever you do, don't mention what I've said, or anything about the key. If there was any money involved, I think he might do anything to get his hands on it. But, then again, I might be just being over suspicious.

Good luck with your life, dear Sarah. I am sorry we have not known each other better, but I hope there is something in this gift from me that you can enjoy.

Your Uncle Charles

X

My heart was racing. I felt cold and sick. Only a few moments ago I had been thinking what good timing it was that David should ring me at that moment. Now, I could not think of any possible worse timing.

I went back over my conversation with David. I heard my own voice excitedly telling him all the things I had found out. I heard his silence, and his sudden ending of the conversation, which now seemed ominous. I remembered his sudden changing of the subject from the break-in to the family history, and with a jolt that felt like I had been kicked in the stomach, I thought of something terrible.

I looked at my uncle's letter again: '. *If there was any money involved, I think he might do anything to get his hands on it.'*

Surely not...

Then I remembered what Greta had said when she had arrived at Justin's house last week. She had told me there had been a phone call from someone who just put the phone down when she told him I was away. She had said she didn't like the voice; that she didn't have a good feeling about it. I had dismissed it as Greta just being over-cautious Greta. But that was because I had just wanted to believe otherwise. Greta was good at hunches. Her instincts were often right.

I thought back to the beginning of my conversation with David. He had asked if I wanted him to come over.

'Oh my God!' I said out loud, 'he's not in Manchester! He's here in London!'

Fear crept around me like cold, icy fingers. I saw David for the first time objectively, letting go of my need for a male companion, my need for someone to take notice of me; I saw him as cold, selfish... and I had to admit it to myself now... Justin had probably been right. He was probably homophobic, and God knows what else. How could I have possibly been so wrong?

Because he was family. Because I had been flattered by his attention. And now, looking back at our first meeting, I realised that his attention was because he knew I had inheritance rights, and he was there when Ada had given me the family tree and he knew I would soon have all the information to find out... what?

I felt sick that I had ever been attracted to him. 'How could I be so stupid!' I gasped.

There was only one person who could have been likely to

break into my house. It must have been David. I suddenly remembered the car that nearly drove into me as I left the house only a few days ago... Was that him too? Or was I now being paranoid?

I turned instinctively to look out of the windows and check the locks. As I looked out, a car was turning into my drive. I gasped, my hands to my mouth.

But in the next second, I breathed with relief as I recognised Justin's car, and in the next few seconds I had run to the front door, opened all the locks and flew out to greet him.

CHAPTER 12

February 1850

Eliza sat on the steps at the front entrance of Drury Lane Theatre, not knowing what to do or where to go next. The world went past her in its busyness; carriages drew up, people got in and got out, and passed her by, along the street, and one or two up and down the steps of the theatre. None paid her any heed. She drew her shawl closer round her. It was cold. But still, she continued to sit.

In her head she relived the conversation she had just had.

Bertie had been surprised to see her. Surprised, but not as delighted as she had thought he would be. He had answered her knock on his dressing room door, and ushered her in. On his table was a half-eaten pie and a tankard of beer.

'Why, Eliza! What brings you here?'

'You do, Bertie. Are you not pleased to see me?'

Bertie spluttered slightly, 'Why, yes... of course! But did I not warn you against coming to London? Sit down, sit down. The cholera is still bad here, you know, and I would not want you to come to any harm...'

'Oh, but Bertie, I had to see you!' she sat down on a chair. 'I don't know where else to turn. You must help me!'

'Why, what is the matter?' he said, his face paling.

Eliza looked down at the floor.

'There is going to be a child,' she said.

'A child? You mean...?'

'Yes.'

'Oh, Lord!' Bertie put his elbow on the table, and his head in his hand.

'Are you sure? I mean, have you been examined by a doctor?'

'Yes.'

He groaned. Under his breath, but loud enough for her to hear, he said, 'This is not good timing.'

'What do you mean, Bertie?'

He looked up at her.

'I mentioned my wife in my letter, did I not?'

She looked at the ground again. 'Yes.'

'Did you not know I was married when we were together in Oxford?'

'No.'

There was a long silence.

'My wife is ill. My work here at this theatre is finished. You were lucky to find me here. The manager is bankrupt, and they do nothing but put on horrendous so-called spectacles to try and pull in the audiences; there is no drama. So, I have no work for the moment, and I need to look after my wife. What is it that you wish me to do?'

Eliza felt unable to breathe. Tears were very close. She thought that Bertie would sort everything out, that he would find an answer, and look after her somehow at the very least. She had thought that he would be nice to her. It had been a terrible blow when she had read his letter and realised that he had been married all along; she had felt angry and confused.

That was before she discovered that she was with child. But she thought that he loved her. She thought that he would find a way for him to look after her and the baby. And perhaps even find a way for them to be together, somehow. But Bertie's reaction to her presence; his tone of voice, and look of horror, told her everything she needed to know. The fantasy she had built up around herself and Bertie was crumbling down around her. She had been a naïve fool.

She could not answer his question. Hot tears spilled down her cheeks and dripped onto the floor.

Bertie sighed and shifted in his chair.

'My dear child, what in Heaven's name were you expecting? I am not a free man, as you know. I am financially harassed at every corner. I need physick for my wife, whom I am very fond of, by the way, and I do not know when or where I will be in work again.'

Eliza said nothing, just looking at the floor, not checking the tears that continued to flow.

Bertie coughed.

'Do you wish to ... find someone who will... ahem ... get rid of the child? It costs money, you know.'

Eliza then looked up in horror.

'Oh no, Bertie! Not that! I couldn't...'

'Then,' his voice became gentler, 'what will you do?'

'I do not know.'

'Have you any family at all?'

'No. Only an uncle. But we are not close. He's a respectable man; he would not...'

'I see. Does anyone in the theatre company know?'

'No. But obviously I cannot continue...'

'No.'

'Perhaps if you told the manager...'

'Oh, Bertie. You know what his policy is. He prides himself on running a respectable company. He has always said that any trouble is our own responsibility, and he would not countenance anything that would put the company in a bad light. He is a good man, but I think he would draw the line at... And anyway, I do not think the company will last much longer.'

'No. Well then. What will you do?'

'I do not know.'

Neither of them was going to speak the words that they were both thinking. The workhouse. But this was the only option that now loomed large in Eliza's imagination. Some dark and dismal building where she would be put to work at some menial and meaningless task, looked down upon as a 'fallen woman', and separated from her child, who would grow up in poverty with the stigma of the workhouse, poverty and illegitimacy upon its head.

In that moment, as she sat on the chair in Bertie's room, she saw her future fall away from her. She knew she had lost the freedom she had as an actress; the joy of performance, of audience appreciation, of living and working within a company of like-minded people. In one stupid decision she had made that day when Bertie was about to leave the company, she had changed her life for ever. Not in the way she had thought, but in a completely opposite and terrible way.

'If my wife were in better health, I would offer to take the child...'

She had then got up and left Bertie's room, leaving him as he had sat there, stammering, 'I...I'm sorry, Eliza...but you see how it is...'

She had left the stage door, blindly walking to the corner of

131

St. Catherine Street, and, not knowing which direction to turn, had sat down on the front steps of the theatre. She had no idea what to do next, not just in the wider sense, but immediately. She had spent her last wages on a train ticket to London and a cab to the theatre, thinking that once she saw Bertie he would look after her and would work out what to do next. But she had not even got around to telling him that she had nowhere to go. She had told Henry Holland that she needed to visit a sick relative for a couple of days, thinking that she would come back and work out the season, and by then have had some sort of plan. But now, she did not even know how she would get back to Oxfordshire. If she did not appear for the performance tomorrow, she would probably be sacked, and she would be immediately destitute.

Wild thoughts ran through her head. If only she could get back for tomorrow night, she would at least have a few weeks before anyone would know her condition, and by that time she might have a plan, or perhaps someone in the company would help or tell her what to do. She could walk back to Paddington Station; she did not know the way, but she could ask for directions, and... perhaps beg... or even steal the money for the fare? But what if she was caught? The fear of prison or even transportation was enough to turn her off that course of action. But how would she get back to Oxford? Was there even a train that would get her back in time?

What an utter fool she had been, thinking that she could come to London and that Bertie would make everything right. If only her parents were still alive. She would have gone to them, instead of coming to London, and they would have known what to do. They had always looked after her.

Tears blinded her, as she fully realised just how alone she

now was.

She did not know how many hours passed as she sat on the steps of Drury Lane Theatre, but the light began to fade, and the bustle of the streets changed in their energy as the daytime workers went home, and those seeking evening entertainments took over. Cabs went by with their lanterns lit, and people in evening dress began to emerge; women in silk or velvet gowns with evening capes, chaperoned by moustachioed men in frock coats and top hats. Audiences, out to go to the theatre or a concert, or the opera, most passing Drury Lane on their way to Covent Garden, or perhaps the Lyceum. Crossing sweepers swept the streets clear in front of them so that the ladies could step out into the road without getting their evening slippers muddy or wet. Only a few were coming to Drury Lane.

An usher from the theatre came down the steps and spoke to her.

'Move along, now, Miss. Let people pass. Come along...'

Eliza rose painfully to her feet. She was stiff and cold. She began to step down onto the pavement, and bumped the arm of a young man passing by, who turned in irritation.

'I am sorry, sir,' she said, dully, turning to walk vaguely in the direction of Covent Garden.

'I say... what the devil?' said the young man, 'wait... isn't that...? Wait! Miss Jayne! I say, do wait...'

The young man caught up with her and took her elbow. She turned then to look at him. He looked vaguely familiar, but she could not think where she knew him from.

'It is you! Miss Jayne – Miss Eliza Jayne! What are you doing in London? Are you going to be playing here? How wonderful!', then seeing that she was having difficulty recognising him, he said, 'it's Turvey, Edward Turvey. I am a great admirer of your work...' He took off his hat and gave a little bow.

'Turvey? Oh yes, of course. You came to the stage door only a few weeks ago.'

'I have followed your career with enormous interest, Miss Jayne. Tell me, are you planning to play here in London? That would be marvellous...'

'No... no... I don't think so. I am at Oxford until...'

'Miss Jayne, would you allow me to introduce you to my friends? We are in town for the opera, but there is no hurry. I would be delighted to escort you to wherever you are going. A young lady like you should not be out alone.'

'Well... I...'

Eliza looked at him again. In the past she had thought him tiresome and rather silly, but she saw that he was not un-handsome, just a little weak around the jaw. His hair was curly, though he had only the whisper of a moustache. But she also noticed now that his clothes were well made and expensive, and he was out with young male friends, not a young lady.

'Of course, Mr Turvey, I would be delighted...'

At first, she had thought to tell him some tale about losing her purse and needing money to get a train back to Oxford, but as they walked her brain worked fast, and she realised that if she went back to the theatre now there was no telling when she would see him again, and then it would be too late.

'Would you like me to call a cab, Miss Jayne?'

'Oh, no... I like to walk. Don't you? Anyway, it would be nice to get to know you better. Please tell me more about yourself. I am staying at... at... near Paddington Station. Is that very far to walk? I'm afraid I do not know London very well...'

'No... well, it is a little way... but it would be most delightful

134

in your company. Perhaps we can find a cab on the way. What jolly luck we should bump into each other like this! Here, take my arm...'

'Thank you. So, Mr Turvey, do you visit the theatre often?'

'Oh yes! But much to the vexation of my dear Ma and Pa, who think I am wasting my time on such things. In fact, if they saw me now, walking arm in arm with an actress, they would be horrified... oh but, not that they should be... I mean...'

Eliza laughed and squeezed his arm.

As he rattled on, she thought very quickly. If she had any chance of saving herself, and her child, she could see that she would have to burn her bridges. Turvey was a foolish, naïve man, but she could see that he was not unkind. What other choices lay in front of her? The workhouse, or the streets... Whatever choice she made, it seemed that she would no longer be able to work as an actress. Even if she tried to go back to the theatre after she had the child, there would be no guarantee that she could get work, especially with an infant in tow, and she knew now that she would not want to give up the child. She already felt the maternal pull towards the child in her belly.

After a while, she 'confessed' to Turvey that she was thinking of giving up the theatre and living a more respectable life. That she had come to London to visit an uncle, who was interested in finding her a husband. She had laughed a little at this, hinting at a string of suitors clamouring for her attention.

She told him, truthfully, of her parents' deaths, about which he was appropriately horrified, dismayed and very kind. In fact, his sympathy almost made her cry.

She made it clear that she was alone. That her uncle, although kind, was rather strict, and not approving of her theatrical career; that she was unable to make up her mind about what to do next and felt the lack of guidance from someone who could be a true friend.

By the time they reached Paddington, having found a Hansom cab on Long Acre, Turvey was stammering a vow of lasting friendship and companionship, hinting at more without being able to voice it, while Eliza bowed her head, as if blushing beneath her best bonnet.

They married in Paris. Edward thought it best to marry quickly and quietly, away from England, before his parents could find anything about Eliza's background. Once they were married, there would be little his father or mother could do about it, even if they did find out.

Even so, they both knew that it would be impossible for someone of Edward's status to be known to be married to an actress. To cover her tracks, Eliza changed her name to Elizabeth, practised the refined elocution of the middle to upper classes (she had done this often in theatrical roles), and brushed up on the little French she knew.

Facing his parents' wrath back in London, Edward explained that Elizabeth's parents were dead, and that she had been brought up by a very respectable uncle, who was now very sick and likely to die quite soon. He told them that they had met in Paris some time ago and had fallen in love, and that Elizabeth had been in danger of being married off to a man she did not love, so he had swooped in and bought a licence, and married her himself before this could happen.

It was not the best of stories, but his parents, knowing Edward to be of a rash and romantic nature, thought it had the ring of truth, and agreed to be introduced to their new daughter-in-law.

Eliza, now Elizabeth, in a modest, but expensive, silk gown bought in Paris, her hair scraped back into an elegant chignon, was brought to her new parents' house in Mayfair. She answered demurely all the questions that they asked her, following the story that she and Edward had devised, performing the role of a young lady at the very height of good manners, respectability and modesty. She even threw in a few French exclamations here and there to give credence to the story of her living in France.

While both of Edward's parents felt a little uneasy about the lack of information they had about Elizabeth's parentage, their fears were somewhat quashed by Elizabeth's decorous demeanour and the respectful and deferential way with which she addressed them. All in all, the meeting was a success, and while Mr and Mrs Turvey were not totally happy with the way the marriage had been arranged, what was done was done, and they welcomed their daughter-in-law into the family.

Edward and Elizabeth rented one of the new houses that had recently been built in the village of Clapham, a rising area just south of London, overlooking the greenery of the Common.

On the first night in her new house, Elizabeth sorted through some of her personal belongings. She had a box, given to her by her father some years ago. Into it she put items that she could not bear to part with: the receipt her father had kept on the night she was born, the review of her first theatrical appearance, a poster from the play at Oxford, the book that Bertie had given her. Turning the beautiful pewter key over in her hands, she finally added that to the box. And, the latest item, a ticket stub. Edward had taken her, as a birthday surprise, to see a play at Drury Lane, starring the great Bertrand McDougal. It had been an evening of mixed emotions. She added the ticket stub to the box, closed it and turned the key. She put the box in a bottom drawer. One day she would give it to her son. Nothing else was left of Eliza Jayne. For the rest of her life, she would play the role of Elizabeth Turvey, respected wife of Edward Turvey, solicitor.

Seven months later, she presented Edward with their first child, born a little prematurely, but thankfully small enough for this to be acceptable, though it raised the eyebrows of her mother-in-law.

She called him George, after her father.

Once, a few years later, she and Edward attended an entertainment, where a stunning negro dancer delighted the audience. Afterwards, she saw him coming out of the stage door as they passed by on the way to their carriage. She quickly pulled her hood over her face, and scurried past as Abe walked by. It would not do for the respectable wife of a solicitor to be seen talking to a negro.

CHAPTER 13

May 1985

'Shouldn't we tell the police?' asked Greta, 'given that we know who broke in?'

'The trouble is,' said Justin, 'there's no real evidence that it was him. How would we prove it? There are no fingerprints, he would just flatly deny it, and none of this would stand up in a court of law. As far as the law is concerned, it's all just too subjective. Circumstantial evidence, I think they call it. Furthermore, it would just make him more angry.'

'What do you suggest?' I asked, pouring myself another glass of wine.

'We shouldn't show him our hand. If we say nothing, it might confuse him. He won't know what we know and what we don't know. We could get ahead of the game.'

'This is a game?'

Justin thought for a moment, and then looked at me with an expression of apology. 'I'm sorry, love. Of course, it's totally up to you. If you think you should go to the police with everything, and let them take over, of course that's what you should do.'

'It's OK. It's just that, this doesn't feel like a game anymore. It did when it was just finding out about my ancestors, but it's suddenly got serious. I mean, who knows how far he might go to get what he wants? If my uncle was right about him being sociopathic, then he has no moral compass...'

'That's true, but if we start accusing David, they might go and question him and then he'll know that we're onto him, but the police will have nothing to go on. At the moment, he doesn't yet know that we suspect anything, as your phone conversation with him was before we did, so we do have the advantage. And I can't see the police being interested in all this family tree stuff. Unless there was some real evidence that there was some money to be got out of it, there's no real motivation for the crime, as it were. They probably don't even view it as much of a crime; there was nothing stolen, and nobody hurt – physically anyway. We're just going to look paranoid and they're not going to spend their time looking into it if they think it's nonsense.'

I wasn't sure. The police were not exactly flavour of the month with Justin at the moment and it was possible that he was negatively biased. I did not say that, however, and I did wonder whether alerting David to the idea that we suspected him was perhaps more dangerous than not saying anything.

Into the pause after Justin's words, the telephone rang, and all three heads swung to look at it, and then at each other.

'Oh dear,' I said, 'I'm almost scared to answer.'

Justin reached for the phone.

'Hello?'

We all looked at his face, but he smiled and shook his head.

'It's OK Sarah. It's your genealogist. She wants to speak to you. She sounds a bit excited.'

'Really? That doesn't sound like her! Hello Georgina. How's things?'

'Sarah? Oh, I'm so glad I got hold of you! Listen, I was going to wait and write this all up, but I was rather intrigued about the connection with McDougal, and so I immediately went over to Somerset House, and I found something that I think is extremely exciting.'

'What is it?'

'Well, Bertrand died in 1865. His wife pre-deceased him, and he had no children from that marriage, and no other family. It seems, though, that he left a will, and that will was never claimed. And here's the interesting bit. From what I've found, he left everything he owned to — hang on, let me just read from my notes... here it is, "my child by Eliza Jayne, actress, currently of Oxford". Of course, because Eliza got married, and was no longer an actress, it was impossible for his executor to find her, and so the will has never been administered. Do you know what this means?'

'Wow. He must have felt really guilty about the way he treated her. But it proves that Eliza's child was his!'

'Yes, yes! But more than that Sarah! Don't you see? The money was never claimed! Which means it's still around, accruing interest. It probably wasn't that much, but the interest... Well, what I'm trying to tell you is that, you might be in line to inherit.'

'You're kidding me.'

'No. Not at all. From what I can see, your line is the line of the first child down from Eliza's eldest son George, and you would be the beneficiary. It would have come down to your great-uncle — but he died in the First World War at the age of 17 without issue. Of course, we have to make sure we can prove it all; gather all the documentation and so on. We do have a problem with Eliza's marriage, of course. We really do need that. But I could carry on looking. Look, I could do all this for you without any up-front payment apart from expenses, certificates and so on, and you could just pay me if and when the money comes through. It's a risk for me, but I'm willing to do it; I've never come across anything like this before, and it's good experience for me, so I'd be happy to go ahead if you want me to.'

My head was spinning. Several thoughts were running through it at the same time.

'Georgina, have you any idea how much it might be? I mean, will it be worth all the effort? And, another thing, my cousin David; would he be entitled to inherit as well?'

'Probably. You might be due for an equal share. I will have to check these things out. I'll get back to you. But I thought you'd like to know. It's exciting isn't it?'

'Oh yes, it really is! Georgina, thank you so much for looking into this. I can't quite believe it's possible, but please go ahead and find out whether it will be worth applying and so on.'

'Will do. Oh, and by the way. I found something else that you might find interesting, but it's rather sad. Eliza's parents were both killed in a train crash. It was not long before she would have married Turvey, so it could explain why she left the theatre and chose to marry. It might have given her some protection in those days.'

I was silent for a few moments, thinking of my own parents, and this terrible thing we had in common. My parents were killed in a road accident, and hers in a train crash. I suddenly felt very close to my ancestor.

'Poor Eliza,' I said.

'Yes, indeed. Well, I'd better go. Cheerio.'

I put the phone down and looked at the others.

'Well, that's an interesting turn up.' I explained what Georgina had said about the will.

'Mazel tov!' said Greta, 'how exciting!'

'Yes, but I'm not going to get too excited yet. We don't know how much it would be, or even if we can prove descendancy. We still don't have Eliza's marriage And I'd have to share it with David.'

'So,' said Justin, 'do you think that perhaps David knew something about this? Could that be the motivation the police would need? Perhaps we really should tell them after all, in the light of what we now know.'

I thought about this. I remembered what David had said about having spent some time in archives, and was rather vague about the specifics. So that's what he had been doing. And if he had been the man in the car that day, it could explain... It made my blood go cold to think he might actually contemplate murder. His own flesh and blood, too. But why the break in and the drastic search for something?

'No,' I said, eventually, 'I don't think the will is all this is about. Even if he knows that there is a will, why would he break into the house unless he was looking for something specific. I think what he was looking for was this,' I held up the key that still hung around my neck, 'this is something else, something that goes further back than Eliza and Bertrand. If David thinks there might be something for him in it; I don't know, some kind of treasure or whatever, then he'll do what he can to get hold of it. If I tell that to the police, what are they going to do? Give me a bodyguard? I don't think so. I think you two are right. I think we've just got to figure this out before he does. The trouble is, he knows now that I'm searching, so he's going to be on my tail, whatever I do. How I wish I'd opened that letter before he rang.'

'Don't worry, doll,' said Justin, 'we'll help you.'

'What about Graham? I'm sure he'd like to be included too.'

Justin looked away.

'Umm... I don't know. I'm thinking of breaking it off.'

'What? You're kidding! Why?'

He looked uncomfortable, and fidgeted a bit.

'Things were moving so fast. If it hadn't been for his being beaten up and everything, I would never have contemplated inviting him over to stay at my parents' so soon, and I just felt it was getting out of my control. I just don't think I'm ready for that kind of relationship. He's sweet, but... Anyway, I don't think he could handle this.'

'Really?' I said, 'I wouldn't be so sure about that, but really, Justin, are you sure? I mean, you two looked so good together.' I sat on the sofa, feeling deflated.

'Yeah,' he said, then, 'No. I don't know. I... we need to take a break, anyway.'

Greta threw her hands in the air and shook her head.

'Sarah's right. I think you're crazy. You two were perfect for each other. You should be careful you're not throwing – what is that saying? The baby out with the bath water? These things don't happen every day. It's a rare thing to find a really good partner in life.'

'You can say that again,' I said, quietly.

'I know...' said Justin, 'I'm just... Can we change the subject? What were we talking about before? Your family tree. What now? What's the next step?'

Greta and I looked at each other and shrugged our shoulders.

'Well, I've asked Georgina to look further into Eliza's family tree.'

'Excellent!'

'These dreams of yours...' said Greta, 'what do you make of them?'

'I'm not sure,' I said, drawing my knees up onto the sofa, 'up until now they were nice and gentle, with a happy, comfortable feeling. But the one last night was threatening and scary. But this man in the cloak, he seems to know me, to have some knowledge, and knows which way I should go. Oh, God, perhaps it's all rubbish. Perhaps the dreams are just my weird imagination; I mean, can I really base my decisions on a dream? Aren't they just manifestations of one's own subconscious doing odd things?'

Greta leaned forward.

'In some cultures, it is believed that our ancestors can return as spirit guides. In my own religion this is a traditional belief. This person in your dream seems to return time and time again, and didn't you say yourself that they were not like usual dreams? Your uncle in his letter says he had dreams that were more like visions...'

I shivered.

'It's just so weird. I'm usually very sceptical about such things. I would never have believed it if someone else had told me... and Uncle Charles said something similar.'

We were all quiet for a few moments. The house was very still.

'What is amazing,' I said, 'is that it seems that we have proof that Bertrand McDougal was my ancestor, and I had that dream with his name above the door before I found that out.'

'If we believe, just for the sake of argument, that this man in your dream is an ancestor, or spirit guide, or whatever,' said Justin, 'then what is he guiding you towards? Surely, there

145

must be something more than just this nineteenth century will; after all, he has – or had – the key, which is much older.'

'Maybe you ought to keep a notepad by your bed,' said Greta, 'you might need to remember those dreams in some detail. If he is warning you of danger, then you need to get every little bit of detail and symbolism.'

I nodded, still not quite convinced, but it certainly seemed wise to take note of the dreams, if they came again.

Over the next few days, Justin and Greta helped me to get the house back in order, and then we visited the Theatre Museum in Covent Garden to see if we could find out more about Bertrand McDougal. There was very little to be found out about his family, however, except that they were theatrical and had come from Scotland, and that his mother had found some fame as a tragic actress, whose Juliet had brought her much acclaim from a young age.

All the same, we had an enjoyable afternoon, looking round the museum at old theatrical costumes and caricatures of old actors, including one of Bertie as a young Hamlet, looking dark and brooding in his black doublet and hose. I had to keep reminding myself that this was my ancestor, giving me little bursts of butterflies in my stomach to know I came from an acting family of some fame, as well as the Jaynes as well. Perhaps I was doing the right thing after all, if it was in my genes. But if only I could convince a casting director that I had it in me. Or was it myself I had to convince?

Afterward, we mooched around Covent Garden Piazza, looked at the artisan stalls and laughed at a comic magician. Then we ambled over to look at Drury Lane Theatre, imagining what it was like when Bertrand McDougal was one of the star players, and ended the day with a meal at Louigi's. It was a pleasant day, and a welcome break from the stress and worry of the last few days, but I felt that I was no closer to any answers, and as I got ready for bed, I could not help a stab of frustration. I wanted – no, needed – answers now, but the research was just taking so long, and how much would it really tell me? And how long before cousin David made another move?

I had carefully laid a notebook and pen by my bed, hoping for more dreams to show me the way, but the next morning I remembered nothing, just like the last few nights, as if in my anxiety to learn more, I was somehow chasing them away.

'I have to go back to work next week,' said Justin the following day over coffee.

My heart sank. Just last week I had been feeling so hopeful, and full of enthusiasm to start the journey of discovery, but now everything seemed to have come to a full stop and Justin would no longer be free to help me. I missed Graham, too. After enjoying his company in Gloucestershire, and seeing how well he and Justin complimented each other, it felt to me now that there was something missing in our lives.

'Sorry,' said Justin, seeing the look on my face, 'I wish I could be free to help, but... what can you do? These things take time. I don't suppose you've heard from Georgina?'

'No. As you say, I suppose these things take a lot of time...'

'Why don't you ring her?' suggested Greta.

'What good would that do? I'm sure she'll ring me if she has news. It was only a few days ago that we spoke, and she said it might be a few weeks. I don't want to make her feel under pressure and annoy her...'

'Oh, for goodness sake!' said Justin, 'this is not an ordinary research case. You're paying her, don't forget, and you need the information quickly. You don't have to be rude – just ask how things are going. She'll get the hint that you're anxious...'

'OK, OK,' I said, reaching for the phone, 'you make a good point. Right, where's that card? Here we are... I'm sure she'll probably be out, so I'll have to leave a message... Oh, hello? Georgina? It's Sarah. Sorry to bother you if you're busy, but I was just wondering how you were getting on with the Jayne and McDougal searches? And the will. Any progress at all?'

Half expecting to hear Georgina sound irritated by my call, I was surprised when she responded cheerfully.

'Sarah? Oh, I'm rather glad you've called. I was just off to the Public Record Office to do some work on your Jayne family. The McDougals will take a while, as the line comes from Scotland, and I'm making some enquiries about local genealogists. As for the will, I'm still trying to find the marriage. I did notice on one of the census records that one of Eliza's children was born in France, so perhaps it's possible they were married there, so I'm looking into that. But I have found out that apparently there are some documents that might concern your Jayne ancestors at the archives, and I thought I'd have a look. I've made a bit of progress on tracing the line back – though I do need to verify that. In fact, if you're really that eager, why don't you meet me there? It will probably take more than one visit for me, and with two of us...'

'What about four of us?' I said, smiling broadly at the others.

'Even better!' she said.

'Where do we go? It's at Chancery Lane isn't it?'

'No. The records we want are at the Kew Centre now. I know that's a bit far for you...'

'No problem!' I said,' just give me the address and we'll see you there later!'

'That's funny,' said Georgina, as we took our seats at the National Archives reading room, 'when I mentioned the surname, Jayne, just now, the archivist said that she remembered someone else asking about that name recently. I only mention it because it's quite an unusual name. A bit of a coincidence perhaps.'

I looked at the others. I knew what we were all thinking.

David.

'Now,' said Georgina, arranging her notebook and pencils neatly in front of her, 'because the Jayne family seemed to move around quite a bit – which is not surprising given their theatrical occupations – I have had to rely on the International Genealogical Index to find the parish register entries. Luckily, as the name is fairly unusual, I think I have found them going back into the early eighteenth century, but I will need to contact the relevant county record offices or churches to see the original copies. But if we're on the right trail, then I think I have found Eliza's grandfather – George Jayne's father, Richard, and then Richard's father, Charles Jayne, who was baptised in London in 1718. So, he would be your six times great-grandfather. But here in the Public Record Office, I believe there are some wills, and – even more interesting – some diaries and notes written by Charles himself.'

'Oh!' I cried, 'how interesting!'

'That really is a find,' said Georgina, 'as these things often don't survive. Now, what I suggest is that you get yourselves reader's tickets so that we can order the documents separately, and perhaps you can read through the diaries while I look at the will. Hopefully, one or either of them will mention family members which will verify what I think to be the case so far.'

It took a while to get settled, go through the process of getting readers' tickets and then wait for the ordered documents. When they came, the diary was in a bundle with some papers and letters, so I said I would read the diary while Justin and Greta looked at the papers. The diary was a book, bound in leather, and on the first page in large hand-writing was written: *The Ramblings of a Strolling Player*, and a little ink drawing of a man in doublet and hose and a small cape, a feathered cap in his hand, and his hands splayed out slightly in front and away from him as he took a bow.

'Oh, but how delightful!' I exclaimed, too loudly, which incurred the irritated looks of other researchers in the room. Reducing my voice to just above a whisper, I said to Justin, 'do you think that's a little self-portrait?'

'Not the man in your dreams, is it?' asked Justin.

'No. The dream man has a beard. This guy is probably in costume, anyway – they're not eighteenth-century clothes, are they? Do you think there's a resemblance?' She looked up, while Justin and Greta looked from her to the picture.

'Difficult to say, as he hasn't really drawn the features in great detail, but there is a definite "twinkly" look about him, which reminds me of you when you're in a good mood.'

I smiled and looked again at the portrait. If Georgina was right, this was my six times great grandfather. Then I turned the page and surveyed the slanting writing. Luckily, it did not seem too difficult to read, and was quite large and bold. All the same, it was going to take a while to go through it.

Taking a deep breath, I began to read.

CHAPTER 14

F ebruary 1751

    I find myself in pensive mood. Last night there was somewhat of a disturbance during the performance, when it came to light that there was some dispute over whether we have proper licence to play. The path of a player is so full of snags. We walk continually on shifting sands, doing our best to keep within the letter of law, whilst doing our best to break its spirit. I found myself apprehensive as to whether I should suddenly find myself thrown into gaol, which would be a severe inconvenience at this time when the time draws near for the birth of my child.

    Oh, I could wring the necks of those crude thieves and brawlers, who put on what they call a 'show' and give those of us who are honourable and honest, a bad name.

    Despite what the law says, I do not see myself, nor any of my fellow players, as a rogue nor a vagabond. What is a rogue? A scoundrel, a knave of sorts. I am thus no more than any man, yet am branded legally as such because I seek to entertain the common people – to corrupt and spread dangerous thought, it seems. Oh, then the lawmen and the politicians are a suspicious band of cowards!

    Then we, in turn, are put into the position of having to cajole the justices – or at worse, outwit them – into giving us a place to play, having to grovel and doff our caps. And if we slip just once, if there is the slightest little disorderliness or irregularity, then the beaks have the authority to come down on us like Zeus with a thunderbolt. We have to become adept at the art of survival, when all we would do is entertain, perhaps even educate, those people whose daily lives are arduous and grim.

Charles put aside his journal and put the lid back on the bottle of ink. His fingers were becoming too cold to write. He pulled the collar of his great coat up around his neck, strode over to the fireplace and stoked up the embers, trying to rekindle a flame.

'Are you warm enough, Liz?' he asked of a large heap of blankets on the bed.

'No,' came the muffled reply, 'can you put another log on the fire?'

Charles sighed. The profit shares from the season here in Norfolk had not been good. The spell of freezing cold weather and snow was keeping audiences away from the cold and empty barns where they were scheduled to play, and the landlord of the house where they were boarding was charging a high price for firewood.

'It's the last one,' he said, 'pray for warmer weather tomorrow, or I will have to sell my father's pocket watch for wood.'

The heap of blankets stirred, and a tousled head poked out.

'No, not the watch, Charles. Come, join me under the blankets and we shall keep each other warm.'

Charles took off his great coat and spread it over the bed, and then joined his wife under the covers, fully clothed. As he did so, the key that hung round his neck swung free of his shirt and hit her on her ear.

'Ow! Do you have to wear that cold piece of metal in bed, Charles?'

'Sorry,' he said, taking it off and putting it onto the small table by the bed, 'I forgot.'

'I would not mind being clouted on the ear by it if only we knew what it opened, and that whatever it was contained a treasure. Then we could have all the firewood we needed. I wish your mother had told you more about it. What good is a key without a lock to open?'

'Sadly, my mother knew nothing herself, except that it was of great importance, given to her by her own mother...'

'...who had no husband and died young. I know, I know. It does seem strange to hold onto something that we have no way of using, whose purpose has been lost in time. We would probably be better selling the key itself...'

Charles said nothing. He had never told his very practical and down to earth wife of the strange dreams that sometimes plagued him; the man in the old-fashioned garb who wore the same key around his neck, and smiled, and told him to never lose it...

Charles sighed and put his arm around Elizabeth, holding her close to warm them both up.

'Who would buy such a key?' he said.

His wife chuckled, 'oh, some fool who would like to keep it round his neck – oh! Now, Charles, there is no need to pinch me so!'

2nd March 1751

Heavy rain has set in, making the walk to Lincoln a miserable one.

My left boot is worn and letting in water, so my foot was continually wet and cold. Liz and the new baby – named Richard as we were playing scenes from Richard II when he was born – travelled on the cart in relative comfort. Now there is the cobbler to pay, and another mouth to feed.

Still, as we walk, we pass new growth, primroses and sweet violets showing on the banks by the road. Spring will soon be here, and with it warmer days, larger audiences and bigger shares, as long as our glorious manager does not find a way of spending on so called 'expenses'.

So many times, Liz and I have asked ourselves why we continue in this theatrical vein, travelling the road in all weathers, playing to empty houses for no money, dodging those who would have us thrown in gaol, or those who would blast us from the pulpit. Why do any of us?

The answer is always the same. This life may have its downs, but it also has its ups. As well as the bad days, we also know the thrill of a full house, a cheering audience and a good profit, a long walk in clement weather, and the occasional riches of a good benefit night. It is only in times of harsh weather and bad houses that we question our lot. But like the gambler, we are forever anticipating the excitement of what may be just around the next corner. A new play, a good part, a high profit. What! Perhaps even an offer in London! What other walk of life has such possibilities? The labourer in the field, the clerk at his desk, know nothing of such highs and lows.

I dreamt last night again. A reminder to keep the key safe, and a voice telling me to pass it to Richard one day. So, it seems, I may never find its mystery, and perhaps it is for my son to do so, or his son. I sometimes wonder why I bother with it, but somehow, I know I cannot let it go. The dreams give me such a strength of

154

feeling that somehow this will one day be important, if not to me, then to someone, and the key itself has some bewitchment about it that will not allow me to give it, sell it or throw it away. What nonsense! Yet, that is the feeling I have, and it is a pretty thing. I remember well my mother talking about it, saying it had some importance to our family, and to the family she came from, and had always told me that I would be the next custodian. Yet, she spoke little of her mother, except that she died young and without ever having married.

Charles paused. His mother had never been able to shake off the stigma of having been base born. She never knew who her father was, and her mother, Ann, had never spoken of him, and had died in her twenty-sixth year of smallpox, when Susanna had been but nine years old. She had been brought up by her grandparents, and it had been her grandmother who had passed the key down to her, as Ann had been their only child to survive into adulthood, so there was no-one else to pass it on to.

Charles turned the key over in his hands and pondered on life and death, and the blood that ran from one generation to the next, and a key that had come from more than two generations before him and would be passed down to the generations after his own passing. What did it all mean?

* * *

I raised my head and nudged Justin.

'Look!', I whispered, pointing to the last entry in the diary; the paragraph about the dream and the key. I watched as Justin's eyes widened, and a broad smile crossed his face.

'What is it?' whispered Greta, who was sitting opposite, and had sensed our excitement across the table.

Justin moved the book to her and pointed out the paragraph.

'Oh mein Got!' she exclaimed, forgetting to whisper, and ignoring the irritated scowls of other people at nearby desks, 'I've just got chills down the back of my neck! The same dream! The key!'

Someone coughed pointedly, and she blushed, and put her hand to her mouth.

'This is very exciting!' she whispered.

I turned back to the diary. There was too much to read in one sitting, so I flicked through to the latter part of the diary.

* * *

February 1793

So war has been declared on England by France, and Pitt's government is in disarray.

I have been watching my little grandson, George, just three years old last month and can already carry a tune, read a few words and recognise notes on my son's fiddle. He is a natural-born entertainer; enjoys making us laugh and being the centre of attention. But I fear for his future in this uncertain world.

He is a bright little lad. This morning, as Richard was playing with him in a kind of cat-and-mouse rough and tumble, the key that was round Richard's neck swung out from under his shirt. For me, I had a moment of sharp emotion. I was almost jealous that the key was his now, and not mine. I gave it to him nearly five years ago, not sure how many years were left to me, and have rarely seen it since. To see it again gave me a jolt.

But this little boy also had a strange reaction to it. He instantly grabbed it with his fat little fist and peered at it with wide eyes, crying, 'W'dat?'

Richard met my eyes, and then turned to his son, saying, 'it will be yours one day,' and George gave him a huge smile, and then, as only children can be, was immediately distracted by a toy soldier.

The toy brought me back to my fears of the future. I am old and feeble now. Of no use to anyone, and only a burden for my son and his wife. I have not walked on a stage for many a year, and spend most of my time in this damned bath chair. Next week I will make the painful annual journey to Liz's grave.

This war will no doubt see me out, and what does the future hold for Richard and Martha, and this little lad? Thank God they need no longer fear gaol, now that the theatre has been more properly recognised, and that Richard is probably too old to go to war, but what will war bring?

* * *

I looked through the last few pages of this journal, but there were only a few more entries, and the handwriting was wobbly and the subjects vague and wandering, and I wondered if his mind had gone in his last few years. The last entry was in early 1795, and I leaned over to Georgina and asked her if she had Charles's death date.

She looked through her notes, and whispered back, '4th June 1796.'

I sighed. As he had foreseen, he had died long before the wars with France had finished, and I wished I could have told him that his grandson lived to produce my ancestor, Eliza. Though, it seemed horribly poignant to me, that after Charles's worrying that war would threaten, George would end up dying in a train accident.

I closed the diary. Although I had only read a few pages, I felt I knew Charles, and was sad that he had died, as though I had been there personally.

I was also fascinated by what he had said about the key; that last sight of it around his son's neck, and his grandson's sudden interest. It seemed that I was not the only one who had a strange reaction to it. I closed my hands around it, feeling the connection between myself and all those who had carried it before me: Eliza, George, Richard and Charles. And before that, who?

CHAPTER 15

At that moment, Georgina, who had been engrossed in a document on the other end of the table, raised her head and leaned over.

'So, what's happening over here? Have you found something?'

I showed her the diary with the notes about the family and the key.

Georgina nodded with a grin of satisfaction. 'For me, what's really helpful here is that it looks as though Charles's mother was illegitimate, which will help with trying to find her birth. But, look here; Charles's mother left a will. I'll just read this part to you...

"...and to my eldest son, Charles Jayne, I leave the pewter key that I always wear, given to me by my mother, Anne Curtis, for him to keep as his own, and pass on to his own son, or until such time as its use is known...." This is wonderful – we know Susanna's mother's name, and that she never married, so she will have been baptised with the name Curtis. We've done well to get this far, but the further we get back the more difficult it will be to find documents. My problem now is that I don't know exactly where in London Susanna was born, and there's always the possibility at these dates that the registers are lost

or unreadable.'

'If we can find Susanna's mother, how far will that take us back,' I asked, 'I mean, in terms of how old the key is?'

'Well, if Charles's mother was in her twenties when she had him, then her own mother would perhaps be born.... mid to late seventeenth century. We're getting closer, but not quite far back enough, I would say.'

'Wow,' I gasped, 'Seventeenth century London. What was happening then?'

'Quite a lot. Civil war, the Protectorate, the Restoration, plague, the Great Fire of London. Of course, Oliver Cromwell closed down the theatres, so your family might have had to find other occupations if they were actors back then too.'

'I never did like the sound of Cromwell,' I said.

'Didn't he ban Christmas too?' said Justin, 'those puritans were not exactly a bundle of laughs.'

I looked down at the diary. 'There seems to have been a constant struggle to keep theatre alive, even in the next century. It's amazing when you think about it,' I mused, 'that the theatre has survived at all. It just goes to show what can happen when people have a passion and love for something, and a determination to keep it going.' With surprise, I found my eyes were prickling. 'Wow. I didn't think this was going to be so emotional. I wish I could keep this diary, but I suppose I can come back and look at it any time.'

I asked if Justin and Greta had found anything interesting, and they showed me a few letters, mostly from Richard, Charles's son, who had been more of a musician than an actor, it seemed, and played fiddle for theatres in London and even at the Royal Court. Justin showed me a letter announcing the birth of George in 1790, and a few other bits and pieces, but there was nothing else that mentioned the key or any other clues.

'Let's go and find a pub by the river and have something to eat,' said Justin, 'I'm famished, and we can talk more freely then.'

It was a pleasantly sunny May day, so we sat by the river in the garden of a pub, and spoke of what we had found. For me, although I was enjoying the relaxed quality of the afternoon, I had a feeling like the last day of school holidays. Through the laughter and the joy of watching the river and its ubiquitous activities, it was as though a small cloud hung over me, and no matter how I tried, I could not shrug the feeling off.

My mood worsened over the next few days, and I had a feeling of severe anti-climax. Justin had gone back to work, and Georgina was ominously silent. I had no dreams, and the house seemed quiet and empty. Every night, I went around the house obsessively checking every door and window, and plugged my telephone into the extension in my bedroom for an extra feeling of security. While I knew it was unlikely that David would try again, the break-in had unnerved me, and I felt vulnerable and alone. I jumped at every little creak and crack the old house made, even though those settling noises had never bothered me before. I began to wonder whether I should sell the house and find myself a flat or something. Yet, I did not feel ready to let my parents' house go. It was too full of memories.

A few days after the Kew visit, the phone rang, and I was surprised to hear Graham's voice on the other end.

'I hope you don't mind me ringing,' he said, his voice wavering slightly, 'I've been wondering whether I should, but

I just need to know something, and you know Justin so well.'

I sat down. These kinds of phone calls could be awkward.

'OK,' I said, 'I'll answer, if I can.'

'You see, I really thought that he liked me, and things seemed to be going really well; we were even going to stay on in Gloucestershire for a few days. But then, when he went back to London, he said that maybe it would be best to slow down for a while – that things were going too fast for him.'

'Hmm,' I said, wondering if Justin had been completely honest with him. As far as I could remember, Justin had said he was thinking of breaking it off completely.

'Well, the thing is, I'm just a bit confused. He's gone completely cold on me, not even answering my calls. And...' he broke off for a few seconds, '...I'm just thinking if I did anything wrong? If he's angry with me for something. Has he said anything to you?'

I sighed. It was difficult to know what to say. Graham needed honesty, but by telling him all I knew, was I betraying my best friend? On the other hand, it seemed that Justin wasn't really playing fair with him. I was in a difficult position, but I decided to go with my gut feeling.

'Look, Graham, it's not anything you've said or done. As far as I can see, you two are great together, and I'm completely mortified that you're not seeing each other at the moment. But, there's probably something you should know, and it will probably explain why he's being difficult, though he'd probably kill me if he knew I told you, so please don't tell him where you got this from. The thing is, Justin was seeing someone for a while, a guy called Mark, and it was getting really serious. They were talking about buying a flat together, and then they found out that Mark was HIV Positive, which developed into

162

AIDS. He died two years ago, and Justin hasn't been serious about anyone since. It completely freaked him out, too. He was tested, and was in the clear, but the whole thing was just devastating. It's taken him a long time to get over it.'

Graham said quietly, 'I wondered if it was something like that.'

'Yes, well, he doesn't like to talk about it. But you should know that the fact that he got so close to you is a good sign. I don't want to give you false hope, and perhaps I shouldn't say this, but I'm going to anyway. Don't give up on him.'

'Thank you. I'm in the clear too, he knows that. But I suppose it makes it difficult to make a commitment. And he knows my history. I'm no angel, as I'm sure you know. We met at the Vauxhall, and I was casing the joint, as usual. But... oh, Sarah, I really like him. It's the first time I've felt like this, like for ever.'

'I know. I think you'd be great for each other too. Look, hang on in there. Give it a while, and I'll see what I can do this end.'

'Thanks so much, you're a sweetheart.'

Another few days later, I had a phone call from Greta.

'My dear, I don't like to impose, but you did offer, and you can say no if you like, but did you mean it when you said I could stay with you for a while?'

'Oh Greta,' I exclaimed, delighted at the thought of no longer being on my own in that big house, 'of course I did! And of course you can! Is Uncle Otto coming to stay with your parents?'

'Yes, it was the least my parents could do, and now he will end his days in some comfort, though God knows, he deserves luxury. When can I come? And don't worry, I will pay rent.'

163

'Really, you don't have to. Whenever you like. I will make up the spare bedroom for you.'

'Silly girl. Of course I shall pay rent, and don't argue. We shall discuss it when I arrive. Will next week be OK? Uncle Otto arrives on Saturday week, and my parents want to redecorate the room for him.'

With a new sense of purpose I went happily to clear out the spare room and air the bed.

But just as I was feeling cheerful again, Georgina rang.

'I have good news and bad news'

'Ok,' I said, 'throw me the bad news.'

'I've searched the available indexes for Susanna Curtis, and I can find no baptism that looks illegitimate. The trouble is with these dates is that the one we want just may not be indexed, and without knowing where in London she was born, it's a needle in a haystack. I'm sorry, but it looks like we've hit a brick wall here. I've searched various Curtis wills and documents but there is nothing that mentions Susanna or Ann, and I don't want to use up your money without having something more concrete to go on.'

'Oh,' I said, deflated.

'I'm sorry,' said Georgina, 'but genealogy is like that. Just when you think you're getting somewhere, it all comes to a creaking halt.'

'So, what was the good news?'

'Ah, yes. Well, we have proof that we are following the right line and Eliza was definitely your ancestor. There was success with finding the French marriage certificate, and the French certificates have far more information in them than ours. They give both parents' names, including Eliza's mother's maiden name, and where and when they died. It all adds up and confirms what we've already found. So that's all good, and it means we can probably apply for probate of Bertie's will, if you can get hold of all the necessary documents going back to Eliza?'

'Yes,' I said, 'my uncle was very efficient in that respect. I have them all.'

'Well, let's go for it. My husband can help with this; he's a solicitor. In the meantime, I'll send you a proper report for what I've done so far, and then you can decide what you want to do with regards to further research, though, to be honest, unless something else comes to light, I don't think there's much else I can do with this line. But I can carry on with the McDougal line of course.'

I had almost forgotten about the Bertrand McDougal connection, though it was purely for interest, and was not likely to have anything to do with the key, which was what I really wanted. Still, it would be worth finding out more about his family. 'Yes,' I replied, 'please send me the report, and then carry on with the McDougals. Thanks for all your help so far, Georgina.'

I sat on my sofa and held the pewter key in my hands, staring at it intensely and touching it lightly with my fingers, as if I could will it to give up its secrets.

Perhaps it was all nonsense. It could be just a wild goose chase. Some ancient legend in the family, sparked off by an idea or assumption that the key was meant to open some treasure chest. To think that such a chest could still have survived after all these centuries was really quite ridiculous. Even if it had, it was probably lying empty in some museum somewhere, or someone's attic, broken into and its contents long since plundered.

I sighed, once again feeling lost. The old feeling of gloomy purposeless descended upon me again. As for the will, I seriously wasn't convinced there would be anything much in it for me, but I'd go through the motions, fill in the forms and do what was necessary, just in case.

I put a Dire Straits cassette in the machine, opened a bottle of wine, and wallowed in the dark profundity of 'Brothers in Arms.'

At 4 am in the morning, I awoke. Fumbling for my notebook, knocking a tube of hand cream off my bedside table, and spilling a glass of water onto the floor, which I ignored, I started scribbling without turning on the light or sitting up in case the dream disappeared before I could write it all down.

CHAPTER 16

London, September 1666

Elizabeth Curtis looked down at the child in the cot. She was fidgeting and grizzling again, a little fist punching the air and the rosebud mouth turning down into a frown. The recent winds that had not yet quietened had unsettled her, and were even now blowing through the streets, rattling the shutters, creating draughts and gusting fretfully against the windows. Elizabeth had fed her, sung to her, made sure she was warm, but still the babe seemed fractious and uneasy, as if sensing something in the unsettled air.

Elizabeth stroked the baby's head.

'Ann – Annie. What is it, my daughter?'

For the third time that morning, she unbuttoned the infant's cotton gown and looked closely at her skin. She had lost her first two children to the plague, along with both her parents, and although the disease in London was now in decline, she still feared another outbreak. She did not think she could bear more bereavement, and she fussed over and closely watched her third child to a degree that drew exasperated comment from her husband William.

Her marriage had suffered over the last few years. The lack of money, the loss of their children and family, had not brought them together but somehow thrown them apart, and even though William now had legitimate work, the damage had been done. He was often quiet and sullen, and it seemed that every conversation seemed to turn to acrimony and bitterness. William spent much of his time in the taverns and inns of west London, leaving her to manage as best she could in the dark and reeking streets of the east.

The child's skin showed no signs of the swollen glands, the dreaded buboes, that were the first sign of plague, nor did the child seem unduly hot. Elizabeth smiled, holding her close and breathing in the sweet essence of her, like a nosegay against the smells that constantly permeated the air of the London streets, and always managed to creep in through the windows, even with the shutters tightly closed. Soot was also a constant menace to clothes and furnishings. Sometimes Elizabeth felt it was impossible to be clean in this part of London, where the soap-makers, bakers, brewers and metalworkers lived alongside residences, all higgledy on top of one another.

Perhaps, now that the theatres had been open again for the last six years, perhaps their life would soon start to change for the better. William was at the new Lincoln's Inn theatre now, working under William Davenant as part of the Duke's Men. Life had been hard during the Republic. Both her and William, and both their parents had had to find work where they could, performing 'pieces' and concerts, even at times performing in secret in a private house or tavern; a dangerous activity that, while sometimes lucrative, lacked any creative joy, for it was impossible to truly practice one's art whilst in fear of being raided by Cromwell's men and being thrown into gaol at any time.

But when Charles II rode back into London to take back the crown that was rightfully his, she and William were there in the cheering crowds. He was to re-open the theatres again, bringing with him the French style of drama influenced by Moliere and Racine. Elizabeth thought that perhaps now they could be happy, and William would be his old self again, until the plague struck, and they lost so many of their friends and family.

But now, the plague had receded, and William was working, leaving early that morning to walk the distance to the theatre. Once they had saved a little money, perhaps they could move from this crowded, reeking area of east London into some-where a little west of here, closer to the new theatres, and start a new life.

It was still early, and Elizabeth moved to the window to let in a little light. Opening the shutters a crack, she heard shouts on the street. It was nothing unusual, but something in the urgency of the voices made her open the shutter wider so she could see out.

Looking down onto the grimy street below, she saw that people in the opposite house were carrying chests and goods out of the building. Were they moving out? But further along, there was more activity. She could see carts being piled high with all kinds of things, from chairs and tables to musical instruments and even, she thought she saw, a large cheese.

Just below her window, a man was knocking on doors. She shouted down to him.

'Good sir, what is happening?'

'The fire, mistress. Best gather your precious goods and get out. The fire is spreading quickly; the wind is blowing it this way, and it's spreading quicker than anyone can contain it!

They have been pulling down houses near London Bridge, but they can't pull them down fast enough to stop it! St. Margaret's and St Magnus and Fishmongers Hall are burned down, and it will be here before long!'

Elizabeth looked towards the east, and now for the first time, through the daily familiar smells of local dyers, brewers and bakers, she caught the acrid smell of smoke in the air, and through the dark streets, she saw an orange glow in the sky to the south east, close to the river.

The wind was blowing strongly down the narrow street so that the shutter leapt out of her hand and banged against the wall. The child in her arms jumped at the sudden movement and started to cry.

'There now,' Elizabeth cooed to the baby, pulling the shutter to, and coming back into the room, 'nothing to worry about. Perhaps we will go and find your Papa, hmm?'

She wrapped the baby up in a blanket, all the time cooing to the child to calm her, but in her head wondering what she should do. There had been reports of a fire over near London Bridge very early this morning, but William had said there was nothing to worry about; it would quickly be contained.

With Ann still fretting in her arms, she managed to tie a hood around her head and went out of their door, down the communal stairs and out onto the street.

There was more activity now than when she had looked out of the window. The sounds of people shouting instructions to those manoeuvring large pieces of furniture out of windows, mingled with the sound of cartwheels hurrying over the cobbled streets and the excited voices of children, bid as runners to gather information about the spread of the fire.

Elizabeth went to the nearest cart and found the carter, busy strapping items down.

'Please,' she said, 'where are you taking these?'

'Across the river, Mistress,' replied the carter, hardly looking at her,' be safe there, if we make it.' He looked up and over his shoulder at the crowded street. 'Too many of us, that's the trouble.'

'But...'

'Some are taking things to the churches, but the way I sees it, like as not they'll have to move them again. That fire ain't stopping with this wind from the east. Look!'

He pointed up, just as a large flake of fire, carried in the wind, landed at the end of the street. Shouts rang out and buckets of water were brought out to quench it.

The carter shook his head.

'Lucky... but not for long. Too much tinder. They'll stop that now and then, but just one of those landing on all this dry stuff...' he pointed to hay bales on the street, 'you'd better get out lady, while you can.'

'But my things! Who can help me? Can you take some of my furniture?'

'Sorry, mistress. I'm overloaded already. No good if it all ends up tipping over on the street, lending fuel to the fire, is it?'

Elizabeth ran to the end of the street, turning the corner onto Cannon Street, where she met a similar scene. She looked around her, trying to find a friendly face to help her, wondering what she should do.

The street was already crowded with carts and horses and people, trying to gather their goods and get them and themselves to safety. A cart drew up beside her, and the carter looked down at her.

'I've got room for a few sticks more, lady!'

'Oh, thank you!' she said, 'how much?'

He turned and spat on the ground.

'Twenty.'

'Shillings?'

'Pounds.'

She stared at him, wondering whether she had misheard through the noise of the street.

'Did you say twenty pounds?'

'Yep. Danger money, see?' He looked at the baby, now wriggling and wailing in dismay at being out in the wind, and held too close.

'Look, I'm not a hard man. For you, fifteen. That's the best I can do.' He looked behind him, 'extreme case. Putting my life at risk. Got a wife and littl'uns too.'

'But... I do not have that kind of money.'

He shrugged.

'Well, good luck to you then. There's people that do.'

He cracked his whip and drove away, leaving Elizabeth staring after him, incredulously.

After standing for a while in a daze, she decided to go back to the house and see what she could carry. If she had to walk, she could not carry the child for very long anyway, and it was getting more unlikely that any carriage would take her across London; the streets were already becoming too busy with traffic.

Back in the few small rooms they had on Bush Lane, she looked around her at their few possessions. Much of what they had inherited from her parents had been sold over the years, except for the old chest full of household linen and a few precious items. She could not carry that. The cheap table and chairs could burn. The bed that she slept in with William, and Ann's cot were precious to her, but would have to stay. She put some of her and William's best clothing into a basket, along with some of Ann's napkins and bonnets. From the pantry she took a piece of ham and some bread. She wrapped Ann in a cloth and strapped her to her back, tying the cloth in front of her. She could carry no more.

Outside again on the street, there was now a palpable feeling of panic. The wind was still blowing, but now it had warmth to it, with the added stench of burning houses and goods. On Cannon Street, carts and carriages were trying to move through the traffic moving away from the fire, west, or south to the river where boats could take people to the safety of the Surrey bank. Their progress was slow, and some people had begun to abandon their goods in fear of their own safety.

Which direction should she take? West to find William, north to Spital Fields, or south to the river? It would be a long walk to the theatre with a child on her back, and the river was closer than either. But what were her chances of finding a boat? And would they not all be taking advantage of the situation to charge excessive amounts, as the carters were?

But she had no choice. The weight of the baby and the basket would slow her down, and would not the fire overtake her? The river would be safer, and she would have to take her chances from then on. She would walk north-west along Cannon Street, and then turn left, following the crowds, towards the docks.

William Curtis was in the Leg and Seven Stars Inn, where he was enjoying an ale and a pigeon pie with his fellow players when the boy burst in.

'London's on fire!' he shouted.

Some of the customers laughed and one told him he'd been dreaming, no doubt sleeping while he should have been doing something else. A few turned round and looked concerned.

'There was a small fire near London Bridge this morning,' said William to his friend, sitting next to him, 'but surely it would be out by now.' He turned to the youngster.

'Boy! Do you not exaggerate sirrah!'

'Not me sir no sir! It's the city, sir, the city's on fire! The churches are burning, and it's reached Cannon Street now!'

William stood abruptly, almost upsetting the table.

'Cannon Street you say? Speak, boy! How do you know all this?'

Me ol' man's a carter, sir. He's been carrying people's belongings from church to church. Every time he puts things down in one, then blow me down if the fire don't come nearer, and he has to take the stuff further on. It's coming from the east, see, what with this wind. It's God's truth, sir. I was helping, and he told me to run home and tell the missus.'

William's friend stood up.

'Will? Is there trouble?'

William grasped his friend's arm.

'My home. My wife and child. We are just below Cannon Street. My God! What do I do, Tom? It's an hour's walk, and who but a madman will take us towards the fire?'

'Calm yourself, man. I am sure your wife has had fair warning, and will have the babe safe somewhere. Here lad!' he flipped a coin for the boy to catch, 'where are people heading to, those fleeing the fire?'

'Some to the north. Some to the river, sir,' he said, pocketing the coin, 'hoping to get lighters across the water. Last I knew, all the lightermen were charging a heavy fee to cross; them's

174

that can afford it will pay it to save their life.'

William felt sick.

'My wife has no money,' he said to Tom.

Tom clapped him on the arm.

'Let us go and see Davenant.'

William Davenant was an elderly man of sixty-two, with the eyes of a man who has seen and suffered much, but still retained a witty sense of humour.

He looked kindly at Will.

'Yes, I have heard news of the fire. And it is spreading quickly, you say? A curse on this wind and dry weather! Yet, should it be raining, I may equally be cursing that for the sake of my poor joints... How can I help you, Will?'

'Please, Sir William, it seems an ignoble thing to ask for money, but my wife is in need of it if she is to cross the river, and I have very little left before next...'

'Say no more,' said William, holding up his hand. He looked at Will, nodding his head as if remembering something.

'In remembrance of the honour in which I hold your family. Of course, I knew your grandfather when I was but a small boy. A man of incomparable talent and good wit. Here, Will.' He opened a draw in a cabinet with a small key, 'take this. There is thirty pounds. Pay me back when you can – I will not press you.'

He gave to Will a pouch of coins.

'But Sir William... That is too much!'

'No... no... You will need to hire a carriage to go and find your wife by the river, and you will need money in the days to come. I am an old man and have little need. You are a young man and have lost much. Take it, with my blessing. I pray you find your wife, and all is well.'

It was not easy to find a carriage. The traffic coming in from east London had begun to crowd the streets. William made his way south. It was not far to the river. Once he got close to the Thames, he would turn east and see if he could find a carriage that would take him to the docks.

He felt the key on its chain under his shirt, and as so often when he did so he felt a sense of reassurance. It had belonged to his mother's father; that was all he knew of it, except that there was some secret that it would unlock. By the time his mother had given it to him, she had already slipped in to senility and could not remember the thing it opened or where it was, only that it had been important to her father and had wanted him to keep it in case something came to light and brought them money. Knowing it had come from his grandfather, whom he had never known, but had mainly been the reason why Sir William had employed him, had always given him hope and a sense of continuity, even through these years of uncertainty and tragedy.

Those years had affected him deeply. He had lost his children, close friends and family to the plague and coming so soon after the miserable years of the interregnum, he had become bitter, he knew, and knew not how to change himself. He had distanced himself from his wife for he could not bear her own grief at the loss of their children on top of his own. He knew not how to help her, so instead, he spent his time when not working in taverns, spending too much of his money on ale, and sometimes a whore's bed, though God knows he regretted it afterwards.

Now, though, his wife was in danger, and Will realised that if he lost her too that would be the end of him.

Even here, he could smell the smoke, borne in the wind, and

looking over to the east there was a visible pall of grey cloud over the city.

He clutched the key tighter.

'By God, I swear,' he said out loud, 'I swear if my wife is saved, I will be a better husband and father. Let me find her, though all our house and belongings may be gone, if I find my wife, I will be a better man.'

She could feel the heat from the fire, and the crowds down by the riverside were so dense, Elizabeth could barely get through, and the child on her back was screaming with being jostled and pressed.

Pressing back, she came onto Thames Street, and made her way further west, along with many others, some pulling carts with their treasured belongings, and hampered in the narrow streets by those who now just beginning to fear for their houses and bring their belongings into the street. She saw four people carrying a bed with an old woman in it and a man carrying a table on his back. It was almost impossible to make much progress, and fear began to grow in Elizabeth that the fire would catch up with her before she would be able to find a way to cross the river. Judging by the looks on the faces of the people around her, they were thinking the same thing. The street was full of warehouses carrying oil and spirits; fuel for the fire. She heard rumours amongst the people of a plot by the French or Dutch because of the current wars, that foreigners had been seen throwing fireballs into houses. Another spoke of a second Catholic gunpowder plot. The suspicions of attack from some enemy added fuel to the fear that was already spreading throughout the streets, itself like a fire out of control.

She turned left again, making her way towards Queen Hythe,

where there would be more boats. She met a crowd of refugees, all desperate to get themselves and their belongings onto the river, safe from the fire.

It was closer now. The smoke was making her cough, and her throat itch, and there was no doubt that she could feel the heat from the east, and turning that way she gasped when she saw flames above the buildings what must only be less than two hundred yards away.

But the rumours she heard destroyed her hopes of finding a place. Just like the carters, the boatmen were charging twenty pounds to take people on board. Only the wealthy were getting into boats.

She stood, unsure what to do next. Perhaps head west...

A great shout went up.

'The King! The King!'

Pushing her way through the crowd, Elizabeth could see the royal barge drawing up alongside the crowds, and the king – yes, the king himself – was talking to the people, giving advice, telling the men to get back and help to pull down buildings to provide fire breaks and assuring everyone of help for the homeless after the fire was over. Some of the men took heed and drove back towards the city.

Elizabeth took her chance and pushed herself further forward.

'Please! I have a child!'

The nearest boatman held out his hand, but it was only to ask for her money.

'I have no money! Please, I will pay you later, but I must save my child!'

'Give the woman a place man! Cannot you see she has an infant on her back?' came a booming voice.

The boatman bowed, and took Elizabeth's hand to help her on board, while she turned to face the kind, heavy lidded eyes of her king. She smiled, but had no room to curtsey, so she bowed her head in gratitude and he nodded, before turning away to continue his business.

As the boat moved out into the crowded waters of the Thames, all eyes were turned to the terrible scene of destruction that was now clearly visible.

Towering flames engulfed the city and soared high into the sky in front of them all the way to beyond London Bridge. The sound of the roar of the fire, the crash of timber as buildings collapsed, the heat from the fire, and the red-orange glare across Elizabeth's field of vision was terrifying. Nearby she could hear women crying. She untied the cloth that held Anne, who was crying fiercely from having been crushed and jostled and was now hungry, and held her tightly in her arms. She watched the city burn, knowing that her home was now gone. She saw the steeples of great churches burning and toppling; a terrible thing to behold. She saw great drops of fire falling onto the river, so that people had to shield their eyes, and these great drops of fire were carried by the wind and falling on houses further west, setting light to them, so the fire was now spreading even quicker than before. She realised that she had escaped with only a short time to spare and hoped her neighbours and all the people on the streets had found safety. She then wondered whether William knew yet of the fire, and where he was.

William stood and cursed.

He could go no further. Already the fire had reached Queen Hythe, and crowds were coming in full force against him.

Around him, men were busy pulling down houses in an attempt to create fire breaks.

If Elizabeth had escaped the fire, she would not have reached here, there would have been no time. If she lived, she must have crossed the river, and so that was also what he must do, though how he was to find her in the crowds of people he could see were crossing the water to safety on the south bank, he did not know.

At St. Paul's Wharf he eventually found a lighter and paid him fifteen pounds to take him across the water. The river was thick with boats, and many people were sitting and staring in disbelief at the terrible conflagration in front of them, and many had their hands in front of their faces as they sobbed.

'Why?' thought William, 'Why? After all we have been through. The closing of the theatres, the plague. To have lost so much, to then see a way forward and better times to come, and now this?' He may have lost everything. To be sure he had lost his home, but perhaps his wife and child as well, and everything he possessed.

He again felt the key against his chest. It was of no value, yet it gave him strength. It had a meaning. Whether there would ever be a time when he or someone else might find the thing it opened, he knew it symbolised something that could never die: family and friendship. He had dreamed it. A riverbank, two friends, a family tie – a bloodline. All vague images and impressions, nothing he could ever grasp hold of fully, but he knew it was all to do with this key, and he must keep it against such time when things might be clearer.

To the west of Southwark Cathedral in St. George's Fields, crowds of refugees from the fire were setting up camp. William slowly made his way through the meadows here, where those who had escaped the fire were attempting to put up makeshift shelters, building fires, or just standing and staring at the flames across the river where their homes and businesses had disappeared in a few hours. Many of them were obviously of some wealth, but had now lost their livelihoods with stock and places of trade all now gone to charcoal and ashes. William wondered how all these people would now be fed and looked after, once the fire was out and the government looked to rebuilding the city.

But for now, there was only one thing that was important to him. Desperately, he searched the crowd for the familiar face of his wife.

Elizabeth buttoned her chemise and bodice quickly. She had managed to find a private spot to sit and feed Anne. She now found something to eat from her basket and sat watching the crowds, wondering what she should do next. Everybody around her seemed to be with someone. They may have lost their homes and livelihoods, but they had family and friends around them. She felt completely alone. Perhaps William would have given up on her, believing her lost in the fire. What would she do then?

With a sudden instinct she turned to look behind her.

She saw him from afar, searching the faces for her.

She did not immediately get up and go towards him. For a moment, she saw him as she had first seen him; a handsome young rogue, rebelling against the restrictions of the Cromwellian regime, a daredevil, risking all to carry on his family's legacy of drama. Looking at him now, careworn and frowning, she knew she still loved him, though she had almost forgotten how over the last few years. And judging by the concerned look on his face, he felt the same way.

Slowly she walked towards him, Anne now sleeping on her shoulder. He saw her. Their eyes met. He smiled.

CHAPTER 17

May 1985

I coughed, still feeling the smoke in my lungs, even though it had been a dream.

Hadn't it?

I put the light on, retrieved the almost empty glass, which thankfully hadn't broken, and drained the last drops of water from it.

The light of dawn was showing through the curtains and I could hear a few birds already beginning to herald the day. Yet, I could still see the terrible orange-red wall of flame and pall of smoke across the Thames, and hear the sickening crash of timber. It was like waking from a nightmare, only I could not shake off the feeling that it had been real.

I threw off the duvet and got up. Going to the window I drew the curtains and opened the windows to get some air. Outside, all was still. The air was cool, and the birds were now getting into their full throttle. I took in a few deep breaths, trying to get back to the present moment, which as yet felt less real than the dream I had just had.

I must not forget it though. I had written a few notes, but there was so much detail.

So William Curtis was the key holder! The father of Ann, the baby in the dream, and Ann must have been the mother of Susannah, who was in turn the mother of Charles Jayne. And... and William's grandfather; his mother's father; the key had belonged to him!

I must find out who it was.

I went back to my notes and filled in some details. The dream had been so strangely real, and yet, like a dream, it had changed from one scenario to another, and sometimes I had been Elizabeth and sometimes I had been William.

And William Davenant had been in the dream! I had heard of him. I must look him up in my *Oxford Companion to the Theatre*.

My heart still beating, I padded down to the living room and found the book I wanted.

'Now, let's see... Davenant...Here we are:

Davenant, Sir William (1606-68)...

So, he had died two years after the fire. I felt sad, as if I had really known him.

English dramatist and theatre manager, reputed to be the natural son of Shakespeare by the hostess of the Crown Inn, Cornmarket, Oxford...

'Good heavens!' I said out loud.

...There is no proof of this, though Shakespeare may have been his godfather....

I read on, muttering to myself. 'OK... blah blah..."plays in the style of Johnson".... fought on the King's side during the Civil War..." no surprise there "...obtained a patent under Charles II under which he opened Lincoln's Inn Fields Theatre. Later built a new theatre in Dorset Garden but died before it opened...'"

All this all tied in with what I dreamed about him. It was interesting about the Shakespeare connection, but that probably meant that William's grandfather was a contemporary of Shakespeare, and Davenant knew him! This was something I must tell Georgina!

Before doing so, I found an encyclopaedia and looked up the Great Fire of London. Everything, from the weather conditions to the refugee sites concurred with what I had dreamt. I had known very little about the fire before, except that it had begun in Pudding Lane, went on for several days and destroyed most of the city. But the events I had witnessed in the dream took place before anyone knew any of that. There was no doubt in my mind that what I had just dreamed was not the fantastical workings of my sleeping imagination, but something real. It was more like a memory. A memory passed down through the blood of my ancestors, perhaps.

'I tell you what,' said Georgina, 'this is the strangest job I have ever worked on.'

I smiled. I was increasingly warming to Georgina. 'What, you mean no-one else has mysterious family heirlooms and historical dreams about her ancestors?'

'Certainly not! I can't say they're always straightforward, but I do pride myself on carrying out professional and scientific research based on documentary evidence. This is... well, if I'd heard about this from anyone else, I would have been incredibly sceptical, but I must say, the way the details all fit... It is very odd, but I can't help feeling you are right about Anne's parents.'

'Is there any chance you could find anything more about William and Elizabeth, now we have their names?'

'It's very unlikely, unless I could find a will for William Curtis. But the further back we go, the chances of finding documents gets less likely. Particularly without knowing what part of London William was born in, if he was born in London at all.'

'What about theatre records? If William's grandfather knew Davenant, then it's likely he was theatrical too, surely?'

'Again, I can't be sure any records would have survived, and William was working mostly during the time when the drama was banned, so the chance of finding anything is pretty minimal. Also, it may be that it was his maternal grandfather, not his father's father, so we can't be sure the name would be Curtis.'

'Of course, I hadn't thought of that. It's a needle in a haystack, isn't it?'

'Quite. If I had a pound for every time I've researched the proverbial needle, I'd be a very rich woman.'

'Perhaps we're going to have to rely on me having another dream again.'

'Perhaps we are.'

'Any luck with the Scottish research?'

Georgina sighed. 'It's slow going. Bertrand's parents were fairly well-known actors, but McDougal is a common name there, as you can imagine, so it's not easy. I'm not holding out much hope we can get very far back there.'

Nothing else came to light after Georgina once again searched records at the Theatre Museum.

At the weekend I met up with Justin and Greta over an

Indian meal in Covent Garden, and told them about the dream. Afterwards we wandered down to Drury Lane Theatre, gaped at the huge foyer, pondered on booking tickets for 42nd *Street*, but decided it was too expensive, and ended up in the *Nell of Old Drury pub*.

'All these places,' I said, 'my ancestors have been here. Played in that theatre. Probably sat and drank a pint of ale in this pub. I love this place; it's in my blood, literally. I wonder if any of them had so much trouble getting work though,' I added with a wry little laugh.

'Are you still unsure about the way forward?' asked Justin, 'or can you imagine your name up there in lights...' he waved towards the theatre across the road with its big neon signs.

I squinted my eyes and nose and tried to imagine it.

'It's all big musicals here, and I can't tap dance! I think perhaps the Barbican's more my goal, or Stratford, or even some little provincial rep. But I'm still unsure I'm on the right path, somehow.'

'What's next on the agenda?' asked Greta, 'any ideas about further research on your ancestors?'

'It seems we've hit more brick walls – on both sides - and all I can do is hope for another dream, but I think I'm wanting it too much. Since the night I dreamed about the fire, I'm having difficulty sleeping, hoping for dreams that won't come. It's so frustrating.'

Apart from the question about my future career in the theatre, Justin had been very quiet all day.

'Seen anything of Graham?' I couldn't help asking.

'Yeah,' he said, staring out of the window, 'he was at the Tavern the other night.'

'Did you speak to him?'

187

'No. He was dancing with some guy and having a good time, I think.'

I doubted it.

Greta made a sort of scornful, snorting noise. She obviously was thinking the same way as me.

'If you ask me,' she said, ' he was trying to make you jealous.'

I couldn't have agreed more, and as far as I could see, it had worked.

After that, Justin changed the subject, and we moved on.

A few days later, I rang Georgina to see if there was any news at all.

'Well... there is something, but it might be nothing.'

'Tell me anyway.'

'On the IGI – the International Genealogical Index – there is a William Curtis baptised in 1640 in Westminster. It's the only one I can find of the right age, but that doesn't mean it's the right one. He could have been born in a parish where the registers didn't survive, but it's all I've got at the moment. The parents are William and Ann, and they married in 1636 in Bishopsgate. William Curtis and Ann Burbage.'

'Burbage....' I echoed. Why did that name ring a bell? 'Ann Burbage? Do you know her parents' names?'

'I haven't got that far yet. Does that name mean anything to you?'

'Actually... yes. But I'm not sure why. Oh, gosh, I have a hunch this might be right. Georgina, could you check her out? It's not a common name, is it? Perhaps you could find more about her, and I'll try and think why that name rings a bell.'

'Ok. As usual, there are no guarantees but...'

'I know. Still, I have a feeling we're onto something...'

With butterflies in my stomach, I looked again at my *Concise Oxford Companion to the Theatre.*

'Burbage...Burbage... - here! "BURBAGE, James, 1530-97...the builder of the first permanent playhouse in London..." Oh my God! And he also built the Globe. Wait – those dates are too early. Let's see... oh, here we are: "BURBAGE, Richard (c.1567-1619), the first great English Actor. Son of James..."

I sat down. My legs were feeling weak, and my skin was prickling all over.

I knew I'd heard that name before! Richard Burbage, who worked with Shakespeare! I looked back at the entry.

'"...created a number of Shakespeare's heroes, including Hamlet, Lear, Othello and Richard III...." etc, etc..."...a high reputation and his name long remained synonymous with all that was best in acting."'

I put the book on the coffee table and sat back with a sigh.

Was it possible? Did I have the blood of the best actor of Shakespeare's era running through my blood?

I sat up as another thought struck me. I went to my bookshelf and ran through all my books on the theatre, but could not find what I was looking for.

'Damn, damn, damn!'

I looked at my watch. Justin might be home from work. I picked up the phone.

'I am so glad you're home!' I said before he had barely had the chance to answer, 'have you, by any chance, got a biography of Shakespeare, or anything on sixteenth century theatre, with pictures?'

'Um... hang on...'

I waited on the phone while he went to look, my foot nervously tapping against the table leg.

'I have a Schoenbaum's *Compact Documentary Life*. It's got some pictures...'

'Does it have any pictures of Richard Burbage?'

'Burbage?' he answered, surprised, 'Wait a minute... let me look through the list of illustrations.... Um... No. Sorry, darling. Is it important?'

'Yes. Well, I think it might be. Damn!'

'What about a library?'

'There'll all be shut now.'

'Wait... let me see... hang on a minute...'

She could hear him going through books again, muttering as he searched...

'Ooh! Hello...!' I heard him say, and I sat up, my hand tightening on the phone receiver.

'Here we are! Hartnoll's *Concise History of the Theatre*. Portrait of Richard Burbage from Dulwich College Picture Library.'

'Can you bring it over?'

'Er... well, I was going out, but I could come over quickly before I go.'

Almost as soon as I put the phone down, it rang again.

'Sarah? It's Georgina. I found a possible baptism for Ann Burb....'

'Don't tell me! Let me guess. The father's name is Richard...?'

I could hardly bear to hear the answer in case I was wrong.

'Richard... yes. And the mother was Winifred. How did you know?'

I let out a long sigh.

'Richard Burbage was a major actor in Shakespeare's theatre and his father built the Globe Theatre on the South Bank. I knew that name meant something.'

'Oh my!'

'Would you like to come over? My friend's bringing over a portrait.'

'You're very kind. I'd love to.'

I had laid out a bottle of wine and glasses, and we sat round the dinner table while I poured us all a drink.

'Let's see it then,' I said, my stomach doing somersaults.

Justin put the paperback book on the table and opened it to page seventy-five. In the upper right-hand corner was a detail from the only known portrait of Richard Burbage, his head and a part of his collar.

I sat back on my chair and grinned. I suddenly felt incredibly calm, a feeling that I finally knew who I was.

I looked at the expectant faces around the table and laughed.

'That's him,' I said, 'that's the man from my dreams.'

CHAPTER 18

D iary of Winifred Robinson

Shoreditch 20 October 1638

I am somewhat grieved to hear of the death of Christopher Beeston, whom I remember well when he played in 'Every Man in His Humour' with my former husband, my beloved Richard. Just last year I went to see Beeston's company at the Cockpit. Perhaps a better manager than he was an actor, and I hope his son does as well in the coming years.

His death hath put me in a contemplative mood. These last few years have been happy ones as Robinson's wife, but I can never forget that I was married to the best actor of the age.

What years those were, yet fortune deals both good and bad cards, and those days I cannot remember without the pain of eight children borne, and six children gone in the plague years, and Richard never to see his surviving two to adulthood.

Thinking of these things, I remembered the thing he gave me, with its contents and the story that surrounds it. It lies in front of me now, and I am wondering what should be done. Almost twenty years have passed since he told me the tale, when he knew he was going to die, and asked, no begged, me to carry on with the search *he had begun.*

I did but try. I went again to that neighbourhood and asked for her, but she was long gone, and only the echoes of what he had already heard remained: she had married a northern man and moved on. How then would it be possible to search even now, when she has passed from memory, perhaps even dead.

And yet, I cannot dispose of it or sell it, even though it could bring us some much-needed money. It would be a betrayal, and not only towards my former husband, but to his closest friend.

What, then, am I to do? For now, I can only keep it.

23 October 1638

Today I received a visit from my daughter, Ann Curtis. She is with child, which sent joy into my heart, for my son William is unlikely to marry.

Despite his namesake, my son has also no interest in the theatre, which hath been a disappointment to myself and his step-father; and a blight upon his family name, but my daughter married an actor whose talents may one day be worthy of the King's Men, God's will they survive if plague and puritans do not have their way.

While my daughter and I were talking, my thoughts returned to the search my Richard had been making for the girl, to give to her what is rightfully hers. I had a mind to give it all to Ann in the hopes that she and her husband might further the search. I am too old now, but Ann's husband is young. If the girl cannot be found, then in truth, would it be wrong to keep it and what lies within? Surely, by law, it belonged to my husband, and therefore to me, and then I am free to give it whom I will?

I told Ann my thoughts, but she was doubtful of ever finding the girl, whose daughter would now be a young woman herself and perhaps married, and God only would know where they might be now, if it was true she had left London and gone north.

I told her then that she was to take the box upon my death, and as for what it contains, then she will make her own decision. I gave her the key as an insurance. It is out of my hands now. I hope that I have done the right thing by Richard, but I trust my daughter more than my own son. She was twelve when her father died and very fond, whereas William was barely three and hath no memory of him. Furthermore, I do not think the matter would be of great interest to him and the nature of the story may be abhorrent to him. It is more like that Ann will be of greater understanding and honour her father's wishes because of the bond there was between them.

London 1653

Ann Curtis reached down into the chest and picked up the key, remembering in an instant her mother's words to her fifteen years past.

'For your father's sake, keep this and take the box upon my death. It meant so much to him – that he had been entrusted with this task, and unable to fulfil it – and if we cannot finish the task for him, then at the least we must keep the thing itself. It's what he would have wanted.'

Ann felt a pang of guilt, but said out loud, 'Oh, mother, if you could have but known what these last fifteen years would bring...'

After discussing the matter with her husband, and making some vague plans, they had all but forgotten it in the maelstrom of the following years. Two sons born, followed by her mother's illness and subsequent death in 1642. In that same year, the country was at war with itself and the theatres were closed, although the King's Men continued with sporadic performances, including Ann's stepfather, Richard Robinson. Because London was for Parliament, she and her husband fled to Oxford, where the king had recently arrived after his victory at Banbury. The following year William had joined Marmaduke Rawdon's regiment. With them came William's spinster sister, Katharine, who was company for Ann, and a help with the young Will, and the infant named Richard for her father. With some of the legacies from her father and mother, she was able to supplement the soldier's pay and find decent lodgings, but it was still a struggle to feed them all; and constantly the need for news, of battles lost and won, of sieges.

Ann and Katherine stayed in Oxford when William was away, and helped out at the temporary Military Hospital at Brasenose College, but while the armies and Royal court were residing in safety in the colleges, the womenfolk had to live outside in what was a strongly Parliamentarian town and were only able to find accommodation in poor students' quarters, finding rooms on the corner of the Corn Market. Because there was such resentment from the town for being used as a Royalist Garrison, labour was scarce, and so Ann and Katherine were both drafted to help in building the defences, taking it in turns to care for the two young children. Nurses were now a luxury and hard to come by.

Life for the two women was harsh and unpleasant at this time. The soldiers barracking in the colleges very often got drunk at night and were often rude and offensive. The women locked their door every night, and sat trying to write letters or darn stockings by candlelight while outside were the noises of swearing, fighting and loud singing in the streets.

The city was crowded, and disease was rife. During the day, the women found themselves tending to cases of typhoid and cholera as much as to the wounds of war. The streets became places of filth, lined with rubbish, sewage and rotting animal carcasses. What little money they had left over from buying food, they used to buy the latest news-sheets, and Anne spent many anxious days waiting for a letter from William. When they came, they were either joyous with victory or bitter with defeat.

After the end of the second siege at Basing House, he wrote,

...at times some men did think that God hath deserted their cause and turned Roundhead. I am very assured that those on the other side equally believe God to be on their side, only to turn coat when things go against them. I speak nothing in such converse for my thoughts are such that might go against me if spoken aloud, but I do not think that God, if he doth exist, would be so fickle.

Dangerous, heretical words to send in a letter, but it made no difference now. After this, his letters stopped coming.

Anne had little time to wonder or worry about this, for soon after this letter the Parliamentary army started to advance on Oxford, and a siege was only narrowly avoided by a combination of some false diversions on the part of the King and his army, coupled with the incompetence of the Parliamentary troops.

Anne and Katherine had watched all these coming and goings from their window and were badly frightened that they had so nearly been caught up in the downfall or siege of Oxford. She feared for her children if Parliament should another time break through. She wrote to William to ask his advice, but no reply came, and after weeks of anxious uncertainty, hearing only that his regiment were once again under siege, she received a letter from his comrade. Poor Will had died during the Second Siege of Basing House, not in battle, but of the smallpox, which had broken out amongst the tired and hungry garrison. After promising to write to his wife, his friend had been severely injured by a cannon ball, losing his leg, and almost losing his life and his wits, only remembering his promise after weeks of recovery in hospital.

When Ann received the letter she collapsed to the floor and Katharine found her there, read the letter and wept with her for her brother.

Without any hope of a safe place outside of Oxford, and not wanting to risk travelling alone with two children, they remained at lodgings in Oxford, where Anne's fears were realised, and they underwent the two dreadful sieges under Parliament over the next two years. She became used to spending her days hungry, feeding the boys before herself, and watching soldiers calving up horsemeat for food while she and Katherine spent days living on small crusts of bread.

Under the Treaty of 1646 the Royalist army were evacuated and Oxford became a more peaceful town, albeit still under Parliamentary rule.

When Charles had been finally defeated and beheaded, and Oliver Cromwell had marched in victory through London, Anne and Katherine wearily began to pack their bags. They both looked older than their years. They had lost much, and seen friends they had made die of cholera under the wretched conditions of the sieges. The news of the execution of the king had been a blow to the spirit that Anne felt she would never recover from. Yet, she thanked God that her two children, and Katherine, had been spared from death, though all had fallen ill at some time over the last few years.

But before returning to London, she asked Katherine to accompany her on a small errand. That small item from the box she had inherited by law from her grandfather she had never felt was really hers, and by rights should return in some way to its original owner. She therefore made a journey and left in a place as close as possible to his heart.

They finally returned to London with a reduced household itinerary and to a smaller house. The city they came back to was a different London, with the theatres closed and Christmas abolished, and Cromwell's cronies claiming that he had been called by God to rule. When Ann read this she spat at such blasphemy, and could only be glad that neither her father nor her mother had lived to see this day. She vowed that she would bring her sons up to love the theatre, and to do whatever they could to rebel against puritan rule.

Looking at the key again now, as she unpacked again in her new London lodgings that she would share with Katherine, she knew it was too late to do anything beyond take care of it and pass it to her son in memory of her father. The thing it opened was still in Oxford, one of the items that she had deemed too bulky to bring back with her, and she had entrusted it to a friend until such time that she could retrieve it.

It was time for her son, William, now thirteen, to continue his grandfather's legacy. While plays upon the stage were now prohibited, she had heard tell of some actors putting music to drama and calling it a musical performance, which was not prohibited under the new law. Some called it 'opera' in the Italian style. But it broke her heart that the King's Men were no more, with many of the actors of the former days now gone to other work, Swanston now a jeweller, and others gone as stationers. These were dangerous times. Actors had been arrested for putting on plays. Charles Hart and others had been arrested in 1648 during a performance at the Cockpit, but she was damned if she would allow her own son, who had been brought up to love the drama, to be intimidated. His wings would not be clipped.

In the meantime, she must find some service, or even apprenticeship for the lad. At the very least, it might cool his spirit, for he was a wild child, fond of apple scrumping, rowdy song and prone to hot-headedness. If she could find a place for him in the household of some performer or musician, she would do it, though she risked him being thrown in gaol if he became a player. If only William Davenant was not currently held in the Tower; he would be the one to help.

Anne found a chain to put the key on and put it round her neck to make sure that she would remember it, and her father, and to pass it on to William when the time was right. When he was more of a man.

199

CHAPTER 19

J uly 1985

I stared at the answerphone. It had been so long since I had heard from my agent, I almost had not recognised her voice.

I pressed the play button once more.

'Hi Sarah. Good news! You have an audition for Oxford Playhouse next Thursday at 11 am. They're holding the auditions in Oxford, so you'll need to find your way to the theatre. You need to prepare a classic and a modern piece. It's to play the part of Elisabeth of Valois in their production of *Don Carlos*. Good luck, Sarah!'

It had been about a month since I had discovered that Richard Burbage had been one of my ancestors. Since then, things had gone quiet again on the family tree front, and my initial thrill at finding this out had faded somewhat. Now I knew who he was, I wanted him to return in my dreams again, but he remained stubbornly absent.

Greta had moved in and we'd had a couple of girly nights out to celebrate. I was busy at the wine bar, covering for staff holidays, and in between, reading *The Stage* for jobs, writing letters to casting directors, and traveling into London for a few classes at the Actor's Centre. A class had come up that was a little bit of a different track for me, a beginner's class in the art of direction, and I wondered whether it might be a line of work that could interest me. There was no harm in trying.

I still had my mind on my family, however, and when the call came from my agent, I had been on my way to the library to see if I could find anything further on Richard Burbage. But now I had a different library errand. The play was one I had not heard of, so it would be a good idea to familiarise myself with it so I could choose some appropriate audition pieces.

In a moment, my ancestors were pushed to one side as I focused all my energies preparing for this audition.

I came out of the stage door of the theatre and walked slowly down the road past the front of house. As always after an audition, I felt dissatisfied and deflated. The days of learning a speech, going over and over it again and again until word perfect, getting the meaning of the piece through and trying to add my own personal interpretation, were gruelling, but enjoyable. For the last week I had felt like an actress again, someone with a job to do, with something to aim for. Then, the anticipation of the morning of the audition, travelling to Oxford on the train, going over my lines, feeling quite confident that I was right for the part and had prepared the right speech (Queen Anne from *Richard III*), until I walked into the waiting room where about six other women were waiting to try for the same part, who all looked far more right for the part and were exuding more confidence than I was. Trying not to let it show, trying to tell myself they were probably all looking at me and feeling the same, but not quite believing myself. Then the audition itself, the adrenalin rush, the meeting with the director and his assistant, putting on my best outward going, confident, 'I am the only person for the part' persona, and then my audition pieces, which I got through as I had practised them, and then the inevitable: 'thank you – we'll be in touch', and I was suddenly outside on the street, feeling like a balloon, which, having been blown up to its full capacity, was now having the air slowly let out of it until it was limp and flat.

I knew I hadn't got the part. I had done enough auditions to recognise the polite smiles of the auditioning panel, unable to act well enough themselves to hide the dismissive 'not quite what we're looking for' thoughts as their eyes look to their sheets to see who's up next. I knew when an audition had gone well; there was an extra energy in the air, a genuine interest in the eyes of the panel while they vainly tried to treat you just like all the other auditionees but could not help that sparkle in the eyes as they knew they've found the right one for the part. No. That had not happened this time.

Hardly noticing where I was, I considered, as I walked, whether I should begin to find some other kind of job, a 'proper' job, one where you got paid regularly and had something definite to do every day, where you didn't have to go through this adrenalin roller-coaster of auditioning, hope and disappointment. I looked up at the windows of offices and imagined myself cooped up all day long at a typewriter, and shuddered.

Perhaps I should do more acting classes. I was enjoying the directing class, but was it really going to lead to anything? Getting work as a director was surely just as difficult, without experience, as getting work as an actress. I felt out of touch. I had been so wrapped up in my family history lately, and so unsure of myself, that I had looked for something other than the same old acting classes. Perhaps I should enrol in some audition preparation courses. I grinned sardonically. Ironic, was it not, that a direct descendant of the great Richard Burbage should find so much trouble finding work and motivation?

The truth was, despite my illustrious ancestor, I still felt lost and unable to choose what direction to take.

I did not feel like getting on a train and going home right away. It was a pleasantly warm day, and Oxford looked charming and inviting in the sunshine. I found myself standing opposite the grand, classical edifice of the Ashmolean Museum, but decided that the day was too nice to spend inside.

I had no plans for the rest of the day; I might as well try and get the most out of being here, rather than going home and moping about my life.

Without any idea of what to do, I followed my nose towards Magdalen Street and turned right, strolling slowly southwards, stopping to look in the shop windows on the right, whilst occasionally getting glimpses of the old colleges and churches through the trees on the left. Passing the Saxon Tower, I stopped to admire the Medieval buildings on the corner of Cornmarket and Ship Street.

It was then that I started to feel lightheaded. My hand reached for the key on my chest, as if for comfort, while I stood, pedestrians pushing past me, wondering why my skin had started prickling all over and I felt like I was not quite all there. A feeling that I had taken a step into another reality.

Shaking my head, I turned, bumping into a passer-by who tutted and stared at me, as I mumbled an apology. Without knowing why, I found myself wandering down St. Michael's Street, and a few doors down, stopped outside the whole-food restaurant called the Nosebag. Mouth-watering aromas floated down the stairs, and I realised that I was hungry.

'Pull yourself together, girl,' I said to myself, 'you just need some lunch!'

Smiling at my own stupidity, I went up and ordered a salmon quiche and salad, and sat by the window, looking out onto the street below.

Despite the food, which was delicious, I continued to feel a little weird. I hoped I wasn't sickening for something, but I had no sore throat, and there was certainly nothing wrong with my appetite.

I mentally retraced my steps, remembering that I had been looking at the old buildings on the Cornmarket when I had started to feel odd. Trying to put what I had felt into words, I realised that it was somehow as if the modern world had started to fall away, and I was seeing those buildings as someone else, in another time...

I shook my head again. It made no sense. I had no connection to Oxford. Except, I remembered that Eliza had played at the theatre at Kidlington, but it seemed unlikely she would have had much connection with the centre of the city, and that period didn't feel right. The sense I had was of another, much older, time; a more threatening, fearful time, and those houses on the corner had sparked it off.

'I need caffeine,' I thought, and ordered a large coffee.

When I came out of the restaurant, instead of turning back towards Magdalene Street, I found myself automatically turning right, for no reason other than I felt that I needed to.

Further down, the street was quieter and there were fewer shops, but on my right, I found myself walking past an auctioneers.

It was in the window.

It only caught my eye at first as a general item of interest; something old and well-used. But I felt breathless, as though someone had punched me in the stomach, and I stopped next to it, staring in through the window, my heart racing.

The pattern on the lock matched the pattern on my key.

'Coincidence,' I said to myself.

Something whispered, 'No.'

Before I could argue with myself, I was inside the shop and asking the auctioneer about the writing desk in the window.

The auctioneer peered at me over his spectacles and smiled warmly.

'Ah, yes, the writing box, you mean. Let me get it for you and you can have a good look at it.'

'Thank you,' I said, breathlessly, instinctively making sure the key was well hidden underneath my blouse.

He put the sloped box onto his desk.

'Can you tell me something about it?' I asked.

'Well, it's oak, probably early seventeenth century; perhaps a bit older. It's in a dreadful condition, as you can see. It's very stained, and the wood is warped here and cracked here and there. But the 'S' scrolling along the front, and the unusual pattern on the lock is quite beautiful.'

'Wh... where did it come from?'

'Originally? I have no idea. It came to us in a house clearance. I think it's been sitting in someone's attic for many years. Probably a rather damp one.'

'Does it have a key?'

'Sadly, no. That's been lost.'

I swallowed.

I reached out and stroked my hand across the wood, and down the writing slope. Chills tingled down my back, and I shivered.

'So... without the key, do you know if there's anything inside?'

'We have had it open; we have a skeleton key for such things, and these old locks are not that difficult to open, really. There was nothing inside.'

'Oh.'

I felt a wave of disappointment. If this was the thing that my key opened (and surely it couldn't be?), then why had I been led back through my family tree, and here to Oxford to find it, only to discover there was nothing inside? None of it made any sense at all.

Yet, I did not want to leave it here.

Noticing my hesitation, the auctioneer spoke again.

'It goes up for auction tomorrow. If you're interested, you can pre-register now, and then come back tomorrow and make a bid.'

'Tomorrow? So, how much...?'

'Well, because of its condition, it's valued at a lot less than if it were in better shape. I would say between £100 and £200. But the bidding will probably start at around £30 to £50, so depending on how much interest there is, you could get a bargain.'

I looked down at the box again. If I had to pay up to £200 or more for it, it would take a very large chunk out of what was left from my mother's royalty payment. I would also have to stay in Oxford overnight and lose the money on my return ticket back to London. But I knew in my heart that there was no way I could leave the auction room and never see it again.

'Yes, please,' I said, before I could start arguing with myself.

Ten minutes later, I stood out in the street, looking for a

phonc box. I nccdcd to find a Yellow Pages and find the nearest, cheapest bed and breakfast that had a vacancy for the night.

Driving along the M40 the following afternoon in a hired car, I could not help but keep looking in the rear-view mirror at the large object on the back seat, wrapped in brown paper.

The bidding process had been relatively easy, despite my never having been to an auction before. There was only one other person bidding, and they dropped out early on, so I was able to buy it at £95. It wasn't until after the auction that I had realised how difficult it would be to take it back on a train. So, I had had to leave it at the auctioneers until I had gone on a hunt for a car hire service and was able to find a little Vauxhall Astra that wasn't too expensive to hire until the following morning, when I could return it to the nearest Vauxhall hire firm in London.

'What have I done?' I kept asking myself, 'Am I crazy?'

Yet, every time I looked at the writing box, I knew it belonged to me. Not just in the sense that I had just paid money for it, but because it did, and always had done.

On the North Circular, I looked at my watch. It was getting on for five o'clock. Hopefully, Justin would be back home from work soon. I decided to take a detour and turn up on his doorstep. I had a need to tell someone about it, and I knew he would be interested, even if he did think I was completely mad.

'So,' said Justin, putting two mugs of tea down on the table, 'let me get this straight. You were wandering around in Oxford, and you saw this in an auctioneer's window, and you think it's the thing the key fits? Did you try it? I mean, why would it be in Oxford, and how would you have just been there at the right time? Are you sure this is it? Wouldn't lots of locks have the same pattern?'

I sighed.

'I can't answer any of those questions, Justin, because I don't understand it myself. I just knew that I had to have this box.'

'Have you tried the key with it?'

I looked at him.

'No. I've almost been too scared to. If I'm wrong...'

'Let's have a look, then.'

Something about the way he said this told me that he was not in the right mood, and I hesitated.

'Hang on,' I said, 'this is really important to me, and I don't want to do this unless we're both really into it, but I'm getting the feeling that you're not quite with me right now.'

Justin sat down, put his elbows on the table and covered his face with his hands.

'I'm sorry.'

I sat down, glancing at my box which I was so eager to open. But the timing was wrong. Friendship was more important.

'Do you want to talk about it?' I asked.

'I think Graham's seeing someone,' he said, through his fingers.

'Well,' I said slowly, 'he does have a right to. You dumped him, remember?'

No answer.

'Justin, since you met Graham, I haven't seen you be so happy since... well, I'm not sure I've ever seen you so happy, even though you have tried to convince me it's not a proper relationship.'

No response.

208

'And since you broke up with Graham, I've not seen you so miserable since... well, for a long time.'

There was a big sigh.

'I know, I know, I know, I know, I know.'

He took his hands away from his face.

'But I am so scared, Sarah. When Mark died, I fell into an abyss, and I thought I'd never recover. And I never want to go there again.'

'I know,' I said, gently, 'but you did recover.'

'But what if...'

'What?'

'What if I get into a serious relationship again, and then something bad happens...'

I was suddenly reminded of a Winnie the Pooh story, where Piglet says, 'Supposing a tree fell down, Pooh, when we were underneath it?' and Pooh replies (after careful thought), 'Supposing it didn't.'

'What if something bad didn't happen?' I said, 'what if something really good happened?'

'But...'

'Look,' I said, dredging up all the stuff I had learned from reading self-help books and reading the occasional New Age article, 'things happen. Yes, bad things happen. My parents died. Mark died.' I thought about my ancestors. 'Eliza's parents died. People get arrested and thrown in gaol because of ignorance and prejudice; people's homes and livings were destroyed in the Great Fire of London. Whole families died in the plague. But, guess what? Life goes on. People survive. Here we are – here I am, despite all of that. And despite all that you've been through, you're here too, still capable of living a life and being happy. And all I know is, that if we spend our lives trying to avoid death or bad things, then we're not living at all, and we're never going to be happy anyway – so you might as well be dead.'

I took a large swig of tea, and put the mug down firmly. I wasn't sure where all that had come from, but it had kind of just spilled out of my mouth before I was aware I was thinking it.

'I know you're right,' he said, 'but it's still hard.'

I had got into my swing and I was taking no prisoners.

'Ring him,' I said.

'What?'

'Ring Graham. Ring him now. Of course it's bloody hard. But that's what it's like, isn't it? Life is hard, it's not meant to be easy. Relationships are bloody difficult. But all I know is that when you're with Graham, you're all twinkly eyed and like a cat with cream, and when you're not with him, you're not yourself at all. Ring him.'

He stared at me.

I looked back at the wooden writing desk.

'I tell you what,' I said, fully into my stride, 'I'm going to leave this here with you because it's not the right time to open it. And I'm going to go home, and you're going to ring Graham and sort things out with him, and then I'll come back tomorrow, and we'll open this together. Because you've been with me on this journey all along, and... and it's important that you're here with me when I open it... and I mean properly here with me, not all moody and distracted.'

'But what if he doesn't...'

I turned on my way out of the door.

'Believe me, he will.'

When I telephoned Justin the next morning, he told me that he had spoken to Graham, and that they were going to meet later that night. Then he asked me if I wanted to come in the evening, before he went out, to investigate the writing box.

I knew not to enquire too much into what had passed between them, so I arranged to go over after he was back from work. I was dying to know whether the key fitted the box, and had barely slept, having woken several times from strange, muddled dreams that I could not quite remember.

I had lain in bed for a while, wondering how it was that I could be so sure about somebody else's life and, and so unsure about my own. Yet, in some ways, when I had spoken to Justin the night before, I had felt far surer of myself than ever before. I had spoken with an authority that was unusual for me. Perhaps something had changed in me after all. Yet, why could I not see the way forward for myself?

And then my thoughts kept coming back to the box. Would my key fit, or would it all have been a big mistake? And, if it did fit, and there was nothing in it, as the auctioneer man had said, what then?

I tried to distract myself by going for a walk on Hampstead Heath, window shopping in the High Street, and then went home to listen again to Dire Straits. As it was nearing five thirty, I went over to Justin's house, and had to wait on the doorstep as he had not yet got back from work.

After he got home, he made us both cups of strong tea and put the box in the centre of his kitchen table.

'Let me have another look at the key,' he said.

I lifted the chain with the key on it over my head and handed it to him, and he looked closely at it, and at the box.

'They definitely have the same pattern, but who knows,

211

maybe that pattern was common. I don't know enough about this kind of thing to be sure. It's lucky the lock isn't rusty, or perhaps the auctioneers were able to clean it up.'

He held the key out to me.

'I think you should do the honours, don't you?' We smiled at each other. The time was right.

I nodded, and took the key, feeling shaky and cold. I sat down in front of the box, and slowly put the key shaft into the keyhole. Then, with a small glance at Justin, I attempted to turn it.

There was an initial resistance, but as I applied just a small amount of pressure, I could feel the internal workings of the lock giving way, until the key had made a 180 degree turn, and the sloping lid of the box shifted slightly as it was released from its tethers.

We looked at each other, Justin sitting back in his seat in disbelief. Without saying anything, I lifted the lid, which was heavy, and creaked with age. A musty, dusty smell; a smell of centuries gone by, rose out of it.

I sat back and looked at the interior of the box, holding my hands across my stomach, in an attempt to quell the butterflies therein. I could hardly breathe.

As the auctioneer had said, it was quite empty.

But across the back of the interior were some shelves, and beneath the bottom shelf, four little drawers.

'How lovely!' said Justin, who had now stood up to come and look over my shoulder.

'Yes,' I said, but could not bring myself to tell him that I felt I had seen this before.

'I suppose they looked in the drawers.'

Justin reached in and pulled the first of the drawers, which of course was empty.

'That's the wrong drawer,' I said, almost without thinking.

'What do you mean?'

'I mean...' I shook my head, 'I don't know what I mean, but I think...'

It was the last, the fourth drawer, that I knew was the right one.

I pulled it open, and it, too was empty.

I frowned. I had been so sure...

'Hang on!' said Justin, 'that drawer has a false back. Look. The drawer seems much shorter than the other one.'

I smiled. Of course.

Justin fiddled with the drawer.

'I think all it needs is a little shove... Yes!' the little false panel gave way to reveal a tiny compartment inside the corner of the box. We both peered in.

'There's something there!' cried Justin, now fully engaged.

My fingers trembling, I reached in and pulled out a thick piece of ancient paper, folded once, which was yellowed and flaking round the edges.

Very carefully, because it felt so fragile it might disintegrate if I unfolded it too much, I pulled apart the two edges.

There was something handwritten on the paper, but I could not read it. The writing was not faded, thankfully, but the words looked so different to twentieth century English, that I could barely make anything out at all.

Justin was looking over my shoulder.

'Oh, Lord,' he said, 'that's going to take some deciphering. I think the first word is "It" and then... I think that's might be "is"...'

'Georgina,' I said, 'she'll be used to looking at old writing'.

'Right,' said Justin, looking at his watch, 'let's hope she's not too busy tonight!'

Georgina stood on the front doorstep.

'You must be the only one of my clients who can tear me away from *Dynasty* on a Friday evening,' she said. 'Come to that, you're the only one of my clients who I'd answer the phone to – on any evening!'

'Georgina, thank you so much,' I said, standing aside to let her in, 'I'm sorry to call you out, but this is so important, and I just couldn't have waited the whole weekend.'

'It's OK,' she said, 'I've left my husband fiddling frantically with the video recorder. I just hope he manages to set it up properly, or heads will roll! So, where is this paper?'

I put the folded paper in front of her on Justin's dining table, with a glass of red wine at a safe distance from the paper, and Justin and I sat opposite.

'Ah,' said Georgina, eyeing the wine, 'well, that will help. And so will this,' she said, rummaging in her bag and pulling out a large magnifying glass, a notepad and pen. 'Well, here goes.'

Carefully holding the paper with one hand, and holding the magnifying glass with the other she began to slowly read the words on the page while we waited, hardly daring to breathe. I watched Georgina's face as she frowned, peering at words that were difficult, occasionally muttering an exclamation such as 'Hmmm...' or 'Ah!', while jotting down word by painfully slow word on her note pad. I resisted the temptation to try and read the notes upside down.

'Wow,' said Justin, 'you must need a lot of patience to do this. I think it would drive me mad.'

'Funnily enough,' said Georgina, scrunching up her eyes and

twisting her head as she tried to make sense of a particularly difficult word, 'I'm not the world's most patient person, but this work has taught me a little more patience, if anything.'

'I don't know how you do it,' I said, 'it looks like a foreign language to me, not English.'

'That's because many letters were formed very differently back then. It's a knack. You have to stop your brain from reading what it thinks is familiar to make an "assumed" word, and instead consciously break each word down, letter by letter. That's why it takes so long. I can charge clients hours of work just to transcribe a two-page will, most of which will often be extremely boring legal jargon, but the interesting bits can prove to be very interesting indeed!'

After another long silence, during which I noticed her raising her eyebrows as something surprised her, she looked at us over the top of her spectacles and said, 'I think we have it.'

'Shall I look?' I asked.

'I'll read it to you,' answered Georgina, 'chances are you won't be able to read *my* writing. Ha! Here we go...

It is buryed nearby where he lies at Holy Trinity
   Amongst a bed of columbine and purple loosestrife
   For safe keeping within a metal box.
   If ever she be found who is the rightful owner,
   That is to saye, the daughter of Agnes McDougall, who was Agnes Smith,
   His ... I can't read the next line – it's across the fold...
   Then it is to be dugge up and returned to her.
   Anne

We all sat without speaking for a few moments, to digest the words, then I said,

'Agnes McDougal?'

'Yes,' said Georgina, taking off her glasses, 'interesting eh?'

Goosebumps had risen all over my skin.

Justin spoke.

'McDougal? But... isn't that the name of that actor who we now know was your ancestor... Bertie, wasn't it?'

'Yes!' Georgina and I said in unison.

'But how...?'

'I don't know!' I said, rubbing my face with my hands, 'I'm so confused. None of it makes any sense. Unless it's just a coincidence.' But in my heart, I knew this was more than that. I recalled the dream with the McDougal name above the door. Why would I have dreamt that unless this name bore more significance than I had thought before?

Justin scratched his head.

'Hang on. This is crazy. If it's not a coincidence,' he said, 'how does a writer's box of the early seventeenth century, somehow connected with your Burbage family, end up in Oxford, with a note in it that seems to relate to another actor who lived three centuries later?'

'Is there any way we can find out?' I asked, 'and also, the writer's name is Anne. Could that be – oh, I'm getting so confused – could that be Anne Curtis? Who was she? Was she Richard and Winifred's daughter? Sorry, I'm feeling a bit tired. It's been a long day, and I didn't sleep well last night.'

'Well,' said Georgina, 'if this is your family's heirloom, it seems likely. Going by the handwriting, I'd say this was written around the middle of the seventeenth century, and the box would be older than that. To answer your other question, what I'm thinking is that the Agnes she mentions was obviously born with the name Smith and married someone called McDougal. When I get back to my desk on Monday, I could check the indexes and see if I can find a marriage. It might lead us somewhere, who knows?'

'Thanks,' I said.

I picked up Georgina's notebook and read the note again.

'"Where he lies at Holy Trinity." Who is "he", do you think? And where is Holy Trinity?'

Justin, who had been looking at the carved 'S' decoration on the writer's box, said, 'Stratford-upon-Avon.'

He looked up at us.

'Where William Shakespeare is buried.'

CHAPTER 20

J ustin went out to meet Graham, Georgina went home to catch up on *Dynasty*, and I went home to sleep. I did not dream that night, but I slept well, and deeply.

The next day I got up late, and sat in front of the writing desk, drinking strong coffee, and wondering what to do next.

Justin had said he would call me some time this morning, but I wondered whether his evening with Graham had gone well or badly, and either way, he might not be in the mood to discuss my ancestors.

But true to his word, he did ring me around 11 o'clock.

'How did it go?' I asked.

'Good,' he said, 'OK, I think. Turns out he wasn't really seeing anyone else, seriously. He was just going out a few times to get his mind of me! Look, I'm dying to talk about the desk and everything, but do you think you could wait until tomorrow? We're er... we're going to spend the day together and see how it goes. Graham's got a day off work and he wants to watch *Live Aid*, so it was a good excuse to get a few drinks in and spend the day here in a kind of relaxed way. You know, not too intense, just sitting together and taking it easy.'

Live Aid! I had completely forgotten it was on today, I had been so wound up in my family history.

'Sounds like a great idea. I'll probably watch it myself. Tomorrow would be great. Greta will be here, and we'll all have a discussion about what I'm going to do next. Um... if Graham would like to come, you can invite him, but I'll leave that up to you.'

I thought that nothing was likely to take my mind off the mystery of my ancestry, but soon after I had turned the television on to watch the concert, I was completely taken over, and as soon as Status Quo took to the stage to sing 'Rockin' all Over the World', I was up and dancing, playing air guitar and making a complete idiot of myself. It didn't matter, though, there was no-one there to see me, and it felt good, letting off steam and having my mind taken over by something else. By lunch time I had sent off my cheque. It was a very warm day, but there seemed to be very few people out when I went down the road to post the envelope. I was tempted for a moment to take another walk on the Heath, but the call of Ultravox and Spandau Ballet was too great, and I rushed back to sing 'Vienna' at the top of my voice.

That evening, as I watched Dire Straits, followed by that legendry set of Queen's, followed by David Bowie, followed by The Who, followed by Elton John, I was in seventh heaven. I ordered a take-away by phone, unable to tear myself away from the screen, and opened a bottle of wine.

At the end of the evening, as I sat in a happy stupor, and looked over to the writing desk, that seemed to be part of a different life right now, the one song that kept going through my head was David' Bowie's 'Heroes.' I had no idea why.

When I opened the door to Justin the next day, I was delighted to see Graham standing behind him on the doorstep, doing a big 'jazz hands' wave. As he came through the door he whispered in my ear, 'Thanks for everything. Justin told me what you said.'

'I'm so pleased,' I whispered and gave him a hug.

Before we started on the topic we had gathered for, we spent some time discussing yesterday's concert, and remembering our favourite bits. Greta had missed most of the day as she had been at her parents for Sabbath, but she had seen some of the evening sets.

'Freddie was just amazing!' said Graham, 'So much energy!'

I had put the box on my dining room table, and after a while, we went and sat down around it, and I got out the note that Georgina had transcribed.

Graham stared at it.

He pouted, 'how could you have all this excitement without me?'

I grinned and handed him a mug of coffee. We were all a bit bleary-eyed after yesterday's TV marathon.

'So, what do you think it all means? Do you really think there's something buried at Stratford, and what do you think it is?'

'I don't know, and I don't know,' I said, 'but even if there is something, how on earth would we find it after over three hundred years? Even if it's still there, the words "columbine and purple loosestrife" is hardly "X marks the spot" is it? There might be loads of that stuff, or none at all. A lot would have changed in all that time. It might even have been built over by now.'

Graham read the note again. 'It sounds like the writer was expecting it to be dug up fairly soon. Probably within her lifetime if this Agnes person was found. If not, then she probably thought it would stay there forever.'

'That's just about what we thought too,' said Justin.

We were all silent for a few moments.

'I don't get it,' said Greta, 'why would something belonging to William Shakespeare be in this desk, and how did it end up in Oxford? Do you think it was his desk, or is that just crazy?'

I sat back in my chair and closed my eyes. The finding of the box, and the transcription of the note seemed like a lifetime ago. But after the gap of yesterday, my mind felt clearer, more objective.

'Well,' I said slowly, 'strange as it might seem, the desk, or box or whatever you want to call it, appears to have belonged to Anne, the daughter of Richard Burbage. As you know, Richard Burbage was a colleague and possible friend of Shakespeare's. Perhaps there was some legacy that couldn't be fulfilled, some object that's referred to in the note, and she buried it, but I don't know why and what is has to do with the McDougals and why it ended up in Oxford. And', I said opening my eyes, and sitting up, 'how on earth was it that I just so happened to have an audition in Oxford when I haven't had any for ages, and how on earth did I just happen to be passing that auction house on the very day before the auction when this thing was to be sold?' I had asked myself this question many times since I had found the box, but it had suddenly only just hit home just how extraordinary this was.

'That is so weird,' said Graham, 'it's almost as if that audition was meant to be...'

'You mean someone up there...' I waved my hand vaguely in the air, '...arranged an audition in Oxford and then led me to the place where I would see it? But it's crazy!'

'What other explanation do you have?' asked Graham.

'Your ancestor again?' said Greta, 'the man in the cloak? What's his name? Burbage?'

I sank back on the chair again.

'I don't know. I think I must be going mad. Do you know, when I was walking down Magdalen Street in Oxford, I was thinking of dropping all this family history stuff and concentrating on my career. I was beginning to worry that it was taking over too much of my life, and then, this happened! It's like it won't let me go!'

'Is it worth going to Stratford,' said Graham, 'and see if there's anything that relates to this clue? Something to dig up?'

I shook my head.

'It all seems a bit unlikely. A bit too cloak and dagger.'

'Then... what?'

'I don't know. I really don't.'

'I tell you what,' said Justin, into the silence that followed, 'if you don't know what to do, it's sometimes best to do nothing. Why don't we all head over to the new wine bar in West Hampstead for lunch? A different location might clear our heads, or we could talk about something different, if you like.'

'Well, it's a plan, of sorts, I suppose,' I said.

I wasn't going to leave the house empty again with the box inside, without making it secure. So, before we went out, I took it into my Dad's old study, which had a lock on the door. But as I was putting it down on his old desk, I gasped as waves of dizziness took hold of me, and I heard someone whispering my name.

'Sarah.... Trust me...'

I sat down on my father's swivel chair, holding my head, waiting for the dizziness to pass.

When it did, I opened my eyes and knew in that moment that I must go to Stratford. I wasn't going crazy. I had listened and followed these voices, dreams and instincts from the very beginning, and had they not always led me to something?

I said nothing to others about my experience in the study, and we all got into my car. As I pulled out of the drive, I noticed in my rear-view mirror a car swiftly pulling out from street parking, but I thought nothing of it. There were always plenty of cars parked round here; people going for walks on Hampstead Heath, or visiting the high-end shops and bars of Hampstead High Street. This one had just taken my attention for a moment because it had pulled out so suddenly.

We entered one of the new trendy wine bars in West Hampstead, and found a table near the window. Despite it being daytime, the setting was dark and candle-lit, the shades drawn, the tables and chairs of old stripped pine with dark, floral cushions, the floors bare, and on the walls black and white photographs of vineyards in Tuscany and the Loire hung on a bare stone wall hand-painted with vine leaves. In the background the speakers played old torch songs from the 30s and 40s.

We ordered a bottle of cold Frascati with some olives, pitta bread and dips.

'This is nice,' I said, 'very relaxed.'

'Very "shabby chic", darlings,' said Graham.

'Yes,' said Justin, 'people will pay a fortune these days for a chest of drawers that looks like it's been vandalised and then left out in the rain for years, but apparently it takes a lot of work to make it look like that!'

I smiled and looked around the room. It was quite busy, a strange mix of yuppies and arty, ex-hippy types, mostly with friends, while a man in a beard and a peaked cap drank alone on the table next to ours.

'Are you OK? You were very quiet in the car.'

Justin's question brought me back to my current world, and I told them of the voice in the study.

'I have to go to Stratford. I've been guided before, like in Oxford. I think perhaps I will be again.'

'Hey!' said Graham, 'don't you mean *we* have to Stratford? I'm not missing out on any more excitement!'

'Graham's right,' said Justin, 'we're in this together, don't forget.'

I grinned.

'Tomorrow, perhaps? But what about your jobs?'

'Damn!' said Justin.

'Well, I've got very little to do in the new play at the Barbican', said Graham, 'No quick changes, and so I'm only sitting around twiddling my thumbs. I can feign a migraine and get someone to stand in for me with no feelings of guilt at all.'

'Is that fake migraine at all catching?' asked Justin, 'I could do with one and get a day or two off work, though I probably *will* feel guilty about it.'

'Shall I come too?' asked Greta.

'Of course!' I said.

'Ooh!' squealed Graham, clapping his hands, 'we're going to Stratford-upon-Avon!'

At that moment, I heard the sound of a piece of cutlery falling on the hard, wooden floor nearby, and I automatically turned my head. The man with the beard was bending down, trying to retrieve it.

A memory stirred in my head. My uncle's wake, and David diving under a table to retrieve a fork he had just dropped. In hindsight, I realised he had just heard Aunt Ada tell me about the family tree and had dropped his fork in surprise at that moment.

With a strange tingling sensation all over, I looked closely at the man as he came back up from under the table. He had a beard, and some sort of cap, and looked out of place in this setting. That was probably why I had noticed him before, without really thinking too much about it. But there was something about his cheekbones...

I leaned over to Justin, putting my head in front of him and speaking directly to him so that the man could not see or hear me speak.

'Don't look,' I said just above a whisper, 'but that man on the next table... I think it's David.'

Justin's eyes widened, and flickered over in the direction of the man, who was sidling out from the table, his back towards us.

I shook my head to signal him to say nothing, and watched out of the corner of my eyes as the man left. Yes, there was something in the man's gait, and his slim figure, even though he was wearing a long jacket.

'Are you sure?' asked Justin.

'Yes,' I said. I was feeling slightly sick, and suddenly cold, even though the bar was warm.

'What is it, what is it?' said Graham, 'you two look all furtive. Do let us in!'

Justin told him what I had said.

'Oh my God! That was David?'

'What was he doing here?' asked Greta.

'There can only be one explanation for him being here,' I said. 'Oh God, what do we do? Should we ring the police?'

'Yeah, I can just imagine what they'd say,' said Justin, 'if we start describing men disguised in hats and beards eavesdropping on our conversation, they'd probably suggest we'd read too many Enid Blyton novels.'

'

'You're probably right. And, to be honest, I wouldn't blame them. I think I'd feel the same thing if someone told me this. But, after reading Uncle Charles's description of him, it's obvious that he is a bit weird... Oh God!'

'What?'

'I've just remembered – someone pulled out pretty sharpish in a car when we left the house. I thought nothing of it at the time, but how else could he have followed us here? It wasn't the car David used to have, but I suppose it would make sense for him to change it, along with his looks. Which means, he's been sneaking around, watching the house.'

'Are you OK, love? You've gone very pale.'

'No,' I said, 'there is something so creepy about this, and it's brought all the feeling around the break-in back to me. I think I'd allowed myself to think he'd kind of given up after that, but obviously that was naïve of me. What am I going to do? Should we go back to the house? I locked the study but...'

'I don't think he'll try that again,' said Justin, 'but again, don't you mean what are *we* going to do? Well, we do have the advantage of knowing that he's overheard us. He heard us make plans to go to Stratford tomorrow. We could steal a march on him and go up earlier. Today?'

'Where will we stay in Stratford? It'll be heaving with tourists at this time of year.'

'I hadn't thought of that. Look, why don't you and Greta go back to your place and start making phone calls, see if you can find a bed and breakfast or something. Graham and I will go and pack a few things, and we'll come over and meet you.'

We all started to move, and then suddenly Justin clapped his hand to his head.

'No! Wait a minute. I've just had a thought. My parents have a camper van. It's one of those early 1970s motor caravans; we all used to go on holidays in it when my brother and I were in our teens. It's up in Gloucestershire of course, but we could drive over this afternoon and pick it up. It's big enough for us all.'

CHAPTER 21

By early evening, all four of us were strolling along the banks of the Avon, through the Memorial Gardens towards the church. It was busy with people; some hurrying to get to the theatre, others, American or Japanese tourists soaking up the river atmosphere after visiting the birthplace of the bard, people still out on the river in boats, and the noise of early evening drinkers across the road at the Dirty Duck pub.

It would have been an enjoyable evening if we had been here as tourists or playgoers, but I felt nervous and unsure of myself. Having dragged my three friends all the way to Stratford, I wondered if this really was an incredibly stupid wild goose chase.

And there were too many people. How could we find the right place without looking suspicious? And another thing was bothering me. I kept looking over my shoulder, half expecting to see David hovering somewhere behind us.

As we approached the church, and climbed up the steps towards the gate into the churchyard, I said,

'I don't know how on earth we're going to be digging something up around here, if we even find the right place. It's all so public! And there's a wall barring access to the riverbank here, which probably wasn't there in Ann's day. I'm sorry guys. I haven't thought this through. I just don't see how this is going to work. We haven't even got any spades for digging!'

'Don't give up yet, hon,' said Graham, 'anyway, it's an adventure! And we're in Stratford. Even if nothing came of it, we can still have a lovely time. I've been dying to come to Stratford for absolutely ages. And now we're all here, thanks to your ancestors!'

I smiled. Graham was one of those people who was always able to put a positive spin on things.

'Didn't your ancestor tell him to trust him?' asked Greta, 'you can't deny that. And you don't ignore what ancestors say to you in dreams.'

But I could not help doubting myself. *What if my ancestor has no idea how difficult it would be to start digging holes in the ground in a twentieth century tourist town? Or what if the whole thing is just my imagination?* But I kept quiet.

We went into the church and stood at Shakespeare's grave, reading the curse that was engraved there:

Good frend for Iesus sake forbeare,
  To digg the dust enclosed heare.
  Blese be ye man that spares these stones,
  And cursed be he that moves my bones.

I shivered. The talk of digging and curses after what I had just been saying did nothing to lighten my mood.

Graham whispered to me, 'do you think he's a relative?'

'He can't be,' I said, 'it's well known that he has no direct descendants. His only son died young, and his daughters' families died off within two generations. Anyway, we know

229

I'm descended from Burbage, not Shakespeare.' I sighed. 'I don't know why we're here.'

Yet, I felt rooted to the spot, not wanting to drag myself away from this hallowed place. My whole life and career were inspired by this man, who lay here at my feet.

After a while we went and looked at the bank of the river by the church, peering down over the low wall that bordered the churchyard. Below was a tangle of roots, weeds, ivy and grass, on a steep, short slope to the water's edge. It was Justin who pointed to the white flower growing amongst it all.

'Isn't that columbine?'

I felt a shiver run down my spine.

'Oh! Yes, she said columbine in the note. What was the other thing? Loosestrife? Anyone know what that looks like?'

Graham was wandering further down.

'Here!' he shouted, 'this purple spiky plant – isn't that it?'

We joined him.

'More columbine too. We're in the right area, but still, I suppose these have been growing here for years and they could be spread all over the place. We're still no closer to where she might have buried... whatever it is. If it's still there.'

Justin looked back up at the church.

'Probably as close to the chancel as possible. That's where he's buried.'

'You're right,' I said, 'that seems the most likely.'

We all wandered back to the bank opposite the west wall of the church and looked down at the inaccessible riverbank. No-one said anything.

Silently, we wandered further along to the south side of the chancel, where an ivy-covered corner sloped down to the river.

I looked down the bank and turned back to the church, and as I did so, I felt dizzy, and the spire seemed to lurch above me, the wall in front of me swaying, as if under water. For a fleeting moment, I saw a short, wooden spire, and then I shut my eyes, my hand on my head.

'Oh!' I gasped, as I felt two sets of hands grab my arms.

'Sarah? Are you all right?'

For a few seconds I could not think where I was or who these people were. Then I opened my eyes, and there was Justin and Graham on either side and a worried looking Greta in front of me. Above me was the solid stone wall and stone spire of the church.

'I'm sorry,' I said, 'Something really odd happened... I... I felt I was here, but not here, and... and...' I looked again up at the spire, '...the spire was wooden.'

Justin looked up. 'It may well have been wooden when it was first built, and in Ann's time. Look, perhaps we need to go and get something to eat.'

'And drink, probably,' said Graham.

'No... no... wait a minute,' I said, 'we'll go for something in a minute, but this is like when I was in Oxford. A feeling that I had been here before, long ago. Well, not me, but... I can't explain it. I think this is it, where we're standing. No – wait...'

I peered over the shallow wall onto the steep bank below.

'Here. It's on the bank.'

'Are you sure?' asked Justin.

'This is where she buried it, whatever it is, I'm sure. Down there.'

We all looked down at the steep bank, at the nettles and jumble of greenery.

'So close to the water?' remarked Greta.

'Well, don't rivers widen with age?' said Justin, 'it probably wasn't so close when she buried it.'

'Er... so what now?' I said.

'Will it still be there?' said Greta, voicing what we were all thinking.

'Why not closer to the chancel, where Will is buried?' asked Graham.

'Bodies,' said Justin, 'too many bones. And too risky to have it dug up again. She was a clever lady. Much safer to bury it a little further away, where there'd be no grave digging, closer to the bank. And thankfully, she said a metal box, not wooden. It won't have rotted away.'

'But how will we find out?' said Greta, 'we can't start digging a hole here in broad daylight!'

Justin turned to her.

'You're right. If we're going to do this, it would have to be at night.'

Greta's eyes widened.

'You want to start digging in a churchyard at night? I'm not sure about that...'

'...and wouldn't it be locked?' I said.

'Look, if you're really serious about this, if you really think this is the place - I know I've been a little sceptical before, but it seems you haven't been wrong yet - then we have to do something drastic. No-one's going to give us permission to dig here, so we'll just have to do it without permission. If it's locked, we can probably get over the wall. I'm up for it if you are.'

Graham giggled.

'Ooh, it's like Agatha Christie meets Bram Stoker. Darlings, I'm *so* excited!'

'Oy Gutt!' exclaimed Greta, 'You're not serious? Digging in a churchyard at night-time?' She shuddered, 'I might have to leave you guys to that...'

Graham put his arm round her.

'Come on, Greta, it'll be fun!'

'Fun...' I echoed, 'My God, I hope so. Oh, Uncle Charles, what on earth have you got me into?'

During a meal at the Dirty Duck, we planned to come back on the Monday night, giving us time to buy spades and anything else we might need the following day at a local garden centre.

During the meal, while both Justin and Graham seemed in high spirits, and Greta resigned to go along with the adventure, I could not shake off my feelings of apprehension. Being a Sunday night, the pub was busy and noisy, and I was developing a headache, so I went easy on the wine. Much of the time I looked around the pub, scouring the tables and bar for that familiar face.

'You're looking over your shoulder again,' said Justin, 'do you think he'll be here?'

'I don't know,' I said, 'but I think it's likely he'll be in Stratford, somewhere. I am sure he heard us yesterday.'

'But unless he was standing nearby when we were at the church, he wouldn't know where to look for buried treasure,' said Justin, 'and I don't remember seeing anyone around that might have been him.'

'That's true,' I said, but I still could not shake off my feelings of apprehension.

The following day, it rained heavily without much let-up, and after we had been to the local garden centre and picked up a couple of spades, a torch and a camping lamp, we went back to the church to suss out the best place for getting into the churchyard at night. We then spent much of the day cooped up in the motor home playing board games that we found in the cupboards. At about 5pm Justin went out and got us all pizzas.

'I hope this rain doesn't go on all night,' said Graham, staring wearily out of the window after the sixth game of Scrabble, and wiping crumbs from his trousers, 'I don't fancy digging in the rain much.'

'At least it will make it easier to dig,' said Justin, 'but I do tend to agree.'

'As long as it's not muddy,' I said, 'we don't want to feel like we're digging trenches in the Somme. God, I hope we're doing the right thing.'

Graham yawned. 'It's an adventure,' he said, 'but I have to admit that it doesn't much feel like one right now, cooped up here, and I'd rather not catch pneumonia while having one either. Shame we couldn't have gone sightseeing, or something.'

'I feel safer here,' I said, 'whatever the weather.'

Justin put his arm round her shoulders.

'I think we should try and get some sleep early,' he said, 'and I'll set the alarm for – what – around two? We want it to be as quiet as possible, so it will probably be the best time.'

Greta shuddered again.

'I don't like it,' she said, 'I don't like it at all.'

I grabbed her hand.

'You don't have to come, Greta. Really, I understand how you feel, and you can stay here and hold the fort, if you like.'

Greta nodded, but said nothing.

After a few moments, while I cleared the Scrabble board,

Greta got up and said, 'I'll make you some coffee and put it in flasks for you. It will be cold that time of night.'

It was only a few hours later that I woke up, shivering, from a confused dream that disappeared like a slippery eel as soon as I tried to remember it. It had left me, however, feeling disturbed and wakeful, unable to relax.

I turned the switch by my bed to turn on the small light and looked at my watch. It was only just after 1am. I lay on my back and listened. The rain had stopped, but a strong breeze was making the van rock slightly.

In the bunk on the other side of the van, Greta stirred, and sat up.

'What is it?' she whispered.

'I don't know. I just feel... I don't want to wait. I think we should go.'

Greta got out of bed.

'I'll wake the boys,' she said, 'we know enough about your hunches now that we need to trust them.'

Not much was said as the three of us who were going out got dressed, yawning and grunting, trying to shake off our warm sleepiness and brace ourselves for the outdoors, which would now be cold after the rain.

'Well done about the coffee,' said Graham, in the low voice of the night, 'this is going to be very welcome. We can drink this while we're walking.'

'Be quiet as you're leaving,' whispered Greta, 'you don't want to wake anyone else on the camp site.'

'Come *on*,' I said, standing at the door while Graham was fiddling with his shoelaces, 'I feel we've no time to lose...'

The night air was cold, and there was a biting breeze, that kept us huddled together as we trekked from the site, carrying our spades. I held the torch so we could see where we were going. Because of the bank of clouds, there was no moon.

We had agreed to approach the church from the south side, getting across the river on the small footbridge close to the weir, which would bring us to the Lucy's Mill side and a short walk to the church, rather than going past the theatre, where there might still be late night revellers, who might look rather curiously at three people in dark clothes carrying spades.

As we walked over the bridge, we could hear the sound of the weir, and I saw that the river was noticeably higher after the rain. Scudding by in the dark, currents from the open sluice causing eddies and gullies, the Avon did not look like the peaceful river that it did in the postcards.

My stomach churned, and not for the first time I wondered what on earth I was doing here.

We arrived on the other side of the bridge and walked up Mill Lane, bringing us to the southernmost gate of the church precinct. We turned right, and up the few steep steps into the churchyard.

As quietly as we could, we crept along the wall of the churchyard towards the river. Lights on the wall of the church threw out a sickly yellow glow, and I tried not to look at the gravestones looming eerily out of the dark.

Justin, who was ahead, stopped suddenly, holding his arm out in front of us to stop us.

Holding his finger in front of his mouth to prevent us speaking, he whispered, 'Listen.'

We stopped still and listened, holding our breaths.

For a moment, all I could hear was the sound of my own

beating heart, but after a moment something else permeated my hearing.

It was the sound of digging.

I looked at Justin, my eyes wide.

'David!' I mouthed.

We stood in silence, staring at each other and wondering what to do next, and as we did so, the digging stopped, and we heard someone grunting and breathing heavily as they attempted to pull something out of the ground.

We can't just stand here while he takes away my inheritance, I thought, and I started to walk slowly to where we had stood the night before, with Justin and Graham following closely behind.

As we approached the low wall, I could see his shadowy figure, standing below us on the bank as he forced open a box, shining a torch to see what was inside it, and taking something out of it.

I climbed over the wall, balancing myself on the sharp rake of the bank, and I could hear Justin following me close behind. David looked up as he heard us, dropped the box and quickly picked something up off the ground. The moon had briefly appeared from amongst the clouds, and I could see a glimpse of reflected light on steel.

'Don't come any closer,' he said, 'I have a knife here, and I'll use it. I've been expecting you, you see.'

'How did you know...?' I began.

'How did I know where to dig? Well, you were all very sure of yourselves, thinking no-one had overheard you the other evening. No-one passed you by, did they? Not on land they didn't.' He laughed. 'But you never thought of the river, did you? Lots of boats on the river, lots of them available for hire, and plenty of trees and greenery to shelter and overhear a conversation. I knew you'd be coming, so I just rowed up and down the river until I saw you. It was a very pleasant afternoon, really.'

He kicked the box towards me, where it landed at my feet.

'Here Cousin! You can keep that. I'll have this. Fair deal. Share and share alike, and all that. But I think this might do me very well. Very well indeed.'

He held it up, and I shone my torch on it.

It was a ring.

CHAPTER 22

As David stood grinning at the piece of jewellery in his hand, I picked up the small box and thought of my ancestor Ann, who had handled the ring, tried to get it to its rightful owner, and then carefully put it in this little trinket box, perhaps her own personal possession, and hidden it lovingly close to the person it had belonged to originally. The box of course was badly tarnished and damaged, but I guessed it was copper, and perhaps she had used to keep her own pieces of jewellery in until she used it to put the ring inside.

A ring belonging to William Shakespeare.

'It doesn't belong to you, David,' I said.

'No?' he answered, 'what about "finders keepers" eh? Oh, and if it's an heirloom from our esteemed ancestors, then by rights it's mine. I'm the sole male survivor of the Turveys. If I sell this, I think it will bring me a nice fortune.'

He again put the ring in the pocket of his jacket, and turned towards the river, where I could just make out the shadow of a rowing boat.

Automatically, I stepped towards him, but David brandished the knife, and I felt Justin's protective hand on my arm.

'Don't come any closer, coz. Nor you, scum!' he said, turning to Justin. 'You'

239

people disgust me – I hope you all die of AIDS, it's what you deserve.'

'And I suppose someone like you would feel the same way about Jews?' came a voice from behind him, a few feet further along the bank.

David swung round to see who had spoken, as a figure stepped out from the shadows on the path above the wall, and as he turned, Justin leapt forward and tackled him to the ground. They rolled dangerously close to the waters.

'Justin!' I shouted.

A shadow flew past me, and now Graham had joined in the tussle on the ground, and was trying to pry the knife out of David's hand. I tried to get hold of David's jacket and find the ring in his pocket, but in the dark, even with the torch, it was difficult to see, and David was stronger than he looked. After a brief struggle, he broke free, and screaming, 'Fuck you, you bastards!' he scrambled to his feet. Pulling the boat towards him, he jabbed his knife at Graham who had been trying to pull his jacket to bring him off balance, and Graham leapt back.

Wobbling precariously, David managed to find the oars and get himself away from the bank, jabbing one at Justin as he tried to make a last lunge for him. In the middle of the river, the boat carried fast by the current, he turned, laughed and said, 'So long, suckers!'

But the sudden movement, along with the fast, churning of the waters coming from the weir and the sluice, overbalanced him, and we watched in horror as the boat suddenly overturned and, in the shadows, he slipped into the water.

'Oh my God!' I cried, 'that water's too fast. He'll be pulled under!'

We peered into the darkness, and I shone the torch down

onto the river, but it was no good; it was too far, and we could see nothing except the waters hurrying fiercely southwards.

We looked out on the waters for a few moments. All was silent, except for the sound of our panting breaths, and the hooting of an owl on the opposite bank.

'Nothing,' said Justin. 'I'm going to go and find a phone, and call the emergency services,' and he ran off.

My knees seemed to buckle, and I sat down on the wall.

Graham turned and came and crouched down in front of me. 'Are you OK, hon?'

I put my head in my hands.

'It's all for nothing,' I said, 'and now David! I know he's a bastard, but... Oh, this is so awful! And the ring. It's gone. All this work and effort to find it, and it's all for nothing!'

Graham put a hand on my arm, and his other hand in his pocket.

'I don't think so,' he said, and held out his hand. Something glistened in the moonlight.

He was holding the ring.

'Oh Graham!' I cried, bursting into tears, 'how on earth...?'

'When I grabbed his jacket, I wasn't trying to stop him, I was getting my hands in his pockets. Getting this back was more important than stopping him. He never knew. The bastard slit the sleeve of my best coat, but I got it.'

I took the ring from him, and then hugged him tightly.

Greta joined us, and we sat holding each other for a few moments.

'Greta,' I said, 'Thank you. If you hadn't have turned up when you did...'

'Well, I sat in that van for a while, wondering what was going on and worrying about you all, and then I said to myself; "Greta

Bukowski, what kind of a coward are you? Why are you not part of this?" So, I came. And when I got here, there he was, brandishing a knife and insulting my friends. I wasn't going to stay silent then.'

'Well, my darlings,' said Graham, 'that certainly was an adventure!'

'Yes,' said Justin, as he returned from making the call, 'but how on earth are we going to explain all this to the police?'

It was hours later when we were finally sitting around the small pull-out table in the campervan.

I took the ring out of the rucksack I had been wearing all evening, and laid it in the middle of the table. It was the first time any of us had seen it in daylight.

'Oh my!' gasped Graham.

It was a thick, gold ring. The band was wide and decoratively filigreed around the setting and on top was a large sapphire, surrounded by seven pearls.

'It's beautiful,' I whispered.

Everyone was silent for a few moments.

'Wait,' said Justin, 'there's an inscription.'

He picked it up, and peered at the underside of the band, holding it up to the light, his eyes squinting with the effort.

'It says, "HW to WS"'. He put the ring down again.

'WS?' said Graham, 'William Shakespeare?'

'Presumably,' answered Justin, 'but who's HW?'

'Yet another mystery,' I muttered.

David's body had been found further downstream earlier that day by a team of policemen dragging the river.

All four of us had given statements to the police, and we had all told the truth, except for the fact of the ring. I did not want to risk it being confiscated, investigated and ending up in some museum. It belonged to me, somehow. I did not know why, but I knew I was meant to have it. The story we told was that we had found a note about buried treasure, David had got there first, wanting it for himself, done the digging, and when nothing was found except an old box, he had rowed off in a fit of pique. Graham even showed them his slashed sleeve, proof that David had been the aggressor. They appeared to accept this story – and it was the truth – and it looked as though the death would certainly be recorded as accidental.

Late on Monday, Justin drove us all the way back to London.

Very little was said, but none of us had wanted to split up and go home separately, so Justin had delayed getting the campervan back to his parents, and he took us all back to my house, where we arrived feeling exhausted and drained.

I had tried to sleep during the journey, but my mind would not let me. A strange mix of emotions kept me disturbed and wakeful.

David had been my cousin. Yes, he had burgled my house, and would probably have killed me to get hold of some expensive heirloom, and a deep relief that I no longer had to look over my shoulder formed part of my feelings. But I was also shocked at the manner of his death, and the part that we had all played in it. He was the last of the male Turveys. I had no other family.

And there was still a question mark over the ring. If my ancestor, Richard Burbage, had led me to it, why was it mine to have? Why had Burbage's family had it in keeping anyway? What did it all mean, and who was HW?

I seemed to have come to the end of the journey of the

discovery of my ancestors. There was nowhere else to go, and I had the thing in my possession that it all seemed to have been leading towards. And yet, there were unanswered questions and a sense of something still left undone.

As we all traipsed into the house, I saw that my answerphone was blinking. Wearily, I pressed the button, and the very excited voice of Georgina instantly started to speak.

'Sarah? Oh, how I wish you were there! I have some really interesting news for you. I – I don't want to just say it on the phone. Can I come over tonight? I *really* hope you'll be free. I think you'll want to know this... Ring me back as soon as you get this.'

I stared at the phone, as Greta sat down heavily on the sofa with a groan.

'Oy, don't you think it could wait until tomorrow?'

I looked at my watch. It was only eight o'clock. It just felt later. It had been a long day.

'She certainly sounded eager,' said Graham.

Justin looked at me. I was biting my nail.

'Ring her,' he said, 'you know you want to. I reckon we could all do with a little lift. Perhaps a take-away and a few stiff drinks would do the trick. I'll head on out in a minute and do the honours.'

I picked up the phone.

'Sorry Greta,' I said, 'it does sound interesting, and I'm not sure I'd sleep tonight if I didn't hear what she had to say.'

Greta lay flat out on the sofa.

'All right then,' she said, 'but nobody speak to me for the next half hour. I'm going to meditate.'

Half an hour later, I gently nudged Greta, who was now gently snoring with her head on the arm of the sofa, and she moved her feet off so that Georgina could now sit down and put some papers in front of her.

I told Georgina all that had happened that day. She was astounded by our adventures, and was intrigued by the ring, which made her gasp and smile broadly.

'Well,' she said, 'you're going to love this. I was intrigued by the name of McDougal in that old note, so I had a look at the marriage indexes for London, and I found that a merchant called Edward McDougal married an Agnes Smith in 1621. I found no children for this couple in London, so I contacted my Scottish genealogist, and asked if she could find a link between the McDougals, who were the Victorian Bertie's family, and this Edward.

'She'd had a lot of trouble getting back from Bertie, because there were too many people with the same surname, but with this extra information, she managed to find several wills for the McDougals, and with that and the patchy parish registers, she has managed to put a tree together.

'To cut a long story short, this Edward McDougal left a will, naming his wife, Agnes, their four children, *and a person he names as "my wife's daughter, Alice."* Because he calls her his wife's daughter, presumably, this is the child that was born in London, the daughter of Agnes Smith, the one mentioned in the note, whom the ring was supposed to go to. She is not of course Edward's daughter, but presumably illegitimate.'

'But...' I started.

'Wait – just let me go on. This daughter Alice later herself had an illegitimate son.'

'There seems to be a lot of that going on,' said Graham.

'Oh, it's *extremely* common,' said Georgina, 'anyway, the

point is, that the name McDougal was carried through her. After Edward's death, Agnes then leaves her own will, leaving a large legacy to her grandson, Thomas McDougal, *comedian,* the son of my daughter, Alice.'

'Comedian?' I said.

'At those times a comedian was often another name for an actor. This was after the Restoration, when the theatre was legal again. I've looked all this up! Anyway, the thing is, the line from Thomas can be clearly researched down to your very own Bertie McDougal, the Victorian actor.'

I blinked a few times, rubbed my face and ran my hands through my hair.

'Sorry,' I said, 'I'm really tired. What does all this mean? The ring was supposed to be given to Alice by the Burbage family, and Alice is the ancestor of Bertie?'

'That's right.'

'So, I'm also descended from Alice?'

'Yes.'

I picked up the ring.

'This ring was meant to be given to Alice, but her mother married and left for Scotland before that could happen?'

'Yes.'

I looked at the ring, and its inscription.

'And we think this ring belonged to William Shakespeare?'

There was a silence in which I could hear my own heart beating.

Graham suddenly grabbed my hand.

'Oh my God! Sarah, do you realise what this means?'

'But wait!' I cried, not wanting to jump to any conclusions that would lead to disappointment later, 'you're not saying, surely, that Alice's father was... was...'

246

'Of course,' said Georgina, going back to her normal professional tone, ' we don't have any actual documentary proof, but I can't think of any other reason why it was so important for the friends of William Shakespeare to get this ring to her. Think of it. Shakespeare did leave a will, but he could hardly be leaving legacies to illegitimate children in it, in a will that would be read to his wife and two daughters.'

'But...' I still could not process it, 'Shakespeare had no direct descendants. That's well known.'

'None from his marriage, no. But he spent a long time living in London, far from his family, and records rarely show the names of the father in the cases of what were called "base-born" children. There's no reason at all to think he didn't have the occasional fling, and there was no effective contraception, to speak of, then.'

I turned the ring over and over in my hand.

'So, that's why it belongs to me,' I whispered. For the first time since I had found it, I tried it on my middle finger, but it was too large. It was a man's ring. I put it on my thumb.

'It was not meant for her originally,' I said, 'and we know from the inscription that someone had given it to Shakespeare. I wonder who.'

Justin got up and went to the bookshelf.

'And the writing box,' I said, 'I suppose that was a gift to his friend, Burbage.'

Graham stood up.

'I feel I should bow, or curtsey, or something,' he said, 'I'm standing in front of the living, breathing descendant of William Shakespeare, the greatest poet and playwright the country has ever known. Oh, but this is so much better than being descended from Royalty – this is literary royalty! His blood runs in your veins, darling!'

'This is my favourite case ever!' said Georgina, giving me a hug.

'Liebling,' said Greta, doing the same, 'I always knew you were special!'

'Oh my!' I uttered, feeling slightly faint.

'Here's a thing,' said Justin.

We had just finished the Indian takeaway that he had got for us, and were lounging replete on the sofas and chairs in the living room. I was still experiencing shivers throughout my whole body every time I thought about the revelations of earlier that evening.

Justin had gone back to the book he had picked up from my shelf. It was a biography of Shakespeare.

We all turned to him.

'According to many historians, it is thought that William Shakespeare had a close relationship with the Earl of Southampton, possibly even a homosexual one. He is thought to possibly be the "fair youth" of the early sonnets where Shakespeare seems to be trying to persuade him to marry and have children, so that his youth and beauty will never die. The Earl was, of course, a financial benefactor to William, and Shakespeare dedicated his poem, *The Rape of Lucrece*, to him, saying "The love I dedicate to your lordship is without end... What I have done is yours; what I have to do is yours; being part in all I have, devoted yours." It was the language of the day, of course, but still...'

Graham leaned over to look at the book.

'Is that the Earl's portrait?'

'Yes.'

'Well, if he wasn't gay, I'd eat my leather biker cap, darlings. Look at that mouth, all pursed up like a cat's backside!'

I laughed, looking over his shoulder.

'That's a slight exaggeration, but I do see what you mean,' I said, 'but what has he got to do with my ring? Or were you just reading that out of interest?'

'Ah,' said Justin, 'no. You see, the thing is, the Earl of Southampton's actual name was Henry Wriothesley.' He looked up at the four faces staring at him.

'Risely?' I queried?

'No, with a W. W-R-I-O...'

I sat up.

'H.W.? His initials are H.W.?'

'The very same,' said Justin.

CHAPTER 23

Stratford-upon-Avon, April 1616

S It was late afternoon when Richard Burbage entered
Stratford. He was exhausted by the journey from
London, and in need of ale and a rest. But he had a more
pressing concern to see to first.

As he approached the door of New House, he met Doctor Hall
on the threshold. They nodded to one another, but Hall's face
was grim.

The house was dark and silent. Anne met him in the hall and
smiled wanly.

'It is good of you to come,' she said.

'Is there any hope...?'

She shook her head.

He nodded in response. He had known as much in his heart.

She signalled for him to go upstairs.

He crept softly into the room. It was dark, the shutters closed
to keep out the harsh daylight, and only a few candles flickered
near the bedside. All was silent except for the rasping breaths
of his friend, and Richard sensed the presence of death, lurking
in the shadows, waiting for its moment. The smell of sickness
hung heavy in the air, giving it an almost palpable density.

He sat in the oak chair next to the bed, newly vacated by the doctor. He could not tell whether he was sleeping, but after a few moments his head moved as he turned to look at him.

'Ah,' said the weakened voice, that he had once known booming around the wooden O of the Globe, 'I must be sick. My friends come from all corners of the earth to visit me. Ben was here but yesterday. I have not seen so much society since last I was in London.' A laugh turned into a cough, and Richard handed him a handkerchief. 'Even so,' he continued slowly, 'it is good to see you, old friend. How goes it with you?'

'I am well, Will,' said Richard, 'but while I would have come as soon as I heard the news of your indisposition, it was you who called me here, so my appearance should not be any surprise to you.'

There was silence from the bed for a few moments, and Richard leaned closer to see if he had fallen asleep. William's eyes met his.

'Yes, 'tis true. I did ask for you to come. I wanted to see my dearest friend before... before I pay my final debts and sleep my final sleep.'

'Surely, it is possible you...'

'Shh' William put his finger up to his lips. 'Let us not fool ourselves with idle forswearing. I feel death's approach day by day. The room grows cold, though my wife stokes the fire by the hour. He waits here, in this very room.'

Richard reached out his hand and laid it on Will's arm. His eyes stung.

'My dear friend...'

Will turned his head towards him and he was smiling.

'We have had some merry times together, have we not?'

'Some merry, Will, some sad.'

They were both silent, as they thought of the dreadful night that the Globe Theatre, their pride and joy, had burned to the ground. It was soon afterwards that Will had returned to his family in Stratford.

Will coughed again.

'There is a matter of some urgency I need to discuss with you. I am tiring, and it cannot wait. Friend Richard, close the door. I do not wish my wife to overhear.'

Richard obediently got up and closed the door, so the latch engaged. Before he could sit down again, Will pointed to something in the corner of the room.

'Go to my desk, my writing desk, there on the table, and open it. In the drawer on the right there is a...' he stopped, breathing heavily.

'William? Do you need something?'

Will waved him away impatiently.

'No, no! Have you found it?'

'The drawer? There is nothing in it.'

'It has a false back.'

'Ah. I have it.'

Richard reached behind the false backing, and found a ring. He looked at it, gasping at its beauty and the quality of its making. He brought it back to the bed and sat down again, handing it over to William, who rolled it over and over in his hand.

After a few moments, he said, 'I have oft spoken to you of times past, of my time in the company of the young Henry, my patron. You know too, that I have often sought out the company of women, beyond the realms of the marital bed. You and I have indeed enjoyed a little competition in that respect.'

Richard was silent, but smiled to himself, remembering

the friendly rivalry between them for the affections of one young woman or another, women excited by the dashing and dangerous men of the stage that their mothers had warned them against.

Will sighed.

'Henry gave me this ring. He was beautiful in his youth, Richard. He could turn the heads of both sexes...'

'Yes,' muttered Richard, 'I have read the sonnets.'

'Ha! Indeed, love taught me to rhyme, and be melancholy. I did love him, Richard, as an ageing man loves youth and beauty, and I do believe he loved me as a young girl can love an older man. Love takes on many guises, but the world doth not look kindly on all its faces. I have loved before, and I have loved since. I cannot speak for him. Yet it was necessary for him to marry.'

Richard remained quiet.

'He had this made in Italy. He had our initials engraved on it, see. For remembrance.'

Will lay his head back on his pillows. He was tired after so many words.

'My wife would not look kindly on this. I need to dispose of it, but it cannot be named in my public will. You understand.'

Richard nodded.

'There is somebody I wish to give it to.'

'Who is it, Will?'

William smiled, and waved to him to wait. He needed space to breathe.

'Thereby hangs another tale, my friend.'

Richard waited, watching with pain his friend's laboured breathing.

There was a knock on the door, and Anne half entered,

standing in the dim light, the candlelight flickering across her worried face.

'He will be getting tired. Perhaps you can return later...?'

William turned to her. Richard noticed how his hand had closed around the ring.

'My love, I have important things to discuss with Richard. He will not keep me long, and then please make sure he has food and drink. He has come far.'

Anne glanced at Richard and then back to her husband.

'Yes, of course. But no more than ten minutes.'

She shut the door behind her, and they listened to her footsteps down the wooden staircase.

William lay his head back again and sighed.

'Poor Anne. I have not always been a good husband to her. But at least she will not starve after I am gone.'

He shut his eyes, and for a while Richard thought he had fallen asleep again.

'Will? The ring?'

Will opened his eyes.

'Ah yes, the ring.' He closed his eyes again for a moment, and then continued.

'In White Lion Yard, close by the Spital Fields, there lies the house of a widowed tailor I have oft used for my doublets. He has a daughter. She and I have spent much time in each other's company. A strong-willed woman, and full of natural wit. I found her company pleasurable.'

Richard smiled.

'Our mutual affection grew to mutual intimacy. She had a child. A girl.'

'You have seen the child?'

'Yes. Her name is Alice. Agnes's parents agreed to help with the girl, but I fear for her future.'

Richard leaned closer. Will's voice was growing weaker.

For a moment, Will held the ring to his lips, and then he handed it to Richard.

'I wish her to have this ring. To remember me. Or she can sell it if she needs money. It makes no odds. I want her to know that I thought of her. Before I departed. She will understand... its sentiment. Given and received... freely... in love.'

'Given and received,' repeated Richard, 'I understand, Will.'

William grasped his hand. Though his hand shook, his grasp was surprisingly strong.

'It is important, my friend. Please will you do this for me? It is my wish...'

'Of course. White Lion Yard. Agnes, the tailor's daughter. I will deliver it.'

Will's hand relaxed.

'Thank you. And, Richard...'

'Yes, Will?'

'My writing desk. Take it. It's yours.'

'But Will...'

'Please. It is not in the will, but I have told Anne. Words I have written on that desk have come transformed in eloquence from your mouth. I am truly grateful. It means more for you to have it.'

'Thank you,' said Richard, moved beyond words.

Will sighed a deep sigh.

'That's it,' he said, with a small grin, 'the rest is silence.' And then he laughed at himself, bringing on a cough.

Richard waiting for the coughing to ease, and then touched Will's hand.

'Will... my friend...'

'Richard. Thank you for all. Live happily. I will die in peace. I think, first, though, I would like to sleep a little.'

Richard could not help a smile. Will was always quick with a joke, even at such a time.

'Good-bye, my friend, and thanks for all the words,' he whispered.

A slight smile hovered on Will's lips, but he was now soundly asleep.

CHAPTER 24

August 1985

I woke up from another dream. It was hazy and fading fast, but as I lay in bed, looking at the trees outside my window which were now tinted with autumn gold, I knew I had been visited by Richard Burbage for the last time. He had fulfilled his purpose and delivered the ring and had come to say farewell.

I smiled, thinking back over all my ancestors who had never known their true heritage. What would Bertie have thought, had he known that he was the direct descendant of the man whose words he had spoken on stage so often? Eliza had offered him the key, but would he ever have been able to find the truth as I had done? How extraordinary, I thought, that fate had brought Eliza and Bertie together to provide the union for the two lines to mingle, the Burbage and the Shakespeare blood.

Diluted by other lines, of course, but perhaps some lines can be felt stronger than others. I had always loved Shakespeare; the structure of the words, the timeless philosophies and the depth of knowledge of human relationships. Now, of course, I felt closer to him than ever before. And to also be the descendant of one of his closest friends brought an extra dimension to that feeling.

What was I to do with this new-found knowledge?

I sat up, and taking the chain that had the key on it from my bedside table, I released the key, and threaded the ring onto it. I got dressed and put the chain around my neck.

As I prepared my breakfast and got ready for the day, I contemplated what I should do. Would I tell anyone that I was the direct descendant of Shakespeare? Should I take the ring to a museum, have it analysed? It would certainly be worth something, though it was doubtful that I would ever be able to prove to anyone that it had been Will Shakespeare's. What evidence was there? A very shaky genealogical line and some dreams. That was not going to be enough for a sound provenance.

Instinctively, my hand went to the ring and held it, as if to protect it. I realised then that I did not want anyone to know except my closest friends. No matter how much money I needed, I knew I would never sell it; it was too personally significant and had taken so much to find. My illustrious ancestor had wanted it to be delivered to his own daughter, and his friend, my other ancestor, had not rested until he had fulfilled his promise to deliver, even though it had taken centuries. If anyone asked about it, I would just tell them it was an heirloom, which of course it was.

And there was something else about it too. It had somehow altered the way I felt about myself, and what I wanted for the future. I had no idea how I would achieve it, but an idea was growing in my head, giving me butterflies in my stomach and a smile I could not wipe off my face.

I had already started to clear out my parents' wardrobes, sorting stuff to throw out, or take to charity shops. It was time to let go of the past. Perhaps it was time to move too.

Later that morning, I heard the letterbox flap and bending down to pick up the three letters there, I noted a telephone bill and a gas bill, both of which I chucked onto my desk unopened. The other, after looking at the postmark and frowning in puzzlement, I opened and read the single letter inside.

Sitting down very suddenly on my sofa, I clapped my hand to my mouth and sat there, frozen, for several minutes.

Eventually, I slowly put the letter down on the table, and sat back, closing my eyes.

'Thank you,' I whispered.

That evening, when I walked into the restaurant, Graham did a double take.

'My God, darling, you look fabulous!'

We had all planned to get together to celebrate my heritage by going out for dinner at Joe Allen's in Covent Garden. I had spent the afternoon shopping, and walked through the door clothed in a Laura Ashley blue velvet dress, low cut, fitted round the waist, and flared out almost to the ankles. I had adjusted the chain so that the ring sat just above the neckline, allowing the blueness of the sapphire to sing out above the blue dress. In my hair I wore a blue velvet ribbon. I was also wearing a pair of high-heeled Gucci shoes.

Justin stood up and pulled out a chair for me.

'You look like a million dollars!' he said.

'Funny you should say that,' I said, smiling in what I hoped was a mysterious way as I sat down.

Before anyone could speak, I called the waiter over and ordered a bottle of champagne.

'OK, what's going on?' said Justin.

I sat with my hands on the table, and looked at them all looking back at me; Justin, Graham, Greta and Georgina.

'Well, my lovelies, do you remember the will that Bertie left?'

'Of course,' said Georgina, 'do you mean to say...?'

'And how!' I replied, 'I'm the sole heir, and with interest, it comes to a very large amount. I'm rich, folks!'

Graham and Justin got up and rushed to my chair to hug me, while Greta grabbed my hands from across the table.

'Mazel tov! Oh, that is fantastic news Sarah!'

'I knew it!' exclaimed Georgina, banging her fist on the table, 'I'm so delighted for you, and I am more than pleased that it was me that helped you to get it!'

'Oh, I can't tell you how grateful I am,' I replied, 'and I'm so glad that you're here tonight – I really think of you as a friend.'

'We'll all drink to that!' said Graham, as the champagne arrived, and we all cheered as the cork popped.

Later, while we were scraping the last bits of cheesecake or chocolate mousse from our plates, and the last dregs of wine had been shared out around the table, I told them that I had another announcement to make.

I looked at all my friends around the table, all staring back at me.

'The last six months have been...' I was going to say 'amazing', but it sounded so trite, so I said, '...weird...'

Everyone laughed.

'...and incredible, and extraordinary, and...' I sighed, unable to find the words.

'I know I've been grumpy and grouchy at times,' I continued, 'but that's partly because I'm impatient, but also because I've been trying to work out what to do with my life. I've told myself it's just because I'm not working, not getting acting jobs. Being out of work in any business is always difficult, but I've come to realise it's more than that.'

I took a sip of wine.

'I don't think that acting itself is quite enough for me. Oh, I love it, don't get me wrong, but it's like... do I want to spend the rest of my life playing parts, spouting someone else's lines, while audiences come and watch, applaud, and then go away and completely forget about me. I think I need something more. I mean something that isn't just about me.

'I've had this idea growing, but with no idea how to put it into action. And now, this money has arrived, as if to say, "well, get on with it, then!"'.

'We are all ears, hon,' said Graham, 'what is it?'

'Well, I've been thinking about this all day, and it's a little vague at the moment, but I've been thinking about how important things like drama, and any arts, are in people's lives, and mostly people don't even realise it. Look at how theatre has survived down through the centuries, despite it being banned, and despite actors being thrown in gaol, and sometimes shunned by society. And now, people can't get enough; we have film and tv as well as theatre. And, I was thinking how it can help people when they are having a bad time. I know that, for me, doing drama at school and then later at the youth theatre, really helped me when I was being bullied. It helped my confidence and self-esteem, and gave me belief in myself.

'So, what I want to do is give that feeling to other people who are going through some kind of crisis or trauma. A centre for using drama, and other creative outlets, to help people through difficult times. And it's not just about being able to express yourself, it's about getting involved with a group of people who are working towards the same end.

'I mean, Graham, I've noticed how quickly you recovered from that horrible thing that happened by getting involved in my little family project...'

'That's very true,' he said, his face serious for once.

'And Greta, just imagine if your great uncle had had something, some place where he could have expressed all his trauma and anger, instead of being forgotten about in some bedsit in Birmingham.'

Greta nodded, tears in her eyes.

I sat back in my chair. Now I had said it out loud and I had heard my own words out in the air, I felt a bit silly. All day, while these thoughts had been running around in my head, they had seemed so right and completely achievable. But now I had shared them with an audience, they seemed unrealistic and naïve.

I slumped a little in my chair.

'I suppose you think I'm crazy. Perhaps it's not...'

'Of course we don't think you're crazy,' said Justin, 'my God, Sarah, it's a marvellous idea. I won't say it would be easy to set up. You're going to need some sort of financial backing – some funding – to keep it going after you've invested your own money in it, but I love the idea. You know, if it hadn't been for you, and those art and drama classes, I'm not sure how I would have got through school with any kind of belief in myself. I say go for it. Your ancestor would be proud of you!'

I smiled at that.

'For me, it was music,' said Georgina quietly, 'when my first husband was abusing me, and I finally got the courage to leave with two young children and a load of debt, it was joining a choir that really helped me get through those dark days until I met Stephen.'

I stared at her. I had always imagined Georgina as having a solid, perfect life with no money problems and a steady marriage.

'Wow… sorry, Georgina, I had no idea.'

'It's not something I talk about very often,' she said, 'but I do think you've got something here. Not everyone has access to such an outlet, and if they do, it's sometimes by accident that you find it's a help. Most creative activities are seen as just a bit of fun, not actively focused on helping you through a trauma.'

There was a lull in the conversation after Georgina's revelation.

'You're going to need a team,' said Graham.

'I'd love to be part of it,' said Greta.

'Me too!' chorused Justin and Graham, and then turned and smiled at each other.

'My husband's a solicitor; I'm sure he could come on board,' said Georgina.

'Oh, you're all marvellous,' I said, 'but I probably won't be able to pay anyone.'

'We wouldn't expect that, darling,' said Justin, 'and if you can set it up as a charity, you'd need part-time volunteers anyway. That is, if you're not expecting people to pay for the service.'

'No, no…' I said, 'I think it should be free for all; not exclusive in any way. Oh gosh,' I said, feeling suddenly overwhelmed, 'do you think it's possible?'

'Anything is possible,' said Greta, waving a spoon in the air, 'if you really want it.'

EPILOGUE

March 2019

Anything is possible, but it doesn't happen overnight.

I was reminded today of that evening over thirty years ago by a journalist who asked me how it all began.

The image was so clear in my mind. Me in my blue velvet dress from Laura Ashley, the ring heavy on the chain round my neck. My four friends sitting round the table all looking at me as I unfolded my ideas.

'It began with friendship,' I said, 'a restaurant in Covent Garden and a few glasses of champagne.'

I smiled, and the journalist chuckled in understanding. He knew about restaurants and champagne.

What he didn't know, and I wasn't going to tell him, was that it had started earlier than that. With a legacy. A key, a dream and a journey through my ancestry. And, yes, friendship as well.

I have told no-one about my ancestry. Only Justin, Graham, Greta and Georgina know, and they have sworn to secrecy.

For one thing, no-one would believe me. As Georgina has said, the documentary evidence is at times shaky, and at others non-existent. Even today, when searching family history has been made so much easier by the internet, it would be difficult to come up with the necessary documentation. I only have my dreams and visions as evidence, and you can imagine what people would do with that. In today's social media world, the trolls would have a field day.

But the question made me nostalgic. I've been writing a daily journal for some time now, keeping a note of every day's activities, but today I'm looking back at that summer with almost a sense of longing for those times gone by. I know I was impatient and cranky that summer, and I know that days went by where nothing happened and I thought I would never solve the mystery, but looking back all I remember is a blur of activity, racing up and down to Justin's parents' house, the house at Hampstead, the auction house at Oxford, and the adventure at Stratford.

And David. If only he hadn't been so greedy and ended up taking himself out of the equation, he would have had a share in the pay-out from the will.

Well, my heritage has remained a secret, but they are all with me. Shakespeare, Burbage, and all the others, behind me, whispering encouragement and telling me not to give up.

It has not been an easy ride. It took years to get the charity off the ground. Justin, Greta and Georgina became trustees, and Graham – bless his heart – became manager of the first centre, and my right-hand man.

There were so many obstacles to overcome, protocol to be adhered to, piles of paperwork and meetings to attend. The paperwork alone could have discouraged me right from the start, distracting from the creative heart of my idea, but Justin was brilliant with all the practical matters, while Georgina's husband, Stephen, became our representative and adviser in all legalities.

Our first centre – no more than a room in a community centre in Camden - opened in 1987 as the Globe Arts Project; a nod to the theatre my ancestors had built and lost. Within weeks we were over-subscribed. I remember so well the first session I held there, with a heady mixture of excitement, enthusiasm, and gut-knotting, bowel-curdling fear. The group was a cross-culture mix of ages, genders, races and social backgrounds. My main fear was not being able to control things if anything got out of hand, volatile emotions and character clashes in the group. But while things were slow to get started, and some were slow to trust and commit to the project in hand, over a period of six months we managed to bring together that disparate group of mis-matched, damaged souls and slowly bring out their own creativity into something solid. A performance piece, written, designed and performed by themselves, under my direction. Those director classes had come in useful after all. In the end, they found they had something to be proud of, and a sense within themselves of something worthy. By the end of the project there were friendships forged, including one or two romances, new careers begun, and most with a new sense of purpose and a feeling of value in society.

From that beginning, I have slowly extended the charity, opening new centres every few years. I moved out of the house at Hampstead and turned it into an office and rehearsal rooms for the north London branch. We now have Lottery funding and my charity is a household name.

Some of the projects that have been created have gone on to become TV serials and films, the profits of which have gone straight to the charity. As the head of the charity, I now earn a salary, but I continue to be creatively involved with as many of the projects as I can. I was never going to be a desk person.

As for Justin and Graham, they got married five years ago, just a few weeks after gay marriage became legal. My memories of that day are very hazy, but I do remember lots of colourful balloons and cherubs, and Graham wearing a large pink hat. The amount of champagne we got through could have sunk the Titanic.

It seemed that things had changed for the better, but recent political developments have shone a light on how divided we still are, with the Far Right becoming more active, and the election of an openly racist and homophobic president in the US. In many countries, being gay is still illegal and those communities are constantly in danger from violence, often with legal and governmental systems that actually encourage such behaviour. As a global community, we still have a very long way to go.

In the late 80s, Greta met an artist, whom she moved in with and they now own a farmhouse in the Lot Department in France, along with three large dalmatians, and an attached gîte, which they rent out every summer. I stayed there myself last year, and spent a glorious few days shopping at Cahors and Toulouse, and visiting the huge cathedral at Albi.

Georgina and Stephen are now retired, living in a bungalow in Hampshire, where Georgina cares for her husband, who has dementia.

As for me, I have remained single. I like it. Gone are the days of the pressure to be part of a couple. I have the occasional fling, and nights out, but I realised a long time ago that I do not need a man to feel complete. My life's work brings me that – and, of course, my friends.

After all, who was it that said, '*I count myself in nothing else so happy As in a soul remembering my good friends.*'

Oh yes, of course. It was an ancestor of mine.

Acknowledgements

I'd like to express my gratitude for some of the people who have encouraged and helped me with getting this story to the point of publication.Special gratitude goes to my dear friend, Clara Reeves, for her support, for reading each chapter as it came off the printer, and for all our writing conversations. Also, I'd like to thank my sister-in-law, Sharon Bott, and my friend Amanda Collins for their encouragement and support. I'd also like to thank my Advance Team for their feedback on the draft copy. And, last, but by no means least, a big thank you to my niece, Eliza Bott, for another brilliantly designed cover!

Have you enjoyed this book?
If so, may I request a favour?

For a self-published writer like myself, reviews are one of the most important tools for helping me to sell my books. Advertising costs are far beyond the budget of most writers, and so we rely very much on readers like yourself who are willing to spread the word. Honest reviews of my books will help to bring them to a wider audience. If you have enjoyed this book, I would be extremely grateful if you could spend a few minutes leaving a review on my book's Amazon page.

Thank you very much!

About the Author

Rosamunde Bott is the author of several historical and semi-historical novels, often including an element of mystery or fantasy. She has also written a children's fantasy adventure novel. You can find out more about Rosamunde and her writing at her website, and you can connect with her on Facebook and on Twitter (see links below). You can also email her at info@rosamundebott.com.

Rosamunde is also a professional genealogist, and has provided an ancestry tracing service for many years. If you would like to find out more, please visit her genealogy site, shown below.

You can connect with me on:

🌐 http://www.rosamundebott.com

🐦 https://twitter.com/writerros

📘 https://www.facebook.com/WriterRos

🔗 http://www.tracingancestors-uk.com

Subscribe to my newsletter:

✉ https://www.rosamundebott.com/list-page

Also by Rosamunde Bott

All of the following are available on Amazon.

Isobel Brite

Isobel Brite (Historical Novel) When the travelling theatre company comes to town, young shoemaker's daughter, Isobel Brite, is entranced by the idea of a life on the stage, and also by the very handsome and charming lead actor, Frank Douglas. Life as an actress in the 1840s brings freedom and independence, but it is also full of challenges, and she will find that the line between fame and obscurity is a fragile one.

Out of Time

When frustrated writer, Catherine Burns, buys a country cottage on a whim, she also becomes strangely fascinated by the nearby manor house. But it is when she meets the enigmatic musician, Will Days, that things really begin to get weird. For there is more to Will than meets the eye; he is a little older than he looks, and he is about to help Catherine go on a journey through her family's history. *Out of Time* is a multiple timeline novel about ancestry, women's history and the connections between the past and present.

The Light of Drombar

Transported by a magic stone to the land of Drombar, four children find themselves on a quest to save its people from the darkness that is creeping over the land. They must travel to the most dangerous place of all the source of the darkness and the evil Lord Saedor and restore the light.

Tracing Your Ancestors in the UK (non-fiction)

Would you like to trace your UK ancestors, but have no idea how or where to start? My step-by-step process will enable you to trace your ancestors using professional techniques and the most important sources in genealogy. It will also help you to avoid many of the pitfalls that the amateur genealogist often falls into.

Printed in Great Britain
by Amazon

57907368R00166